The Trail of Money

A NOVEL

PETER DAVID SHAPIRO

PenLane Press
11 Wachusett Drive
Lexington, MA, USA 02421

For information please write: PenLane Press, 11 Wachusett Drive, Lexington, Massachusetts USA 02421

www.thetrailofmoney.com
www.peterdshapiro.com

ISBN 978-0-9839244-2-5 (pbk)
ISBN 978-0-9839244-3-2 (ebk)

Cover photograph and interior Hong Kong photographs courtesy of Kate E. Searle.

FIRST EDITION 2012

ACKNOWLEDGMENTS

Special thanks to Bernadette Nelson, a patient muse and honest critic, Gabe Robinson, an editor who made this a better book, and Kate Searle, whose photographs show us Hong Kong.

AUTHOR'S NOTE

Readers familiar with Hong Kong will realize that I have taken liberties in describing well-known landmarks and other particulars. For example, the Furama Hotel really did exist but by the time of the events recounted here it had been demolished and replaced by an office tower. In this respect, the Furama's fate reflects a higher truth in Hong Kong – sentiment never stands in the way of making money.

BEIJING -- A long-running dispute between farmers and local officials in southern China exploded into open rebellion this week after villagers chased away government leaders, set up road-blocks, and began arming themselves with homemade weapons, residents said.

-- "Village Revolts Over Inequities of Chinese Life," Andrew Jacobs, *New York Times*, 15 December 2011

HONG KONG -- When mainland Chinese buyers bid up luxury home prices, "the high end affects the mid-end of the market, and it pulls the whole thing up," says Ms. Lau, who has asked the government to investigate allegations of money laundering.

-- "China's Money Leaks Are Felt Offshore," Jonathan Cheng, *Wall Street Journal*, 23 November 2009

BEIJING -- Execution for corruption is proportionate and accords with "China's national condition," a senior official said Thursday, as a disgraced former party chief from Shanghai, now confirmed to be behind bars, awaits trial.

-- "Beijing defends execution of corrupt officials," *New York Times*, 2 August 2007

HONG KONG -- Whenever the Central Government in Beijing is embarrassed by a scandal involving tax evasion, smuggling or corruption on a significant scale; the money trail invariably leads straight down to Hong Kong.

-- *Hong Kong: the Money Laundering Risk*. Pacific Risk Limited, Peter A Gallo, 15 September 2004

BEIJING -- Hu Changqing was executed Wednesday, after the Supreme People's Court rejected his appeal a day earlier. The Communist Party newspaper -- The People's Daily -- says Hu Changqing was made an example to warn other corrupt officials. It says his execution shows that no one can escape the punishment of the law.

-- "China Corruption," Voice of America, Roger Wilkison, 8 March 2000

Prologue

*1994 - Pudong District, Across the Huangpu River from
Shanghai, China*

THE DEMO SQUAD'S pickup truck bounces and swerves
along the gullied, pot-holed dirt road, spewing up yellow
dust in its wake. The workers who are holding on tight in
the back, coated by the dust, look like six very
uncomfortable terracotta warriors.

Finally their truck comes to a stop at the village they
are assigned to destroy. No people meet them in front of
its mud-brick and wooden buildings, just a few chickens
picking in the dirt, and a short-haired dog that glances at
them warily before sidling off out of sight.

The village is too small and too poor to have a proper
name. On the demo squad's hit list, it's referred to only as
"Number Four."

Squad foreman Wang Yinpeng clambers down from
his relatively comfortable passenger seat and stretches to
ease his bones back into their sockets. "It shouldn't take us

long to flatten this sorry pile," he tells his crew. "Get yourselves ready while I walk ahead to see what we've got here."

The driver of the second truck in the convoy attaches ramps at the back of his trailer to unload the squad's bulldozer. Meanwhile, the drivers of the last two trucks, a front loader tractor and a dump truck, sit cross-legged on the ground beside their vehicles, smoking cigarettes and awaiting further instructions.

As Wang Yinpeng walks past the village's outdoor toilet that's shielded by a rough fieldstone enclosure and a swinging thatched door, and an abandoned pigpen right next to it, large black flies rise and swirl above both, and then settle again.

Nearby he notes a dirt-floor patio with several outdoor wooden tables and stools, apparently Number Four's restaurant.

Farther along, inside a windowless shed, he sees plain wooden tables and benches lined up in front of a blackboard on which "We Stand for Self Reliance" was scrawled in crudely written characters.

Wang Yinpeng had heard that the rebellion in Number Four started when Communist Party cadres came by to announce confiscation of the villagers' land to provide space for New Shanghai. Villagers were informed that they'd be compensated by the Pudong Centre for Land Reserve and that some of them, the more able-bodied, could apply for construction jobs. When they discovered how little money they'd receive, they accused the cadres of corruption, pelted them with pig dung, swatted them with pig-herding sticks, and chased them out of the village, hurling rocks after their retreating vehicles. Then helmeted police descended on the village and beat everyone within their reach. A man who resisted his beating was dragged off. His body turned up later in a Pudong District hospital with bloodied nostrils, broken thumbs, and burnt skin on his feet and genitals. He had died unexpectedly from a heart attack, according to official reports.

One of Wang Yinpeng's crew yells, "Fuck!" and calls out to him, "Foreman Wang, you must see this!"

He retraces his steps to the village restaurant where his crew has now gathered. They stand aside for him to enter the cooking area, a small space with a dirt floor, a bare table, and an iron grate resting on a semicircle of fieldstones over charred wood and ashes.

The mortal remains of a man and woman hang on two ropes strung from hooks in the ceiling, their bare feet motionless above tipped-over wooden stools.

Ten years later, in 2004 - Hong Kong

THE ONLY SON of one of the richest men in Asia takes little satisfaction in the world-class view from his fortieth floor office window. As he gazes down at Hong Kong's bustling harbor, all he could think about is the phone call that he will have with his father.

No-one but Edward Woo understands how lonely it is to be the son of Woo Jian-Min.

Although people greet him with smiles, behind his back they scoff, "The good luck of his birth gave him all that he possesses; his big house on Victoria Peak, his country house in Bali, his top-of-the-line Mercedes, the business his father bought for him to run."

It was time for Edward to prove that he is more than just the son of a rich man. He will be respected. And, he will be feared. The old man seemed inclined to live forever. It was almost too much to bear, to have to grovel for money that is rightfully his.

Edward's desk-phone buzzes and he jabs the intercom button, "Yes."

"Your father's assistant is on the line."

"Put her through."

"Is this Mr. Woo?"

"Yes."

"Please hold for your father."

Then Woo Jian-Min's voice comes on, blunt and to the point, as usual, "Edward, is there a problem? Your message said it was urgent. How is the family? The girls?"

"They are fine, Father."

"Is there a problem at TelePhase?"

"No, the business is doing well."

"Good, Edward. Why then…?"

"Hong Kong Wireless rejected the buy-out offer from the Singapore group."

Silence on the other end.

"So HKW is in play."

More silence on his father's end. Edward asks, "Are you still there?"

"Edward, you must know that I can't comment on such a rumor. I am on the HKW Board."

"It's more than a rumor."

Silence.

"Father, if HKW is in play, I wish to buy it."

Silence.

"I am inviting you to join me as an equity partner."

"You mean, you want me to finance your bid."

"It's a good business opportunity. You'll make money. I'll make money."

"There will be other opportunities that are more manageable for you."

"You think that I can't handle this one?"

"That's what I'm telling you."

Edward suppresses an angry rejoinder that would only cause Woo Jian-Min to grow cooler and, Edward is convinced, more contemptuous towards him. So he strains to speak calmly without revealing the resentment that burns in his throat like acid.

"Father, this deal is important to me. Buying Hong Kong Wireless will earn me respect."

"You are respected now, Edward."

"Not like you."

"You must be patient."

More silence on his father's end. Edward waits out the silence and finally Woo Jian-Min says, "Edward, I am proud of the way you have taken charge of your life. You are running a real business now. By all accounts, you are controlling your drinking, and you stopped acting the fool with gamblers and whores. You have become a good family man."

"You said once that my wife was one of those whores."

"She is the mother of your two children, my grandchildren. People can change."

"Including me."

"Yes, including you."

"Father, I need your answer, will you join my bid for HKW?"

"No, Edward. My answer is no."

"Why not?"

"Because Hong Kong Wireless is too important to Hong Kong. The government will take an interest. Difficult questions will be asked."

"We'll answer their questions."

"Just run your business. Learn."

"Father, I am bored as dirt with my business."

"There will be other deals, Edward. Wait."

"If you won't join me, I'll find another business partner. There's plenty of money on the mainland that's seeking investments in Hong Kong."

"Take care, Edward."

"What do you mean?"

"Not every investor in China is a suitable partner."

"Money is money."

"Some money leaves a stain that you can't wash off."

"You don't need to worry about that. Who I pick for my business partner will be my decision."

Silence.

"Last chance, Father."

"My answer is the same."

"Then I'll go ahead without you."

"If you do, you will regret it, Edward."

2005 - Shanghai

ACCOUNTANT CHEN QIWEI walks out of the Shanghai medical clinic a dying man.

During the time he has left, he resolves that he will exact revenge on the criminals who destroyed his village in Pudong, among so many other villages that they also destroyed, and then erected their shiny new city over the ruined lives of the displaced villagers and farmers.

But he can't kill them all. Even if he makes it past the bodyguards to reach one or two of them, he'll surely be stopped, and the others will escape justice.

There's another way. The greed that made them rich also makes them vulnerable. They could never explain to the Authorities how they amassed so much wealth once it was exposed for everyone to see.

Chen Qiwei knows that the criminals have "invested" their money in the New China Properties Fund, which they've set up to hide their money while it provides them with well-laundered returns.

Chen Qiwei also knows that it would be useless to approach the Authorities directly with his information. He's only an accountant of limited means, and he looks it, being thin and sickly and shabbily dressed in his worn-out suit. For accusing his betters, he might well be sent back to labor camp where he would surely die, having accomplished nothing.

However, the Fund itself can be counted upon to create the opportunity that Chen Qiwei needs. Always hungry for its next business deal so that it can launder more dirty money, before long it surely will find one that's as big as its appetite, big enough to attract public notice. Then he will present his information about the criminals in a form and manner that no-one can ignore.

Unlike Chen Qiwei, these arrogant cadres and officials, and their sleek businessmen paymasters, and the strutting families so proud of their exalted status, and the politicians spinning their webs, are not tormented by the ghosts of Pudong.

But soon they will be.

Then Chen Qiwei can die in peace.

2005 – Hong Kong

Takeover Bid for Hong Kong Wireless

HONG KONG - Edward Woo, Chairman of Telephase, has announced a bid to acquire Hong Kong Wireless, Hong Kong's leading mobile phone operator. The multi-billion-dollar deal will be financed by an equity investment from the Shanghai-based New China Properties Fund.

--South China Morning Post

One

2005 - En route to Hong Kong

AFTER MY SIX HOUR FLIGHT from Boston and ninety minute layover in the San Francisco International Airport, the next stage of my journey to Hong Kong would add fourteen more hours in the air, and I was keen to get on with it.

Eventually my United Airlines' Boeing 747-400 was opened for boarding. I showed my boarding pass to a flight attendant standing just inside the doorway, climbed the stairs to the upper deck to take my window seat, stowed my carry-on, blue blazer, and laptop, and settled in.

A woman arrived to claim the aisle seat beside me. She appeared to be in her mid-thirties, slim, good-looking, with red hair that was cut short gamine style. She noticed my glance and said, "Hello," smiling politely. I replied, "Hello," and returned to leafing through my copy of UA's glossy *Hemispheres* magazine, thinking less about its words and pictures than about my new seatmate's emerald green eyes.

We took off over San Francisco Bay and then turned west to clear the South San Francisco hills. Soon we had climbed high above the wispy clouds and the fog layer that covered the Pacific like white felt.

Once we reached cruising altitude, two flight attendants worked their way down the center aisle handing out warmed cashew nuts and our choice of beverages for our first feeding of the flight.

I selected a channel on my personal video screen showing a trailer for the recently-released comedy *Wedding Crashers*, where Vince Vaughn sprawls groaning on the ground having been upended during a spirited touch football game by an over-bred New England "Lodge" played by Bradley Cooper.

"I love that movie," my seatmate said, looking over at my screen. "Especially the Isla Fisher character, Vince Vaughn's girlfriend."

"Is that because she has red hair?" I asked.

"That's not the only reason," my seatmate said. "I won't spoil it for you."

In-flight etiquette does not require chit-chat with your seatmate. On most flights, I exchange no words at all with whomever the airline reservation system has appointed as my close companion for our shared journey thirty-six thousand feet above the ground. Even when one of us needs to squeeze by the other in order to get to the aisle, our request is likely to be communicated solely through apologetic gestures.

However, now that my seatmate had broken the ice, I asked, "Are you staying in Hong Kong or just connecting through?"

"Staying in Hong Kong," she replied.

"For work or pleasure?"

"Work, but I hope some pleasure too."

Our conversation lagged, then she said, "My name is Erin Haig," and put out her hand, and I shook it, my arm raised to avoid the half-full glasses and small bowls of cashew nuts on the seat divider between us.

"Harry West."

"What do you do, Harry?" Erin asked.

"I'm a consultant, specializing in telecoms. We have a project in Hong Kong. I'll be there for about a week, depending on how it goes."

"Who are you with?"

"Blair West International."

"Named after you."

"I'm a co-founder," I said. "What about you, Erin? What do you do?"

"I'm a research editor for the *Asian Business Journal*."

"Really? I just read one of your articles on my PC."

"We have a reader! What's the article about?"

"A takeover bid for Hong Kong Wireless."

"I did research for that article," Erin said.

It was pure coincidence that Erin was my seatmate on our flight to Hong Kong but I would have seen her article in any case, given its topic.

The project for which I was on my way to Hong Kong was to help the Director of the government's Communications Department, our client Shih Chai-Ming, to evaluate the same proposed Hong Kong Wireless deal.

When my business partner Stephen Blair had called me about the project, he told me that the takeover bid for Hong Kong Wireless had been sitting on Mr. Shih's desk for a several months. "He put it off as long as he could," Blair said. "Now his higher-ups are demanding a decision, either bless it or reject it. He's in a bind because the would-be purchaser is Edward Woo, son of Woo Jian-Min, one of the richest men in Asia. So Mr. Shih has to tread carefully."

I always start a new consulting project by assembling a Casebook, a digital compilation from Internet searches of articles, papers, and snippets that shed light on the project's key players and issues.

The keywords "Edward Woo," "Hong Kong Wireless," and "Woo Jian-Min," had produced numerous hits.

One article, "Woo Princeling Swoops In," reported that Edward Woo's offer caught Hong Kong Wireless by surprise, after HKW had just rejected an earlier bid from a Singapore investment group. The article profiled Edward

Woo as an ambitious second-generation businessman eager to expand his telecoms business, called Telephase, beyond its fiber optic cable to China and its paging service in Hong Kong. It noted that acquiring HKW would make Edward Woo a leading player in Hong Kong business circles.

Articles about Woo Jian-Min, Edward's father, invariably reminded readers about his great wealth and pointed out that his holding company, Beaver Hall Holdings, managed assets in Asia, Europe, and South Africa.

In Erin's *Asian Business Journal*, the article titled "Woo Bid for HKW Raises Concerns" noted that corrupt mainland Chinese officials were acquiring assets in Hong Kong as a way to launder illicit money. Thus, it was cause for concern that Edward Woo's bid to acquire Hong Kong Wireless would be financed by the New China Properties Fund, a secretive equity fund based in Shanghai that had attracted the attention of anti-corruption investigators in Hong Kong.

I said to Erin, "You imply that the HKW bid is a front for money laundering."

"That's why I'm going to Hong Kong," Erin said, "to help with research so that we can connect the dots. More articles are coming."

"I'll keep an eye out for them," I said.

"Thanks. So, Harry, tell me about your consulting project."

"We've been engaged to evaluate a proposed telecoms deal."

"Which telecoms deal?"

"Well…"

A golden rule for consultants is not to talk with strangers about your projects, especially when the person asking is someone like Erin who is attractive, friendly, and clearly interested in what you choose to reveal to her.

"So, you can't tell me," Erin said. She shot me a sharp sideways look. "You're not working for Edward Woo, are you?"

"No."

"Is that the truth, Harry?"

"Yes, it's true," I said. "Blair West International has not signed on with the dark side."

"OK."

"Although if the dark side offered to pay us enough, we'd definitely consider it."

"Spoken like a true consultant," Erin replied, still sounding a bit miffed.

Erin's gaze drifted back to her video screen and I returned to *Wedding Crashers*. Events continue to unfold at the "little place on the shore" to which the privileged Cleary family retreats on weekends to escape the pressures of Washington, D.C. Vince Vaughn is seated at the Cleary dinner table next to Isla Fisher and she has taken matters – his matters – in hand under the table while he tries and fails to maintain his composure and Isla grins naughtily beside him.

I paused the movie when the flight attendants rolled their carts down the aisle distributing pre-dinner-service appetizers and dinner menus. After consuming our dinners, Erin and I each pushed back our seats and turned off our reading lights. Erin slipped on her eye-shade and I re-started *Wedding Crashers*.

Rattling noises jerked me awake. Flight attendants were assembling breakfast trays in the galley. Soon our cabin lights came on, a service cart was in the aisle, and the flight attendants were asking in low voices for passengers' breakfast choices.

Outside my small round window, the sun had cleared the horizon above the clouds and fog that still carpeted the Pacific just like when we had departed San Francisco.

Erin removed her eye-shade and raised her seat-back. She stretched, to the limited extent that was possible while still in her seat.

"I guess I was tired," she said.

"Only five hours to go on our flight."

"Yep," she said, yawning.

"Where are you staying in Hong Kong?"

"At the Sheraton in Kowloon. What about you?"

"I'll be at the Furama in Central, across the harbor from you," I said. "You can see it from Kowloon."

17

"I'll look for it when I'm taking in the view," Erin said.

"I may have free time while I'm in Hong Kong," I said. "Would you like to get together for coffee or dinner if a time opens up?"

"Sure," Erin said. "I'd like that."

Just before we arrived in Hong Kong at 7 P.M. local time, Erin handed me her business card: Erin R. Haig, Research Editor, *Asian Business Journal*, 1212 Broadway, New York, phone and fax numbers, her email address ErinH@ABJ.com, and on the back, she had written, "Sheraton Kowloon, Nathan Road."

"And the 'R' stands for…?" I asked.

"Rose."

"Erin Rose Haig," I said. "That has a nice lilt to it."

I handed her one of mine: Harry F. West, Ph.D., Principal, Blair West International, Inc., Suite 301, Andleman Building, 599 Massachusetts Avenue, Cambridge, Massachusetts, phone and fax numbers, and my email address Harry@BlairWestInternational.com.

"The 'F' is for Forrest," I said. "In case you're curious."

Erin put my card in her wallet.

"Call me," she said. "Harry Forrest West."

Two

I'm a different man now than the Harry West who took that flight to Hong Kong.

But I never expected my fifteen minutes of fame in the blogosphere. Achieving celebrity as "Hero Consultant" was the last thing on my mind.

I only did what I had to, to get a start on making things right, and that's the plain truth.

My path was set for Hong Kong on a grey December day five months ago at MCI-Concord, a state prison twenty-three miles west of Boston, Massachusetts.

Inmate William Harrington was seeking early release after serving two years of his sentence, and my ex-wife Alexandra Ben-Tov and I were invited to MCI-Concord for his first Parole Board hearing, under the "victim access" program.

He had killed our baby daughter Ariel.

Stinking drunk, driving on a suspended license, he ran a red light and slammed into Alexandra's Camry. Our

Ariel, buckled lovingly into her car seat on her way to day care and chatting merrily with her mother just before the collision, died before reaching Mount Auburn Hospital.

The black hole of our grief swallowed our marriage and sucked the joy out of my life.

After Alexandra moved out, I continued to live by myself in our house while most of its rooms, empty and unused, collected dust.

I gave up trying to sleep at night. Instead, I slouched in front of the TV watching old movies, comedies, action movies, war movies; it didn't matter.

At least the judge at Harrington's trial wasn't among those in our great Commonwealth who wink indulgently at DUI offenders. She sent the fucker away for eight years.

Alexandra arrived at MCI-Concord a few minutes before I did, and was waited for me in the prison reception area.

She looked to me as striking as ever, with her athletic figure, olive complexion, and intense dark brown eyes. But her jaw was clenched and she stood stiffly as if braced for an ordeal. I felt the same way. Soon we'd hear, see, and breathe the same air as the man who killed our child.

"Are you OK?" I asked.

"As OK as can be expected," she said. "Let's get this over with."

Normally, Alexandra appeared on top of any situation. As founder of ABTDigital, a successful online video provider, she spoke frequently at conferences and appeared often in *Boston Globe* articles and on local radio and TV stations. She exuded presence and style. But right now, she just seemed like someone who would prefer to be anywhere else.

As we entered the hearing room, I touched Alexandra's arm and whispered, "Showtime!"

She nodded.

Harrington rose to his feet in front of the Parole Board panel, two men and one woman. Pale, balding, and sweating, he did not cut an impressive figure. "I've learned my lesson," he said. "If you allow me to return to my family and my community, I pledge to you and also to the West family that I will never drink again."

West family? There was no West family, any more, because of him.

Then it was our turn. I presented a photograph of Ariel that I had age-progressed so that she appeared as if she'd lived until she was six, juxtaposed against her original picture as a toddler just before she was killed. In both pictures, Ariel came through as a captivating small version of her mother. "This is the life that he destroyed," I said.

Alexandra recited Harrington's expressions of remorse in his prior Court appearances. "He has given these same pledges many times before," she said. "Nothing stops him from driving drunk, putting all of our lives at risk. For the sake of our daughter, whose life he stole, and for those of us who loved her, whose hearts he broke, he must serve his full sentence, every hour, every minute, and every second."

The chairwoman of the Parole Board panel, a thin middle-aged black woman wearing large horn-rimmed glasses, thanked us for our comments. We would be informed of the Board's decision by the Victims Notification Unit.

I returned to my office at Robert L. Week, Inc., a large consulting firm headquartered in Cambridge, where I led RLW's telecoms consulting practice. I was proud of the consultants in my group. Despite the turmoil in my personal life, I continued to bring in consulting projects and to complete them on time and on budget. My group continued to beat its performance targets. In short, I liked working at RLW and I had no immediate plans to leave.

And yet, I felt compelled to respond to my most recent email from our CEO, Glenn Robertson. I'd ignored previous emails from Glenn that he'd addressed to me and other Group Leaders but I couldn't let this one go. My crap deflector shield must have been disabled that morning when I hugged a tearful Alexandra goodbye in the MCI-Concord parking lot.

It didn't perturb Glenn that the consulting product he was pushing, a weightless marketing concoction called Innovation Learning Process, offered nothing of value to our clients. His email urging us to "get on board with our ILP strategy" closed with, "I expect weekly reports from every Group Leader on your sales contacts for ILP – NO exceptions."

To which I replied, "Glenn, I can't in good conscience promote ILP to our telecoms clients. Doing so would jeopardize our client relationships."

Hence the phone call from his assistant, Sue-Beth Eastland, "Harry, can you come to Glenn's office?"

My meeting with Glenn did not go smoothly. I told him what I thought about ILP, he reminded me that he was CEO, I replied that he was destroying our company's reputation, one thing led to another, and when I got back to my office, I met two RLW security guys waiting outside my door. I had seen them around for years, walking the grounds, checking the parking lot, and lounging inside the main entrance on weekends watching TV.

"Mr. Robertson asked us to help you move out," the taller one said.

My removable possessions amounted to three box loads. The security guards had brought with them empty cardboard boxes and a steel dolly which I used to roll the boxes out to my car, under a steadily falling snow.

Late that night, unemployed for the first time since graduate school, and as usual unable to sleep in my silent, empty house, I called Stephen Blair's number in Hong Kong.

A lifelong expatriate Brit, Blair was born in Singapore where his father served as a military attaché in Her Majesty's embassy. Despite his easy confident manner, which he'd learned from English aristos with whom he hobnobbed at Balliol College at Oxford, he felt ill at ease in England. He missed the stifling heat and tropical downpours of Asian cities, their bright colors, surging crowds, glossy new towers and multistory indoor shopping malls. So he returned to Singapore to open and manage an RLW local office, and a few years later, just before we met, he did the same in Hong Kong.

Like his colonial forebears, Blair ventured out happily in the tropical midday sun dressed for business in a suit and tie, clasping his double-strapped leather briefcase at his side. At the end of the day, he repaired to the cool refuge of exclusive private clubs as a convivial guest of the oligarchs who were his good friends.

All that changed when he married Tung Mei-Ling, a well-connected member of one of Hong Kong's prominent families. From that point on, Blair forsook the pleasures of the clubs to spend his leisure time with his wife, a choice easily understood by anyone who has ever set eyes on stunningly beautiful Mei-Ling.

Blair and I kept in touch after we worked together on projects in Hong Kong and in Kuala Lumpur. As fellow Group Leaders, each with front row seats for our CEO's follies, we commiserated about RLW's prospects and mused about life-after-RLW. And, he was one of a treasured few who laughed at my jokes.

"What's going on, Harry?" Blair asked when he took my call. "You're up late." The clock on my laptop said 11:45 P.M., which translated to 11:45 A.M. the next morning in Hong Kong. "Are you calling to wish me a Merry Christmas?"

"Sure, Blair, Merry Christmas!"

"Thanks, same to you."

"I resigned from RLW today, or was fired, the details are a bit fuzzy."

"What happened?"

"Glenn and I disagreed about the merits of his pet consulting product."

"The infamous Innovation Learning Process."

"He wanted me to push it to our telecoms clients and I refused."

"Good for you."

"Glenn was displeased. He had me evicted from the premises by security guards."

"Hmm," Blair said. "What are you going to do?"

"I have an idea."

"Uh oh."

"It involves you."

"OK."

"Let's start our own company."

"The two of us?"

"Sure, why not? You've been talking about leaving RLW."

"True."

"You'll serve our clients in Asia from your base in Hong Kong and I'll cover the US. I'll get Jerry Seligman to join us here in Cambridge."

Jerry was the most senior member of my group. He loved consulting and was beloved by his clients, but he'd grown discouraged by recent trends at RLW. "I'm out of here," he'd told me. "I need a break from all the nonsense."

"Jerry's a good egg," Blair said.

After a pause, he continued, "You're right, Harry. RLW's no fun anymore. Let's do it. It's time."

"Excellent decision!"

"We'll need working capital to get us started," Blair said.

"I'll finance our start-up costs in Cambridge with a bank loan," I said. "I can use my house as collateral."

"Risky."

"I'll pay it off as soon as we get clients. Shouldn't be a problem."

"Alright, I'll see whether Mei-Ling will agree to cover our initial costs in Hong Kong," Blair said. "Actually, I know she will. She'll be delighted. She's been after me to get out of RLW."

"I've thought of a name for our new global consultancy that's both iconic and descriptive," I said.

"I'm waiting with breath bated."

"How about... *Blair West International?*"

We'd picked a tough time to launch a new consulting firm. Because of the sputtering economy, clients' budgets for consulting services had been slashed by corporate number crunchers, putting all new projects on hold. Despite making numerous calls, listening hard, and spreading copious amounts of a consultant fertilizer known in the trade as FUD, for Fear Uncertainty and Doubt, our days turned into weeks, and weeks stretched into months, without producing a whiff of revenues.

By the time t-shirts, shorts, and open-toed sandals had returned to the sidewalks of Cambridge, my branch of Blair West International was running out of cash.

In Hong Kong, Blair reported a similarly bleak situation. "Lots of meaningful discussions. Several leads that could pop at any moment. No actual dollars."

"I'm older than either of you," Jerry said. "I've been through dry spells before. Eventually they come to an end. Not to worry." He posted a sign on his desk quoting the Polish generals in World War II who confronted Hitler's Germans in the West and Stalin's Russians in the East, "Wonderful news! We are not yet defeated!"

On the other hand, it was *my* house and not Jerry's that would be lost when the grace period expired on my bank loan and I was unable to make the loan repayments.

"You're always welcome to live in our basement," Jerry said, his thick eyebrows jumping and bouncing like Groucho Marx's. "Our dog Suzie would love the company."

Blair's call came just in time.

"We have a project! How soon can you get over here to Hong Kong?"

Three

AFTER CLEARING CUSTOMS in the new airport on Lantau Island, I caught an Airport Express high-speed train which delivered me in precisely twenty-three minutes to the Hong Kong Central station.

I craved fresh air, having spent a day confined in planes and airports, so I decided to walk to the Furama Hotel rather than grabbing a taxi. It wasn't far, and in general I'll choose walking over riding whenever possible, one reason that I'm reasonably fit and carry no more weight at thirty-seven than I did when I played competitive intercollegiate squash as a student at UC Berkeley.

I was walking along Chater Road past the old Mandarin Oriental Hotel when I first noticed a humming, chirping sound, which grew louder as I approached Statue Square. It emanated not from a flock of birds but rather, as I soon discovered, from Hong Kong's Filipina maids on their Sunday break, chattering in their thousands in Statue Square and nearby Chater Garden. They occupied all of the park benches and spread out on blankets covering almost all of the grass and pavement, a reminder that I wasn't in Massachusetts anymore. I maneuvered around them to get to the Furama on the other side of the Garden.

My room at the Furama faced the harbor as I'd requested. On the coffee table, a letter from the General Manager welcoming me back to the hotel was propped against a basket of fruit, next to a white ceramic bowl filled with Godiva chocolates wrapped in gold foil. And on my phone, the message light was blinking.

It was a message from Blair, "Welcome to Hong Kong. Let's get together this evening so that I can fill you in about tomorrow."

Blair was still dressed for business in his suit and tie and carrying his leather briefcase when we met a half hour later in the Café Chater, the Furama's coffee shop.

"We've finally got you back here," he said. "It's been almost five years…"

On my earlier visit to Hong Kong, Blair and I had helped our client Mr. Shih to select a cable TV operator when the politics of picking one bidder over another got too hot for him to manage on his own.

Blair said, "You look about the same. No grey hair."

"So do you," I replied.

Blair's round face was still mostly unlined although I had the impression that a bit more grey had been salted into his otherwise dark hair.

"How is Mr. Shih?" I asked.

"As usual very busy, just trying to get the job done. We'll meet with him first thing tomorrow. He says he needs to give us our marching orders."

"I thought we already had our marching orders, to evaluate Edward Woo's takeover bid for Hong Kong Wireless."

"I thought so too. He wouldn't say more on the phone. We'll find out tomorrow what he has in mind. Next, I'll show you our Blair West International Hong Kong office where you can say hello to Elizabeth."

Blair and his administrative assistant Elizabeth Li had sub-let excess office space from an accounting firm that recently suffered a round of lay-offs.

"Based on the pictures you've sent me, our space is almost as elegant as your Suite 301," Blair said.

Admittedly, our office in the venerable Andleman Building in Central Square, a lower-cost part of Cambridge, looks in serious need of updating, with greenish walls scarred by long jagged cracks and pockmarked by nail holes, and wood laths exposed underneath the sagging, split ceiling plaster. But that's why, when the realtor led me up to the third floor of the Andleman Building and apologetically opened the door to Suite 301, I thought it was perfect. It had just what I needed to negotiate a break on our rent. I figured that we could raise our living standard once we had paying clients.

"Our Suite 301 possesses a *je ne sais quoi*," I said.

"It certainly does," Blair agreed.

"What's our plan for the afternoon?"

"We have an appointment with Edward Woo."

"I've read a lot about him, but what's he like, personally?"

"Well, let's see. He can turn quite nasty when he doesn't get what he wants. It upsets him that people rate him a cut below his father. He's smart enough but not as brilliant as he thinks. And he hates to be touched, like your old countryman Howard Hughes. On the other hand, he does have a colorful past. He earned quite a reputation for wild behavior when he was younger, always in the papers, whooping it up in Macao casinos with loose women on each arm, being arrested for one thing or another."

"So how did he become Edward Woo, prominent Hong Kong businessman?"

"He was arrested for drunk driving after an accident in which his passenger, a young woman, was seriously injured..."

"You know my opinion about drunk drivers..."

"I do, indeed. You've told me before."

"...that they should be shot and their bodies left to rot at the side of the road as a warning to others."

"I understand why you hold that view, Harry."

"How did the Court decide his case?"

"It never went to trial. There was a settlement involving a payment to the young woman."

"So Woo got off."

"From the legal system, yes, but not at home," Blair said. "His father laid down the law, get serious or face exile from the family. To his credit, Edward did cut back on his drinking. He got married, and took a job in the family business, managing Woo real estate properties. Then he won his father's backing to start his telecoms company."

"Have you met him?"

"Indeed I have, at social gatherings with Mei-Ling. She's very close with Cynthia Woo, Edward's younger sister. I've even met Woo Jian-Min, again through Mei-Ling. She calls him 'uncle.'"

"I read that Woo Jian-Min is a major shareholder in Hong Kong Wireless."

"He's more than just a shareholder. He's on the HKW Board of Directors."

"While his son is bidding to buy the company?"

"Doesn't seem to bother anyone here."

After we finished our evening snack, Blair said, "I'll get out of your hair so that you can get some rest. I'll pick you up outside the Furama at 8:45 A.M. sharp at the back entrance on Connaught Road. Watch for a black E300 Mercedes."

Back in my room, exhausted but not sleepy, I clicked through the English-language TV channels offered on the Furama Hotel TV. One station was playing an old BBC sitcom with dumpy characters, zinger catch-phrases and a manic laugh-track. The Furama's own TV channel highlighted the hotel's amenities in the lobby, cafeteria, exercise room, and business center. On another channel, a man in traditional peasant dress held up objects and pictures and spoke the words for each in Cantonese, Hong Kong's Chinese dialect. The pay movie channel offered soft porn and day-before-yesterday hit films. CNN and BBC were repeating their cycles of headline news stories, and a sports channel presented a nail-biter soccer match featuring Bolivia versus Guatemala.

I selected CNN to find out what had happened in the world during my day of travel. A CNN presenter based in Hong Kong, identified at the bottom of the screen as Janice Huang, caught my full attention when she mentioned Woo Jian-Min.

Woo Jian-Min's Beaver Hall Holdings had just announced that it would build a massive electronics recycling plant in Wuxi, a city on the Yangtze River about eighty miles west of Shanghai. She said that the plant would extract valuable metals from electronic waste such as discarded PCs, TV sets, and mobile phones, and then safely dispose of remaining toxic components. She reported that Woo Jian-Min had selected the site after personal consultations with the Secretary-General of Wuxi's Municipal People's Government. Janice Huang also reported that police in Wuxi arrested protesters who doubted official assurances that the toxic materials would be disposed of properly. The CNN video showed police

34

wading into a crowd, pummeling protestors with batons, including some who were on the ground with their arms held protectively over their heads.

Ms. Huang then segued to Edward Woo's bid to purchase Hong Kong Wireless. She reported that the HKW Board of Directors was advising shareholders not to tender their shares to Mr. Woo pending completion of evaluations by a special committee of the Board and by the Hong Kong government. She said that Edward Woo's company, TelePhase, had issued a statement that its bid had been under review by the HKW Board and by Government for several months, and there was no reason why it should not be approved without further delay, since it was in the best interests of everyone concerned.

Janice Huang's last story covered the appointment of a new prosecutor in Shanghai, a gangly woman with short straight hair, glasses, no make-up, and a severe expression. She was shown addressing an auditorium filled with attentive party members. According to the voice-over translation, the new prosecutor said, "Our Strike Hard campaign will find and punish officials who have violated the trust placed in them by the people."

The video showed cadres in the audience avidly following her remarks and then standing and applauding enthusiastically when she finished.

Four

MR. SHIH'S COMMUNICATIONS DEPARTMENT was housed in a grey-stone mansion nestled behind a high stone wall, just across Garden Road from the Peak Tram's base station terminus. It still looked as stately and as imposing as when it served as the official residence of Britain's colonial Governors before Hong Kong's transition to Chinese rule in 1997.

A guard at the gate checked Blair's Hong Kong identity card and my passport, and then stepped aside to allow us to drive onto the grounds.

Mr. Shih greeted us in the hall outside his office on the second floor. "Welcome, my good friends Blair and Harry," he said, warmly shaking hands with each of us. He spoke with an English accent in a voice that was surprisingly deep for someone of his slight stature.

Mr. Shih's office was appointed modestly as befitted an honest, hard-working, public servant. It was equipped with a faded red cloth sofa backed against the wall across from his window and, in front of the sofa, a low glass-topped table and well-worn leather easy chair. A plain wooden bookcase on one of the sidewalls was packed with reference books and technical reports. His desk, by the window, overflowed with piles of folders and loose papers. Mr. Shih outstretched his arm to guide us to the sofa while he took the easy chair.

Blair led off, "Mr. Shih, as you requested, our engagement letter was written in very general terms without any details. But when we talked yesterday, you said that you have more specific marching orders for us."

"I do," Mr. Shih replied. "I want you to undertake a task that is too sensitive to put in writing."

Here we go, I thought. Scope creep, the bane of fixed-budget consulting engagements! Possibly noticing my apprehensive expression, Mr. Shih added, "If this task requires more time than you anticipated, I will of course cover the additional cost."

Blair said, "Please tell us what you have in mind, Mr. Shih."

Before he replied, Mr. Shih got up to shut his office door which had been left slightly ajar. Then he said, "I've delayed issuing a decision on Edward Woo's proposal in the hope that he'd find cause to withdraw it. Unfortunately, Edward has persisted, and I have run out of time. I want you to find evidence that will justify rejecting his proposal, either outright or by requiring additional review by the Securities and Futures Commission."

37

"So you've already decided against his proposal," I said. "Why is that?"

"His proposal is not the issue. The issue is Edward Woo himself."

"What about him?"

"Let me start with some history. For example, did Blair tell you how Edward acquired his fiber optic cable to mainland China?"

"Actually I don't know that history," Blair said.

"The cable was built by two Australians in the 1990s with backing from a big telecoms equipment supplier. Businesses headquartered in Hong Kong used it to connect with their factories in China. About three years ago, Edward offered to buy it. The Australians turned him down. Then they began to suffer problems with their connections in China, such as service outages, and telecoms operators in China demanding much larger payments to complete their connections. Still the Australians held on, that is, until one of them disappeared. A hiker discovered his body in the Tai Po Kau forest in the New Territories. It was burned almost beyond recognition. Soon afterwards, the other Australian sold the fiber cable business to Edward and left Hong Kong. He declined to speak publicly about the transaction or even to respond to our private inquiries."

"Did the Hong Kong Police make any arrests?" Blair asked.

"No. And they haven't made public who their suspects are. But the result was that Edward Woo acquired the fiber cable, as he wanted. You can draw your own conclusions."

"I read an article in the *Asian Business Journal* that referred to an investment fund based in Shanghai, the New China Properties Fund, as Woo's business partner," I said.

"The Fund is a very secretive group," Mr. Shih said. "When we asked Edward Woo about it, he declined to respond to our questions. Instead he named the contact person there as a Mr. Xie Sien, but we have been unable to reach him. Edward's lawyers offered to pass our questions along to Mr. Xie. We submitted them as instructed and have received nothing in return."

"I'm confused," I said. "Why not just make it clear to Edward that his bid will not be approved unless he answers your questions?"

"That's not so easy, Harry. He has supporters in the government, as does the New China Properties Fund. To give you an example, when an inquiry concerning the Fund was initiated last year by the Independent Commission Against Corruption, the leader of the inquiry, a respected lawyer on the ICAC staff with many years of experience, was re-assigned. When she protested, she was fired. The inquiry was shelved."

He leaned forward in his chair. "The reason that I contacted Blair, and why you are here, is that I suspect that the New China Properties Fund is buying assets in Hong Kong in order to launder money for high-level officials in

China. If so, Edward's proposed purchase of Hong Kong Wireless would become the largest money laundering transaction ever in Hong Kong, and a major setback in our battle against corruption."

"So, the evidence you want us to find relates to money laundering."

"Yes."

"Hmm," I said.

"Also, you should know that triads may be involved with the Fund."

"By 'triads,' you mean organized crime? The thugs covered in tattoos?"

"Yes, Harry, triads both in mainland China and here in Hong Kong may have invested in the Fund and triad members may serve as its foot soldiers. This is difficult to prove, of course, since people are unwilling to step forward as witnesses."

Bribes? Embezzlement? Money laundering? Dead body found burned in the forest? Triads? Foot soldiers! Holy shit!

"Why have you picked us for this task, Mr. Shih? Why not let the police handle it?"

Blair had grown increasingly restless with each question that I raised, shifting in his chair, clearing his throat, and giving me hard looks. He was stirred now to comment out loud, "I'm sure Mr. Shih has his reasons, Harry."

Mr. Shih replied, "I have to assume that members of the government, including police officers, have taken money from the Fund, and possibly also from Edward. I don't know whom I can trust. However, I am confident that I can rely on you, my friends."

While I was pondering this, Mr. Shih added, "But, if you are unable to accept this assignment, please let me know now."

Blair replied quickly, "We do accept your assignment, Mr. Shih." He was looking at me rather than at Mr. Shih, awaiting my confirmation.

I had decide, *yea* or *nay*. The project for which I'd come to Hong Kong was not what we expected. Mr. Shih's task would be unlike anything we'd ever done. We weren't private detectives, or ex-military. We had no training, no tools, and no relevant experience to draw upon, in order to deal with what we might face.

On the other hand, while Blair shouldn't have responded to Mr. Shih's question so quickly and without checking first with me, he'd done so. I preferred not to embarrass him in front of our client. Declining the project would send me back to Cambridge empty-handed; Blair West International would collapse; and I would lose my house to the bank.

So, I chose what I thought would be the lesser of two evils. I accepted the project. "Mr. Shih, I agree with Blair. We'll take this on."

"Thank you," Mr. Shih said. "I know that you will not disappoint me."

I was glad of his confidence but I didn't have a clue how to find evidence of money laundering. "Do you have any suggestions where we should start?"

"Ask questions," Mr. Shih said. "Be obnoxious."

"That's Harry's strength," Blair murmured.

"Stir the cloudy water and see what rises to the top. Put Edward Woo and his Shanghai partner on the defensive. If we're lucky, they'll make a mistake."

Once we were outside the building, Blair turned to me, and said, "What the fuck!"

"What?"

"Your whinging almost cost us this case. When you kept asking Mr. Shih 'why us?' he started to wonder the same thing."

"I noticed your meaningful looks."

"I was trying to signal you to back off."

"Blair, we're management consultants."

"I'm aware of that."

"We read stuff, interview people, run financial models, write reports. What we don't do, typically, is ask questions that will annoy dangerous people, and that could cost them their freedom, even their lives. We have no idea what we're getting into."

"You're over-dramatizing, Harry. We just need to be careful, that's all."

"I don't carry a weapon. Do you?"

"No."

Martial arts training?"

"No."

"This could get us hurt."

"It's too late to have second thoughts."

Blair was right. We were committed. But to be brutally honest, I doubted my physical courage for what might come our way. *This could get us hurt.*

Blair parked his Mercedes in his reserved slot in an indoor garage on Harbour Road and we walked from there to the China Resources Building where Blair West International (Hong Kong) had its offices. It was a block away, a long block that felt even longer in the enveloping heat and humidity.

"You're making me sweat, Blair," I said. "Do we have a shower at the office?"

"Don't fight the heat, Harry. Just relax, and you won't even notice it."

The office space that Blair and Elizabeth Li had sub-leased (*sans* shower) was on the twelfth floor, ten floors down from their former RLW offices in the same building.

"It's a month-to-month deal," Blair said. "We'll camp there until we're taking in enough income to sign a lease on our own place." Blair led the way past a vacant receptionist desk and a row of empty cubicles towards a corner where Elizabeth sat at a desk in front of a pod of two offices.

Elizabeth stood to greet us. She was trim, in her fifties, with short dark hair. "Welcome back to Hong Kong, Harry," she said. "What do you think of our office space?"

"I like it."

"Elizabeth deserves all the credit," Blair said.

"Blair pays me in compliments," Elizabeth replied.

"Plus, don't forget the salary IOUs," Blair said.

"Both are almost as good as Hong Kong dollars."

Fortunately for us, Elizabeth could afford to work for IOUs and compliments. Her lawyer husband had become wealthy by accepting his fees in the form of equity shares in his clients' property developments. They had no trouble paying US$50,000 each for citizenship in the Dominican Republic so that they could escape Hong Kong if the PRC made life too uncomfortable. Given that they had no intention of actually living in the Dominican Republic, they also bought a beachfront condo in Vancouver, British Columbia, which they visited several times a year.

"We're starting to see real dollars now," Blair said. "Soon the money will flow."

"Of course it will," Elizabeth replied.

My temporary office was equipped with a desk and a small round table for meetings. The view from my window was partially blocked by other tall buildings, but I could see the harbor through the gaps.

When I turned on my laptop to check on email, I found a message from Bill Schmidt, which he'd also copied to Blair. "Heard you were in HK. Let's get together while you are here. I'll get Emily to join us as well."

Bill, an expat like Blair, in his case from Australia, had been hired by Blair for RLW's office in Singapore and then followed him to Hong Kong. Emily Wong was recruited by Blair to join RLW Hong Kong after her year-long internship in my group in Cambridge. A native of Hong Kong, she always exhibited the self-assurance of a person who seldom meets others smarter than she is.

Blair was pecking at his laptop keyboard when I knocked on his open door. "Did you see the email from Bill?"

"Yes, he and Emily are good about staying in touch."

"Do we have time to meet with them?"

"We're running tight right now. I'll set up a lunch for later in the week. Meanwhile, let's grab a bite before we go to see Edward Woo."

The cafeteria order line moved fast. Behind the counter, a woman dressed in a pink pantsuit tapped our lunch orders into a handheld terminal device. She asked for our first names and then transmitted our orders to the food preparers, other women who also were dressed in pink pantsuits. Our first names – Harry and Stephen – and numbers assigned to each of our orders were displayed on a large screen which resembled a timetable of Arrivals and

Departures that you'd typically see in a train station. Each customer's order was labeled as "In Preparation" or "Done." Our sandwich and beverage orders were ready for us within two minutes, as pledged on the cafeteria sign, "Two Minutes or Free!"

"Hong Kong hustle," Blair said, when one of the jumpsuit-clad women placed our sandwiches on the counter in front of us and rang a cowbell to celebrate that yet another order had been filled.

We brought our trays with our sandwiches and bottled fruit juices to a lobby table and ate quickly, fueling up Hong Kong style. After what seemed like just a few minutes, Blair had piled his plate, cup, cutlery and napkin on his tray for disposal, and looked at me, tapping his watch.

"Let's go, Harry," he said, as I collected the remainder of my lunch on my tray to be tossed on our way out. "It's bad form to keep Edward Woo waiting."

Five

TWO MONTHS AFTER a forty million (US) dollar renovation of the historic Hong Kong Flagstaff Hotel was celebrated in the Hong Kong press, Woo Jian-Min concluded that he would make more money renting office space rather than hotel rooms. So he demolished the hotel and built an office tower in its place.

All that remained of the hotel was its name, modified slightly to Flagstaff Tower, and the former centerpiece of its lobby, a ten-foot-high white marble ball balanced artfully on smaller marble stones and bathed in a continuous fountain spray, which was now the most noteworthy object in the atrium of the new building. "When someone says let's meet at the Flagstaff Ball, this is where they mean," Blair said, and indeed several men in business suits were standing next to it, checking their mobiles and trying not to look like they were waiting for someone.

We rode an Executive Express elevator to the fortieth floor where Edward Woo had his offices. On our arrival, his assistant, a woman wearing a stylish white jacket and light-weight skirt, showed us into his office, telling us that Mr. Woo would join us shortly. "I'm instructed to let our visitors know that Mr. Woo prefers not to shake hands and that they should not feel insulted. It's just his personal preference."

"We understand," Blair said.

We trekked across a lush Chinese oriental carpet to a thirty-foot wide, ten-foot high plate glass window. It was quite a view, encompassing Victoria Harbour below, and Kowloon across the harbor, and beyond Kowloon, looming in the haze, the first green hills of the New Territories that extended to the border with mainland China. The harbor put on its usual colorful show. Vessels of all types and sizes including ferries, freighters, tugs and barges, police cruisers and fishing boats, and an ornamental junk for tourists, plowed in all directions through the choppy water. On the Kowloon side of the harbor, lighters bearing freight to and from the dock at Yau Ma Tei swarmed around the big cargo ships resting at anchor. At the far outer edge of the cargo ship moorings, a massive grey US destroyer rose high above the water like a giant steel sculpture.

The heavy wood door opened silently and Edward Woo entered so quietly that I didn't realize that he had joined us until I saw his reflection in the window through which we were admiring the view. He had already reached his chair behind his desk when we turned to greet him.

Blair said, "Hello, Edward. Thank you for meeting with us on short notice."

Woo nodded, unsmiling, and Blair said, "This is my colleague, Harry West." He nodded again generally in my direction, avoiding eye-contact. Blair placed both of our Blair West International business cards on his desk. Woo glanced at them briefly.

"What would you like to know?" he asked.

Woo was in his early forties. He wore his dark straight hair slicked back in the style of a silent film movie star. His open-necked striped blue shirt and the large gold Rolex that hung loosely on his wrist established that he possessed high enough status to reject the stodgy uniform – dark suit and tie – worn by lesser Hong Kong businessmen. "Let's make it quick, Blair. I have another meeting coming up."

"We'll work within your schedule," Blair said.

"Work," Woo said. "That's a joke." Although one not funny enough to amuse him, judging by his dark expression.

"Sorry, Edward, I'm not following you."

Woo scowled. "Do you think I don't know that your client Shih Chai-Ming is plotting against me?"

"Sorry..."

"He refused to act on my proposal for months. Now that he's been instructed to make a decision, he's trying to block it."

"That's between you and Mr. Shih," Blair replied.

49

"Government doesn't need consultants to understand my proposal," Woo said. "I'm offering a fair price for Hong Kong Wireless; I'll provide good services for customers; and I'll make enough money to repay the debt and provide a reasonable return for me and my partners. It's not complicated."

"The HKW board doesn't seem enthusiastic about your bid," I said.

Ignoring my jibe, Woo asked Blair, "Are you going to help Shih to block my project?"

"We're doing our job, Edward."

"Sure you are," Woo said. "Just tell me what you want."

"Alright, Edward," I said. "We'd like to see the details of your proposal, your plans for Hong Kong Wireless, the financials, and so on."

"You'll get all that from my lead bank on the deal, Standard Portside. Anything else?"

Woo's phone rang and he picked up. "I told you not to disturb me," he barked. He listened for a moment and said, "Oh, alright, put him through," and to us, "I have to take this."

"Do you want us to leave?" Blair asked.

"No stay where you are. This won't take long."

Whatever Woo was saying during the call in his stream of rapid-fire Chinese, his angry tone betrayed that he was displeased. Several times, Woo inserted "fucking" and "fuck" to make his points, and it didn't sound like he was talking about making love. He hardly paused to take a breath, let alone to listen. After more loud Chinese words, another "fucking," and more loud Chinese words, he slammed the phone.

"Can't get good help these days," he said. He extracted a cigarette from a pack on his desk, waved the pack perfunctorily in our direction and when Blair and I shook our heads, he lit his cigarette with a gold-plated lighter. "Where were we?" he asked, after taking a deep drag. He sucked on it a couple more times and then jabbed it out in an ashtray. "Trying to quit," he said.

"You asked us if we wanted to know anything else," I said. "And the answer is yes, we do."

"What, then?"

"We need to know more about your financial partner for the deal, the New China Properties Fund."

"That's none of your business."

"We think it is our business," I replied.

Blair said, "We need to evaluate who your partners are, in addition to the details of your proposal."

"Why? I'm the controlling partner."

"Just the same," Blair said, "can you give us any more information about the Fund? We've been told that a Mr. Xie Sien is the contact there. If you give us his current contact information, we'll follow-up directly with him."

"I have already offered to pass along any questions."

Continuing to play *bad-consultant*, a role for which I am naturally well suited, I refused to be fobbed off.

"Edward, we need to communicate directly with the Fund."

"I have nothing to add on this topic."

"We'll get the information we need one way or another."

"No you won't. The New China Properties Fund is off-limits. As people in Hong Kong can tell you, you should listen to what I say."

Being told to back off causes my testosterone to kick in. I was preparing a defiant response, my tail feathers flaring, when Blair intervened in his role as *good-consultant*. "How do we obtain the Standard Portside analysis?" he asked.

"My assistant will set that up," Woo said. "Do you need anything else from me?"

Blair replied, "No, Edward, I think we are done for now."

"Fine," Woo said, and then he added, "I hope Mei-Ling is well."

"Yes, she is, thanks." Blair replied.

"Family ties from the old days," Woo said, looking towards me like he was sharing a friendly anecdote. "She and my sister were at school together."

"So I've heard." Seeing his eyes directly for the first time caused a shiver to run down my spine. Notwithstanding Woo's sudden bonhomie, his eyes looked as cold as a shark's.

Blair stood to leave, and I followed his example. Woo stayed seated behind his desk. "Anything I can do, just ask," he said.

"We will," I replied, as I pulled Woo's door shut behind us.

Outside Edward Woo's office, his assistant told us that she had scheduled our meeting with Standard Portside. "Tomorrow morning, 9 A.M., on the forty-eighth floor of the Standard Portside tower in Central. Elizabeth Li confirmed you are available then. The bank will email you copies of its financial model for your review this evening. Please ask for Mr. Rowland Bridges." She wrote the meeting time, place, and contact information on a sheet of white note paper which she handed to Blair.

"You're very efficient," I said.

"That's how Mr. Woo prefers it."

"It's always better to do what the boss prefers."

"Always," she agreed, glancing at his office door, which was closed.

Back at our office, my thoughts, wandering, settled on Erin Haig. Not only on her remarkable green eyes, nicely-proportioned figure, and appealing personality, but also on the fact that her *Asian Business Journal* was investigating Woo's proposal to buy HKW. We could learn something from Erin that would help us with our project for Mr. Shih.

I called her room at the Sheraton. Her phone went unanswered and I left a voicemail message, "This is Harry West. I'll have a break this evening. Perhaps we could meet. Look forward to seeing you. Let me know." I gave the Furama Hotel phone number and my room number. Then I emailed the same message to her using the e-mail address on her business card.

A few minutes later, my laptop pinged with an incoming email from ErinH@ABJ.com, "Hi Harry. I'll be back at the hotel later this afternoon. How about 6 P.M.? See you soon, Erin."

Blair was on the phone when I looked into his office so I sent him an email to let him know that I was heading back to the Furama, that I planned to connect later in Kowloon with Erin Haig, an *Asian Business Journal* writer whom I had met on my flight to Hong Kong, and that I would to try to learn what I could from her about the upcoming ABJ articles.

Six

THE NEXT STAR FERRY TO KOWLOON was waiting at the dock with its engines idling so I was able to board right away.

Crossing the harbor on the ferry's upper deck provided a refreshing break from Hong Kong's heat and bustle. Air flowed in through the window that I'd opened in front of my seat, and the water splashing and slapping under the bow provided a nice counterpoint to the steady thrum of the engine.

On Kowloon-side, I started down the Tsim Sha Tsui Promenade along the water's edge, and then cut through a theater complex abutting the Promenade to get to Salisbury Road.

The first of several hotels on this portion of Salisbury Road is the Peninsula, an imposing *grande dame* set back from the road behind a fountain and a circular drive. Dark green Rolls-Royces are stationed on the Peninsula's drive to cater to the needs of the superior class of guest who stays there, persons of high status attained through birth, marriage, expense account, or criminality.

Farther along Salisbury Road, across the intersection with Nathan Road, sits Erin's less-pretentious Sheraton Kowloon which, unlike the Peninsula, opens its doors directly onto the crowded sidewalks.

I called Erin's room from a black hotel phone in an alcove near the Sheraton's registration desk. After three rings, the phone was answered.

"Hello?" Her voice sounded muffled.

"Erin?"

"Yes."

"This is Harry."

"Who?"

"Harry West, from our flight over."

"Oh, right, Harry! Sorry, I'm still half asleep. Where are you?"

"In the Sheraton lobby. We'd arranged to meet about now. Is this a good time?"

"Yes, of course. Sorry."

"Do you want me to come by later?"

"No, no, it's OK, I need to get up. Can you give me a few minutes? I'll meet you down in the lobby."

Fifteen minutes later, Erin emerged from one of the lobby elevators. The way that she stood out from the others, dressed with basic elegance in a calf-length lightweight skirt and open-necked cotton shirt, carrying a fabric bag on her shoulder, she looked to me like she'd just stepped out of an American Express advertisement depicting an alluring woman surveying the scene in the lobby of her large international hotel. "Member since 2002… Are You A Cardmember?"

"Hi, Erin," I said.

"There you are, Harry. Hi. Sorry again for making you wait."

"No problem."

"I just lay down to close my eyes for a moment..."

"I understand. Jet lag takes a while to shake off."

"How're you doing?"

"Doing fine," I said. "I had my nap before coming over. Would you like a late afternoon tea, or coffee?"

"I'd love tea. I need something to help me wake up."

"How about at the Intercontinental?"

Commonly known as the Intercon, the Intercontinental Hotel, one of Hong Kong's landmark luxury hotels, is located just past the Sheraton on Salisbury Road, directly abutting the harbor with only the pedestrian Promenade between it and the water.

We walked up the Intercon's short driveway and across a small parking circle at the top that was graced by a large black Bentley limousine, the Intercon's rejoinder to the Peninsula's Rolls-Royces. A doorman bowed us into the lobby.

Inside the lobby the air was much cooler and it was quiet except for the murmur of conversations in the café on the far side of the lobby's shiny white marble floor. A restaurant hostess led us to a table next to the glass wall through which Hong Kong's busy harbor was presented like a huge live mural. Just outside the glass wall, a skateboarder rolled past on the Promenade while on the harbor's choppy water, boats large and small plowed purposefully at typical Hong Kong full throttle. Across the harbor, red, green, and white neon signs on harbor-facing buildings were already lit, advertising NEC, Canon, Bank of America, Sony, Cathay Pacific, Panasonic, and my own Furama hotel, while behind them rose Victoria Peak, now mostly in shadows with its higher levels shrouded by a light mist.

Erin watched as I poured from the Intercon's silver teapot. When I was done, she asked, "What have you been up to, Harry?"

"We got started on our project, a couple of meetings, beginning with our client this morning."

Erin took a small pastry from one of the porcelain plates on a silver rack in the center of our table. "These are tasty," she said, swallowing it in one bite.

"What about you?" I asked. "How are things going at the *Asian Business Journal*?"

"Well, we're definitely ruffling feathers."

White powdered sugar from the pastry dusted Erin's upper lip. I thought that she looked as delectable as the sweet she had just eaten. "Hold still," I said, as I reached over with a paper napkin to brush it off. "Just a bit of sugar."

Erin jerked back when the napkin touched her but then she relaxed, saying, "Thanks, I'll do the same for you sometime."

"You're welcome."

"So, tell me about your meetings. Who were they with? What did you find out?"

"A reporter at work!"

"I already know about your project. There's no point in being cagey."

"What do you know?"

"The government's Communications Department issued a press release announcing that it's hired the international consultancy, Blair West International, to assist in evaluating Edward Woo's bid to purchase Hong Kong Wireless. Am I getting warm?"

"You are indeed. So much for client confidentiality."

"So we do have interests in common," Erin said.

"Yes."

"And, like you said, you're not working for Edward Woo."

"Like I said."

"What have you learned about him?"

"We met him today. He didn't seem all that pleased to see us."

"He wouldn't be, would he? He has secrets to protect."

"How about you, Erin?" I asked. "What can you tell me about Edward Woo?"

"I'll tell you what I know when you tell me what you know," Erin said, with a bright smile, fluttering her eyelashes at me. "We could join forces."

"I don't see why not," I said. "We're both investigating the same business deal. I'll check with my partner and with our client. Will your managing editor agree?"

"He will. When I told him that we'd meet, he said I should suggest it."

By now there were only a few crumbs left on the small plates and we'd had as much tea as we wanted. "Let's take a walk by the water," I said.

There must have been something in the air that evening on the Promenade, perhaps the sweet smell of flowering shrubs and hedges, or the soft light given off by lampposts as the evening sun sank below the horizon, or the sound of the chop sloshing against the rocks along the Promenade wall, or the view of the neon-lit office towers on Hong Kong Island.

Whatever it was, couples stood pressed together side by side at the railing, gazing out at the harbor; they strolled with arms wrapped around each other's shoulders and waists; and they canoodled on benches, their foreheads touching, oblivious to everyone around them.

A gust from the water pressed Erin's shirt against her chest and her light dress flapped against her legs. Her face shone in the light from Promenade lamps. The light brought out the green in her eyes, and it caused her red hair to glint like spun copper. "What?" Erin asked.

"Enjoying the view."

"Are you flirting with me, Harry?"

"Absolutely not."

Putting her arm through mine as we walked along the Promenade, she said, "Talk to me."

"Sure, what about?"

"Tell me about yourself."

I told Erin about my time at RLW, about co-founding Blair West International, and about my marriage to Alexandra and how it all ended after our daughter Ariel was killed.

"Oh, Harry," Erin said, squeezing my arm.

"I think of Ariel a lot," I said, my throat suddenly constricted. "I know that Alexandra does too."

"Are you and Alexandra…"

"Except for the drunk driver's Parole Board hearing, we haven't really stayed in touch. The way everything fell apart… there are just too many bad memories for each of us."

We walked in silence for a while, and then I said, "Now it's your turn, Erin."

"My nickname was 'Irish' when I was in High School."

"People called you that?"

"Yes."

"Kids can be so cruel."

"Also, I'm lacking a 'significant other' at the moment."

"OK."

"Until recently I was living with someone in Brooklyn but that ended when he left to take a job in Chicago."

"So you came to Hong Kong, to get away from it all."

"You're mocking my pain."

"No, I'm listening and responding."

"Well, I did need a change. But also, when Robert Leung invited me to join our team in Hong Kong, he promised that I could write by-lined stories rather than just doing research in the background."

"Is he keeping his promise?"

"I'm helping now to write our next article in the series."

"What's Robert Leung like as an editor?"

"He's stubborn, but in a good way. He locks onto a story and won't let go. He'll follow it wherever it leads. He is not deterred by threats. In fact, they only make him more determined."

"What threats? Have you been threatened?"

"Robert gets threatening emails. We believe our office is being watched."

"Who do you think…"

"Edward Woo. He's made no secret that he doesn't appreciate anyone questioning his proposed deal."

"What are you doing about it?"

"Robert reports the threats to the police."

"Including that you suspect Edward Woo as the source?"

"Yes. But the police just say we should take precautions. So we do. Robert has set up security rules, about calling in frequently, things like that."

"Tell me more about the threats," I said.

"'We know where you are' and 'stop or die' are two that Robert showed us."

"They would get my attention."

"They're getting our attention too."

"Including Robert Leung's?"

"He says that the threats prove that our work will make a difference, and that they come with the territory of being a journalist."

In the gentle fragrance of the evening, with Erin holding my arm as we walked back to the Sheraton, I was reluctant to say good-bye just yet, but there was work to be done to prepare for our meeting next morning at Standard Portside.

"I'd propose that we find a place for dinner but I have to get back to my hotel," I said. "Duty calls, unfortunately."

"No problem," Erin said, looking neither disappointed, nor relieved, just responding factually. "I'm still beat. I'll just grab a snack and then crash for the night."

"We should talk some more about how we can work together," I said.

"Yes, definitely."

"Also, I enjoy your company."

"Likewise," Erin said. "When did you have in mind?"

"How about dinner tomorrow?

"Harry, you have a date!"

Through the Sheraton's glass door, I watched Erin walk across the hotel lobby until she disappeared around a corner. Then I returned to the Star Ferry terminal for my journey back to Central, to my room in the Furama, and to the Standard Portside's financial model that awaited my attention in my email box.

Seven

ROWLAND BRIDGES, SENIOR VICE PRESIDENT for Project Loans, greeted us just outside the door of the conference room when we arrived next morning for our meeting. Red-faced, with a big belly barely contained inside his white shirt, he looked like he'd had a rough night.

"Welcome to Standard Portside Bank," he said, adding, in a raspy whisper that smelled strongly of breath mint, "I have been asked by Mr. Woo to serve as your liaison."

When Blair whispered back that we looked forward to our meeting, Bridges responded, "good, good," and opened the door.

The grey-haired grey-suited banker inside was introduced to us as Ronald Sun, leader of the bank's project team for Edward Woo's proposed deal.

"Splendid," Bridges said. "Let's start. Before I turn the floor over to Ronald, let me say only that we will do what we can to help your evaluation for the Communications Department."

Ronald Sun removed his rimless glasses and placed them carefully before him on the table. "I believe that Blair West International already has received a copy of our financial model."

"We have," Blair said.

"And you have had an opportunity to review it?"

"Yes."

"Good. Then I'll just summarize our conclusions." Blair and I listened politely as Ronald Sun explained why the Standard Portside was comfortable providing debt financing for Edward Woo's deal. Then, to prove that we'd paid close attention, we asked a few pertinent questions about the assumptions used in the bank's calculations.

With those formalities accomplished, I embarked on the strategy laid out for us by Mr. Shih, to go forth and be obnoxious. "Rowland, what can you tell us about the New China Properties Fund?"

"You mean, the Fund that's providing equity financing for the HKW deal?"

"Yes."

"Nothing, I'm very sorry to say." Bridges replied, peering at me over his glasses. "We're involved only with the debt side."

"You don't care who owns Hong Kong Wireless in addition to Edward Woo?"

"Mr. Woo will control the company," Bridges said. "That's all that matters. And his credit is good."

"Does it matter to you that the Fund was the subject of an anticorruption inquiry here in Hong Kong?"

"That inquiry was terminated," Bridges said. "Nothing came of it."

"Do you know why it was terminated?"

"No."

"Not because of strings being pulled? Improper influence?"

"Not to my knowledge."

"Are you aware that the Fund is suspected of laundering money for corrupt officials in mainland China?"

"I've heard the rumors. I haven't seen any evidence."

"So you're just assuming that the Fund will not exploit the HKW deal to launder money for its investors."

"I told you, I know nothing about that."

"Rowland," I said, "it sounds like Standard Portside is willing to participate in a money laundering scheme."

"Why would that be the case?" Bridges demanded. His face was glistening now with sweat.

Blair said, "Because you're providing debt financing that enables the deal to take place while the major source of equity financing for that same deal is a suspected money launderer."

"None of that has been proven," Bridges said. "The New China Properties Fund has not even been formally accused. Mr. Woo is a reputable businessman and the Woo family is a valued client, and my bank has a long and honorable history in Hong Kong. I don't appreciate these accusations. You must not repeat such statements."

I asked, "What do you know about the Fund's investors?"

"That information has not been published."

"Why not?"

"You'll have to ask the Fund. But it's not so unusual. Even in the US, some limited partners in private equity funds are trusts that don't reveal their ownership."

"We've heard that government officials and police may have taken money from the Fund."

"Again, you are repeating slanderous rumors. You should take care what you say."

"So," I said, "to your knowledge, none of these rumors that we've repeated about the New China Properties Fund is true?"

"As I told you, I cannot comment on the New China Properties Fund. We are focused on providing debt financing. Standard Portside Bank is not involved with other aspects of the deal."

Blair was checking an email on his BlackBerry. He looked up, "Well, Rowland," he said, "we appreciate your time for this briefing. We'll get back to you and Mr. Sun if we have more questions."

Rowland Bridges rose quickly to his feet. He escorted us to the elevators, pushed the button for one heading down, and stood silently with us until it arrived and he was sure that we were on our way.

After Blair had handed his ticket to a valet to retrieve his Mercedes, I said, "I'm not sure what we achieved, apart from making Rowland Bridges uncomfortable."

"I know. I felt guilty about the way we were flaying the poor fellow."

"To give him his due, he did stand his ground," I said.

"Actually he didn't claim that our statements about the Fund are untrue, just that he was unaware of evidence to support them," Blair said. "Rowland will report back to Edward Woo about our meeting. We may yet learn something from the way that Edward reacts."

"Stir the cloudy water and see what rises."

"It's a good enough strategy until we've got a better one."

"You cut our meeting short right after checking your email. Anything interesting?"

"Mr. Shih wants me to call him. Says it's urgent."

On his call with our client, Blair provided a brief update about our meetings with Edward Woo and at Standard Portside, and then remained mostly in listening mode before concluding, "I understand, Mr. Shih. We'll do what we can."

Once we were on the road, Blair said, "The Singapore group which dropped out of the bidding for HKW is back again, this time with a higher bid. Edward Woo is screaming that Government's review of his proposal is causing unnecessary delay, that his deal would be agreed by now if Government – read Mr. Shih and his consultants – were not raising unnecessary questions."

"What does Mr. Shih want us to do?"

"Work faster."

"Work faster? We've only been at this for one day."

"He doesn't know how long he can hold out against Edward's partisans in Government. He wants us to find out quickly whether there is fire under the smoke. Otherwise give him an all-clear signal so that he can stand down gracefully."

"How does he want us to deal with the Singapore bid?"

"It's not within our remit, not yet anyway," Blair said. "However, there is one thing about the Singapore group that's raising eyebrows. It now includes Woo Jian-Min."

I pondered that new angle while Blair turned into the parking garage on Harbour Road. Were father and son conspiring to ensure that the Woo family would acquire HKW, one way or another? Or did the old man just see an opportunity to make more money and he didn't care how that affected Edward?

Blair was thinking along the same lines. "I doubt that Edward and his father are working together. Otherwise why would Edward react so vociferously?"

"It could be all part of the act."

"Edward says what he thinks without much filtering. Not much of an actor." Then, changing topics, Blair asked, "How was your date last night?"

"Erin offered to share information about Edward Woo if we and the *Asian Business Journal* agree to combine our efforts. I think we should. It would save each of us time."

"Good idea," Blair said. "I'll get back to Mr. Shih to get his agreement."

Back at the office, when I searched on the Internet for stories about the New China Properties Fund, I found an article about the aborted Independent Commission Against Corruption inquiry that Mr. Shih had mentioned to us. As reported in the *South China Morning Post*, ICAC was planning to investigate allegations of corruption in connection with an investment by the Fund in a shopping and entertainment center to be constructed on new landfill in Kowloon Bay near the former Kai Tak Airport. When asked why the inquiry was terminated, a spokeswoman for ICAC cited "other priorities" and declined to elaborate.

Concerning the more general topic of shadowy investments from mainland China, I found a story titled "Fueled by Secret Money" about the ongoing boom in Hong Kong real estate prices. The article described a newly-built dwelling perched high on Victoria Peak with stupendous views of Hong Kong and its harbor, shaded by trees, surrounded by a hanging garden, and protected on three sides by a high fence. According to a source described as a real estate professional well placed to know the facts, it was built soon after 1997 at a cost that exceeded thirty million (US) dollars. Its owner was believed to be a party leader from Beijing. "It has never been occupied," the source said. "The government in Hong Kong is trying to take it over in lieu of unpaid taxes. The party boss seems unwilling to be identified. Or, he may be under arrest, or dead. One thing is known: He is not enjoying his new house on Victoria Peak."

"Proof that crime doesn't always pay in Hong Kong," I said, pointing the article out to Blair, who had appeared at my office door.

"Sometimes it doesn't," Blair replied. "But there are other houses on the Peak that mysterious owners are occupying quite happily." Then he added, "About the *Asian Business Journal*, I checked with Mr. Shih and he would be glad for us to work together. He'll take anything he can get from us, the sooner the better."

"Excellent. I'll let Erin know."

"Also," Blair said, "Mei-Ling wants to see you while you're here in Hong Kong."

"That makes two of us," I said.

"She has arranged for us to have dinner this evening at one of her favorite restaurants. Are you available?"

I told Blair yes, of course.

Which was an understatement. When Blair called me to come to Hong Kong, my first unspoken thought after "I won't lose my house!" was that I would see Mei-Ling again. I was relieved that she'd taken the initiative. I'm not be the most sensitive person around but even I could foresee that asking to see Mei-Ling while I was in Hong Kong might be taken the wrong way by Blair.

"It's been a long time," Blair said.

"It has, indeed."

"Mei-Ling is looking forward to it."

"Me too," I said.

Recalling my date with Erin, I asked Blair, "How about I invite Erin to our dinner with Mei-Ling?"

"I'll let Mei-Ling know to expect her," Blair said.

My email inviting Erin was answered quickly. "Delighted," she wrote, "where is the restaurant?" According to Blair, it was in Central, only a few blocks from the Star Ferry terminal. I arranged to meet Erin at the terminal at 7:25 P.M. and we'd walk from there.

Eight

I KNEW MEI-LING first, before Blair, before RLW, before Alexandra, before everything.

We met in London at Mrs. Rees's, a hostel on Park Road across from Regent's Park that catered to young travelers. Mrs. Rees's has disappeared now, replaced by a row of upscale flats, but back then her place was a magnet for backpackers, students, and low-budget travelers, in short, for people like me, and like Mei-Ling before her family became as wealthy as it is now.

I'd been in London about a week and had returned to Mrs. Rees's following dinner at a nearby Indian restaurant, planning to read in the common room for a few hours. The common room was empty except for a woman curled with her legs underneath her in one of the stuffed easy chairs by a window. She was flipping through pages in a magazine. She looked Asian, possibly Chinese, or Vietnamese; in any case, she seemed to me an astoundingly beautiful creature. Her face was at the same time delicate and strong, her skin porcelain smooth, her body slender and supple. She was so beautiful that just looking at her, I fell helplessly under her spell, entranced, breathless, a goner, in proverbial love at first sight. Even while she was absorbed in what she was reading, she looked as imperious as a princess and, with her full lips tilted gently in amusement, as alluring as an emperor's concubine. She put aside her magazine, stretched sinuously, fixed me with her enthralling brown eyes, and smiled the brightest, most devilish smile I had ever seen. "Hello, bearded one," she purred, referring to my full curly beard which back then signified that I was be a student, or deep thinker, rather than, as might be assumed today, a crazed terrorist. "My name's Tung Mei-Ling, and who might you be?"

I could only croak, "My name's Harry West."

"Glad to make your acquaintance, Harry."

Mei-Ling said that she'd arrived that afternoon from Greece where she had stayed with friends on one of the Greek islands. "It's my first time in London," she added gaily. "I've come alone."

"I could show you around," I blurted, before I had a chance to think.

"Harry West, I accept your kind offer," Mei-Ling replied, with another enchanting smile. "You will be my guide."

In Mei-Ling's company, the usual things that everyone did in London became, for me, remarkable. Mei-Ling drew smiles from passersby while she walked beside me, as gorgeous as a flower, chatting, laughing, taking everything in. I doubt that anyone who saw us together would remember much about the young man whose arm Mei-Ling was holding, except that he was bearded, skinny, and appeared to be unreservedly happy.

We walked. We talked. We lay on our backs under the late September sun on the green grass of Regent's Park, rowed a small boat on the Hyde Park Serpentine pond, and watched the changing of the guard at Buckingham Palace. We kicked at pigeons in Trafalgar Square, frequented noisy, cheery pubs for fish & chips and lager, and wandered the aisles in Harrods. And, in the visitors' gallery of a court-room at the Old Bailey, we witnessed a judge wearing a floppy grey wig send a sad-eyed thief to prison.

What each of us had to say was appreciated by the other as insightful, amusing, or deeply felt, and therefore worthy of the most respectful consideration. We talked about books and movies, about Mrs. Rees, about places we'd seen or wanted to see, and about UC Berkeley where Mei-Ling had recently graduated with a BA in Fine Arts, and I with a BA in Economics and where, amazingly, it seemed to us now, our paths had never crossed.

About her past, Mei-Ling would say only that her family had escaped Shanghai for Hong Kong when she was still a baby. "It was a bad time," she said.

About her future, all I knew was that after her two weeks in London, Mei-Ling would re-join her fiancé in Germany and then they both would return to Hong Kong.

We walked hand-in-hand back to Mrs. Rees's hostel after our last dinner together. Mei-Ling's flight to Munich was scheduled for the following day. I had sunk into a melancholic mood. Soon she'd be gone out of my life, leaving me nothing to look forward to, a dismal prospect that I hated to contemplate. I didn't know how I could bear it. Mei-Ling also was quiet. Traffic on Park Road was light that evening and the loudest sound in my ears was that of our footsteps on the sidewalk.

There were two dorm rooms in Mrs. Rees's hostel, one each for men and for women, or boys and girls, which is what most of us still were at the time. The boys' dorm on the second floor had five double bunk beds. Each of us chose our beds based on first come, first served. On the third floor, the girl's dorm had the same capacity and layout. Also on each floor there was a shared bathroom. To produce hot water in the shower, we inserted sixpence coins into a meter on the wall, and we brought our own towels.

At the check-in of each new guest, Mrs. Rees recited her iron-clad rule: No boys in the girls' dorm room at night. She warned that violators would be expelled from the hostel. She posted this rule on a card beside the door to the girls' room just in case we hadn't heard her properly, "Note: Men Not Allowed in Women's Room After 8 P.M." Mrs. Rees was stout and matronly, called everyone "dear," and fussed over us at breakfast, but she left little room for doubt that she would enforce her rule without mercy.

Nevertheless, when we arrived at the hostel's front steps and paused for a moment before going in, Mei-Ling proposed that we lie together in her bunk bed on this, our last night. "Just to be close," she said. "No sex." She said the other girls in the room would be asleep and even if some were not and they saw us, they would keep quiet about it.

At 11 P.M., I took a late shower and then quietly pushed the door open to the girl's dorm room. Mei-Ling had told me that she was in the upper bunk just to the left of the door. The hall was lit only with small security lights but when I pushed the door open to the girls' room there was enough light to see dimly inside and to verify that Mei-Ling was indeed in the expected upper bunk, lying on her side facing the door, eyes open, and looking at me. She patted her bed, inviting me to come on up.

I lay on my back with Mei-Ling beside me, her head resting on my shoulder, and her arm across my chest. Her eyes were closed and she was breathing quietly. I, on the other hand, was not sleepy. I had taken measures during my shower to reduce the risk of embarrassment while lying close to Mei-Ling under our No Sex arrangement. These measures proved ineffective. I had a throbbing erection. When Mei-Ling brushed her elbow against it, the shock of her brief touch almost lifted me in the air. She appeared not to notice.

The other girls seemed to be asleep. Several snored quietly. Except, however, in the upper bunk two beds over from us where a blanket was moving up and down in sync with squeaks of the bed underneath. Mei-Ling whispered in my ear, "Don't worry. They do this every night. We just ignore them."

As if overtaken by a sudden storm, the blanket's undulations became more purposeful, intensifying to a crescendo of frenzied thrashing, muffled cries, and hoarse gasps, while the bed swayed and thumped.

"Jeezus!" I whispered to Mei-Ling.

"They're all done now."

"Makes you think…"

She patted gently on the stubborn rise in my portion of our own blanket that I thought she hadn't noticed and whispered, "Be a good boy."

"I'm trying."

Eventually Mei-Ling fell asleep, lying with her back to me. Because of the narrowness of her bunk bed, each of us leaned on the other, and I could feel her rhythmic breathing. We were as close and as intimate as we could be short of crossing the No Sex boundary line, for me even closer because of my nerve endings firing madly excited signals at every point that our bodies touched. From the first until the last hallowed moment that Mei-Ling and I shared her narrow bunk-bed in Mrs. Rees's hostel, I was intensely, precisely aware of her every movement, of the soft pressure of her body, of the smell of her hair, and of the rustling sound she made when she shifted her legs against the sheets. Finally, inevitably, it was time for me to go. As quietly as I could, I slid off Mei-Ling's bed, carefully stepping down the ladder to the floor. Then I padded in bare feet to my own bed in the boy's dorm room.

Each morning, Mrs. Rees and her daughter served breakfast in her large kitchen on the first floor. We hostel guests found places to sit at long shared tables in the kitchen where we partook of hearty English breakfast fare: bangers, rashers, two fried eggs, fried toast, and raspberry jam, with strong black tea.

Mei-Ling was already at the table when I arrived at breakfast. She greeted me with one of her wicked smiles. "How did you sleep last night?"

"It was hard but I did get a few hours," I said. Mei-Ling laughed. Mrs. Rees looked at us quizzically as she handed us our plates. She said to Mei-Ling, "You will be leaving us today, is that correct?" Mei-Ling confirmed that she would check out after breakfast. She thanked Mrs. Rees for her hospitality, and Mrs. Rees replied, "It's my pleasure, dear. You are most welcome to visit here again anytime."

We stood together silently in front of a poster for Madame Tussauds Wax Museum on Marylebone Road next to the entrance to the Baker Street Underground station, where

Mei-Ling would catch the Bakerloo Line to Piccadilly, and then transfer onto the Piccadilly Line to Heathrow Airport. Morning commuters, bound up in their own daily pursuits, brushed by us as we hugged, holding each other hard. Then for the first and only time, we kissed, a long kiss, and it left me light headed when finally we separated, and Mei-Ling whispered, "Good-bye, Harry."

This was before the Internet, before email, before hardly anyone had a mobile phone. I did not know Mei-Ling's address or phone number in Hong Kong, nor even her future married name, nor could I have told Mei-Ling where I would end up after I returned to the US. I expected that our parting at the Baker Street Underground station would be final.

I left London for a rented room in a beach-house near Torremolinos on the Spanish Costa Del Sol where I derived little joy from the sun and the heat and sat for hours on the beach staring morosely at the sea, thinking about Mei-Ling, recalling over and over again every moment of our time together in London, and mourning for what might have been. Gradually, however, scar tissue formed and my gloom dissipated, and life went on.

Fifteen years later, a little more than two years ago now, I was at my desk at RLW on a phone call with Blair, and we were discussing potential clients and other topics of mutual interest when he announced, "I am getting married."

Except that he was a bachelor with friends in many Southeast Asian cities, I was only vaguely aware of Blair's personal life. "That's terrific, Blair. But I didn't realize you were in a serious relationship."

"I have been for quite some time but I'm not sure that she knew, until recently."

"Why not?"

"She was married to someone else when we met. Just got divorced."

"Blair, you are a very mysterious fellow. I had no idea."

"We met when I was still based in Singapore. I was visiting Hong Kong to pitch a client. She was meeting the same client to discuss ideas for his new office space. He introduced us, saying she was the person whom people called when they wanted the best antique pieces. I said that I would soon open an office in Hong Kong for RLW and might need her help to furnish it."

"Very clever."

"It was true that I was opening our office here but I may have exaggerated a little."

"More than a little. RLW would never pay for antiques to furnish an office."

"I'm very ashamed but I needed an excuse to begin a conversation with her, and it worked. We became better acquainted over tea in the indoor garden of her private club. I was completely infatuated. I asked her to join me for dinner but she turned me down after reminding me that she was married. Fortunately for me, her marriage was troubled, and after I heard that she'd divorced her former husband, I contacted her again."

"A real love story, Blair. Congratulations."

"It's true," Blair said. "I have been in love with Mei-Ling from the first moment that I saw her."

Mei-Ling!

As calmly as I could manage, I asked Blair, "She would not be Tung Mei-Ling, would she, by any chance?"

"Do you know Mei-Ling?"

"If her name is Tung Mei-Ling and she is very beautiful, we met in London when we were back-packers just out of university. We met at a hostel near Regent's Park."

"She is indeed beautiful and her family name is Tung," Blair said. "I'll tell Mei-Ling that one Harry West is my colleague at RLW. See if she remembers you."

I was still at my desk ten minutes later when my phone rang.

"Hello, Harry," she said, "How are you? This is Mei-Ling, a voice from the past."

Hearing her then, with the handset pressed hard against my ear, and my eyes closed, transported me back to Mrs. Rees's common room where Mei-Ling sat with her legs curled underneath her, looking up at me from her magazine with her devilish smile. It took me a few seconds to catch my breath and when I was able to reply, my voice was hoarse.

"Mei-Ling, I'm in shock."

"So am I," Mei-Ling said. "I could never have imagined that because of Blair I would once again be talking with you."

"Blair told me your news. Congratulations!"

"Thank you."

"He is a good colleague and a good friend and a good person."

"Yes, I know, Harry. Blair says the same about you. Which of course I already knew."

Mei-Ling told me that after we said our goodbyes in London, she met her fiancé in Germany and, as planned, they returned to Hong Kong and were married, but that their marriage failed after she insisted on pursuing her own career.

I described my own history since my return to the US from London. We talked about my time with Alexandra, and about Ariel.

I told Mei-Ling about the RLW consulting projects on which Blair and I had collaborated in Malaysia and in Hong Kong.

"You were in Hong Kong?"

"I thought of trying to find you," I said, "but I assumed you would be listed under your married name, which I didn't know, and anyway I figured that your husband would not welcome my appearing on your doorstep. 'Hello, I slept with your wife in London, is she at home?'"

Mei-Ling replied, softly, "We only slept. We were so innocent."

By the end of our call, we were chatting like old friends. Mei-Ling called me several more times, each time after I had been in touch with Blair about one thing or another and evidently he had reported our conversation.

Although we had talked by phone, I had not seen Mei-Ling since we parted at the Baker Street Underground station in London. The dinner scheduled for this evening, to which I would bring Erin, would be the first time.

Nine

PASSENGERS WHO HAD JUST DISEMBARKED from the Star Ferry from Kowloon flowed by me as I worked my way upstream towards the terminal. I had almost reached Erin when she saw me and waved.

"You look terrific," I said, noting how nicely her lipstick and make-up highlighted her green eyes and red hair.

"Why thank you, Harry," Erin replied. "You're such a gentleman. For the future, just so you know, I do respond well to flattery."

The Hong Kong Garden restaurant was close by, as Blair had said. It took us five minutes to get there on foot. The restaurant was crowded and noisy, filled with the clamor of diners' voices, the clattering of dishes and cutlery, and the shouts of waiters checking on orders and warning others to stay clear as they pushed through swinging doors to and from the kitchen.

An aquarium extended for almost the full length of the wall from the entrance to a small podium at which the restaurant hostess was standing. I told her that we would be joining Mei-Ling Blair and her party. She replied that they were already seated and assigned a waiter to lead us to their table.

At a mid-size round table near the center of the room, Mei-Ling and Blair sat next to each other, both facing the restaurant entrance. Blair stood as we approached. Mei-Ling stayed seated. She was as beautiful as I remembered her, except that the enchanting girl I had known in London had become an elegant woman; the princess was now a queen. She took my hand in both of hers. I leaned down towards her and we exchanged air-kisses on each cheek. "Harry, it's been such a long time," she said. Then she touched my cheek with her hand. "No beard," she said.

"One of my sacrifices to become a consultant."

Seeing Mei-Ling again, and feeling her fingers on my cheek, however briefly, caused my mind to collapse into a jumble. After an uneasy pause during which I was too muddled to remember that it was up to me to introduce Erin, who, I noticed, when I glanced haplessly in her direction, was watching me closely, Mei-Ling took charge.

"And you must be Erin," Mei-Ling said, turning to my companion. "I'm Mei-Ling Blair." Erin confirmed that she was indeed, Erin, and they shook hands, and Mei-Ling gestured towards the fourth member of our group, who was still on his feet, "And this is Blair, my husband and Harry's partner in crime."

"Crime-solving, actually," Blair said.

Mei-Ling instructed Erin to sit beside her on her left, me to sit beside her on her right, and Blair to move to another chair opposite her, which he did obediently.

Finding my voice again, I told Erin that Mei-Ling was also a consultant, but that unlike us, her field was antiques.

"Everyone's a consultant," Mei-Ling said.

"Who do you consult for?" Erin asked.

"People who want furnishings for their homes or offices. I help them select pieces that work for them. And then I buy the pieces on their behalf and I manage the delivery of these pieces and their placement."

"Where do you find them, the pieces?"

"Mostly in China during my visits to Shanghai. There are many wonderful old treasures that people hid from the crazy Red Guards during the Great Insanity."

Blair said, "That's what Mei-Ling calls Chairman Mao's Great Leap Forward."

"It was a horrible time," Mei-Ling said. "Anyway, some of the pieces date back to the late Ming and early Qing periods and are made of Huanghuali hardwood, really precious."

Then, touching Erin's arm for emphasis, Mei-Ling said, "Now I want to know more about you and about what you are doing in Hong Kong, and about how you met Harry."

"We were seatmates on the flight over. Harry called me to have tea yesterday, and now here we are, on our first dinner date. Of course it helps that he's really hot."

Mei-Ling laughed, and said, "So we're both wild about Harry."

Blair snorted, "Crikey!" and spilled the beer that he was holding. "Sorry, don't know where that came from. Carry on."

This delightful conversation on the topic of Harry was interrupted by waiters who came to our table bearing trays on which were piled plates of dumplings, noodles, soups, sea-slugs, rice, whole fish intact with heads and blankly staring eyes, chicken slices, diced pigeon meat, lettuce leaves, and on and on. Once we were underway consuming the delicacies placed before us, Mei-Ling resumed her interrogation. "How did you come to work for the *Asian Business Journal*?" she asked Erin.

"I was doing freelance research for articles on Asian business trends. The articles were picked up over here, and three months ago the editor of ABJ offered me a job. I work in ABJ's New York office – basically me and one other person – to provide research on how Asian companies are doing in the US market."

"But now you're in Hong Kong."

"I'm here to help out with our upcoming series. Robert Leung, our managing editor in Hong Kong, assigned me to write as one of the by-lined journalists, which for me is a big step up. When we're done with the series, I'll return home to New York."

I felt Erin's shoe nudging mine. I assumed that this was unintentional and I didn't move my foot. She nudged again. I held my foot steady. And again. So this was what they meant by footsie! Now I nudged back. But Erin was cool and her expression, while she talked with Mei-Ling, didn't change.

"Blair told me your series will be about business practices in Hong Kong."

"Well," Erin said, nudging my foot again, "We're trying to expose hidden connections between businessmen and government officials."

"There are always hidden connections," Mei-Ling said. "In China they are called *guanxi*. That's how business is done."

"We want to expose the kind of *guanxi* that involves corruption."

Blair asked, "Erin, do you have any questions for us?"

"I do have a question for Mei-Ling," Erin said.

"Please ask," Mei-Ling said. "It's only fair. I've asked you a few."

"Is it true that you are close to the Woo family?"

Blair looked at me sharply and I shook my head. I wasn't Erin's source about Mei-Ling and the Woos.

"That's true," Mei-Ling replied. "Cynthia Woo is one of my dearest friends."

"And Edward Woo?"

"Of course I also know Edward, although I wouldn't call him a friend."

"What are they like?"

"I love Cynthia," Mei-Ling said. "She is a real sweetheart. Not at all like Edward who was badly spoiled as a child. The only-son syndrome. To put it kindly, he was troubled. A few years ago, though, he did seem finally to grow up, got married and got more involved in the family business."

"What about his father Woo Jian-Min?"

"I think of him as a kindly old uncle."

"Unless you get in his way," Blair said. "Then you best be careful."

"That's applies to most people," Mei-Ling said, looking across our table at Blair. "Even me."

"What about the Woos' Shanghai connection?" Erin asked. "Is it true that they have family in Shanghai who act as local partners for their projects in China?"

"That's true."

"Don't you also still have family members in Shanghai?"

"I do," Mei-Ling said. "Why do you ask?"

"When I checked ABJ's database on Hong Kong business groups with connections in mainland China, I found that the Tung family has businesses both in Hong Kong and Shanghai."

Blair intervened, "Hold on, Erin. If the ABJ is targeting Mei-Ling's family for your articles, we'll need to stop talking now and just enjoy the rest of our dinner."

"We are not writing about Mei-Ling's family," Erin replied. "We're focusing mainly on business groups like

PETER DAVID SHAPIRO

the Woos whose projects require government approvals, because that's where corruption starts."

Mei-Ling said, "The Tungs in Shanghai have partnered with property developers in Pudong but they are mostly merchants, like me buying antiques for interior decorating."

"One of my colleagues, Eugene Suh, told me that he's a distant cousin of yours."

"I don't recognize his name," Mei-Ling said. "I have many distant cousins. The Tungs were well-known for having big families prior to the One-Child policy in China."

"We're trying to learn as much as we can about Edward Woo's financial backer in Shanghai, the New China Properties Fund," Erin said.

"As are we," I said.

"People in Shanghai are well aware of the Fund," Mei-Ling said, lowering her voice, forcing the three of us to move in towards her like a band of conspirators.

"It was set-up for people who have come out on top in the new China, the party cadres, high public officials, military officers, as well as wealthy businessmen."

"How do you get to be an investor?" I asked.

"You need to be invited."

"Like the Mafia," I said.

Erin flashed me a quick smile to reward my attempt at wit. She had kicked off one of her shoes and her foot had progressed to massaging my ankle and calf.

Mei-Ling said, "The Fund is not talked about openly because of the high positions of its investors. In China, bribes are paid upwards, all the way to the top. Graft is tolerated as long as it does not become too blatant, so there are strong incentives at every level to keep things quiet. The Fund provides a good solution for public officials who'd prefer not to be found with large, unexplained sums of money."

It was amazing to hear Mei-Ling talk with such authority about politics, and corruption, and in general about how things worked in China, as compared to the last time I saw her in London when neither of us knew very much to back up our strongly felt opinions. Much had happened to both of us since then. We were different people. Even so, looking at Mei-Ling sitting beside me, I could still see the girl I had once known.

I asked, "What do you think would happen if the Fund's investors were exposed?"

"It depends. If they were exposed in a very public way that could not be easily dismissed, heads would roll, not only in China but here also in Hong Kong if government officials were implicated."

"They might roll metaphorically in Hong Kong but some would roll literally in China," Blair said.

"That's true," Mei-Ling said. "Selected officials and party leaders are executed during anti-corruption campaigns in China to serve as examples. Also their removal conveniently provides openings for others to rise in the hierarchy."

Erin said, "Hearing this from you is incredibly valuable, Mei-Ling. You're validating what we've learned from our sources in Shanghai."

"You have your own sources there?"

"We do. In fact one of our sources has given us a list of names of people who he says are investors in the New China Properties Fund."

Mei-Ling became very still, as if Erin had just laid a loaded revolver on the table. She asked, "How did he obtain such a list?"

"I don't know. Our source must have access."

"He must be very brave. To take a document like that, it's like committing suicide if he's caught."

"Robert Leung says that our sources in Shanghai are risking their lives."

"It's dangerous for you too."

Erin said, "We know that we are stirring up trouble, so we're trying to be careful…"

Mei-Ling cut her off. "Erin, are these articles for the ABJ really worth the risk to you and to your colleagues? These people in Shanghai, they will do anything to stop their names from being published."

"Robert Leung believes that it is our duty as journalists to report what we find out. If we censor ourselves, corruption just gets worse."

"Corruption in China won't go away because of articles in your *Asian Business Journal*."

"But what about in Hong Kong?" Erin asked. "Doesn't money from the mainland spread corruption here?"

"Yes, and you'll find corruption in your own New York City, and in Harry's Massachusetts, and even in Blair's blessed UK. Listen to me, Erin, I can't tell you or your editor what to do. But so what if publishing your articles means some people get punished in China and in Hong Kong? Others will take their place. Meanwhile your editor, by pushing for these stories, is putting you and your colleagues in serious danger."

"I have to trust Robert Leung," Erin said. Then she added, "I'm sure we will be fine."

Mei-Ling wrote on a scrap of paper which she folded and put in Erin's hand, closing Erin's fingers around it. "Here's my mobile number. If you get in over your head, if you feel threatened personally, call me. Don't wait until it is too late. Call me anytime. I can help. I know a lot of people."

"Thank you, Mei-Ling. I appreciate the offer," Erin said, putting the paper in her purse.

After a waiter placed a mango sorbet in front of each of us for our dessert refreshment, a stout man, his cheeks shiny and clean-shaven, his suit and shirt protected by a capacious white apron, approached our table and was introduced by Mei-Ling, "This is my cousin, Martin Li. He owns this restaurant and has been our wonderful host for the evening."

Martin Li beamed at Mei-Ling and said he hoped everyone had enjoyed their meal, and that we would return soon to his restaurant. Blair and I stood to greet him and to shake his hand. Each of us murmured thanks and assurances that we would certainly return.

A waiter brought a bill. Blair scanned it quickly and then handed it back to a waiter with a gold AmEx card.

"Thank you, Blair," Erin said.

"Don't thank me," Blair said. "Thank Mei-Ling. That was her credit card. I only pretend to pay in order to keep up appearances. Mei-Ling says that it enhances my sense of masculinity."

"It is my pleasure," Mei-Ling said.

When we were outside the restaurant, Blair asked whether Erin or I would like a lift anywhere.

I glanced at Erin, who shook her head, and then I answered, no, thanks, we could get where we needed to go on foot.

Mei-Ling and I once again exchanged air kisses, although not totally in the air, as I could feel her lips and warm breath on my cheeks. She said, very quietly in my ear, "I'm glad to see you again." Then she held Erin's hand in both of hers, "Take care," she said.

After Blair and Mei-Ling left to retrieve their car, Erin took my arm for our walk back to the ferry terminal. "Mei-Ling likes you a lot," she said.

"We met when we were both students. This evening was the first time that we've seen each other since then, although we've been in touch a few times by phone."

"She's very beautiful," Erin said.

"Indeed, she is," I said. Suddenly feeling a rush of confused loneliness, I added, "I was wondering if you'd like to continue this evening with me at the Furama. Or at the Sheraton. Either one."

We kept walking. Rather than replying, Erin grasped my arm a bit tighter. "Did you enjoy our game of footsie?" she asked.

"At first I thought you were just trying to stretch. Then I got confused when I felt your foot massaging my leg."

"Yes, wasn't that fun?"

"Yes, it was, and also strangely stimulating."

"I'd love to prolong our evening at one of our hotels," Erin said, "but I have this notion that we'd lose track of time, and I have homework to do."

"Doesn't hurt to ask," I said.

We had reached the Star Ferry pier and I was about the pay to go through the turnstile, when Erin stopped me. "You don't need to escort me over to Kowloon, Harry, but thanks anyway. Perhaps I'll see you tomorrow."

Ten

NEXT MORNING, when I checked email before leaving the Furama for our office, I found one from Erin, "Enjoyed our dinner. Please thank Mei-Ling for me. See attached documents relevant to our dinner discussion. Let's talk later."

One of Erin's attachments, an internal TelePhase memorandum marked "Proprietary and Confidential," indicated that the New China Properties Fund had provided financing for Edward Woo's purchase of his fiber optic cable to the mainland.

Another was a report in the *Hong Kong Standard* about the legal troubles of several officials who formerly were responsible for licensing new factories in Guangdong province. Two of them confessed to accepting bribes and were sentenced to death. A third who protested that she was innocent was nevertheless found guilty and also sentenced to death. Appeals for all three were pending.

I was just about to leave my hotel room when my phone rang. "Glad I caught you," Blair said. "Heard early this morning from Edward Woo's assistant. Edward wants to meet in his club which is right next door to the Furama. Wait for me in the hotel lobby and we'll walk over."

Although the Hong Kong Club occupies the top floor of the Ritz Carlton Hotel, it has its own separate entrance, guarded by two formidable bronze lions, one on each side of the steps that lead up to its heavy brass-trimmed double doors.

A doorkeeper who was stationed inside took my passport and Blair's Hong Kong identity card, promising that we'd get them back when we left. He guided us towards an elevator that would take us directly to the Club Restaurant where he said Mr. Woo was waiting for us.

The Club Restaurant was outfitted like a Victorian-era London men's club, dark wood paneling, dark brown leather chairs and benches, grey tinted windows, yellowing glass ceiling fixtures, and floor lamps at the corners of the room.

Edward Woo sat alone in a booth, nursing a Scotch. He motioned us over.

"Take a seat," he said. "Let me get you a Scotch. I keep my brand here at the Club in the glass cabinet by the entrance."

"What is your brand?" Blair asked.

"Chivas Regal 25 Year Old Original."

"I usually don't drink just after breakfast," Blair said, "but I won't pass up your Chivas."

"And you, Harry?"

"Tea for me, thanks."

Woo raised his hand slightly. A waiter appeared by our table and Woo told him what we wanted.

That done, he said, "Tell me what you concluded from your meeting with my bankers."

"Their analysis looks reasonable," I said.

"Alright."

"Although their financial model assumes your original purchase price for HKW."

"So what?"

"There's a new higher bid from the Singapore group."

Woo asked, "Have you seen the Singapore proposal?"

"Not yet."

"I've seen it and I am not impressed," he said. "Unlike the Singapore group, I offer a vision for Hong Kong Wireless based on local Hong Kong knowledge."

"Your father Woo Jian-Min joined that group," I said. "Wouldn't he provide local knowledge?"

"Sometimes his name is used by underlings without his approval. My father is an old man."

"Are you saying that Woo Jian-Min doesn't know?"

"I don't speak for my father. You need to ask him."

"So you don't plan to change your bid."

"I am reviewing the situation." Woo sipped his Chivas, draining the golden liquid from the ice cubes in his heavy crystal glass. Then he beckoned a waiter to bring his personal selection of Cuban cigars.

A waiter wearing white gloves approached our table carrying a shiny cherry-colored wood-grained humidor. He opened it, and Woo selected a large, long cigar. "Want one?" he asked Blair. Blair declined. Woo turned to me, "How about you?" I also said no thanks, adding that I could get all the cigar smoke that I wanted from the other smokers in the room.

I wondered how many decades had passed since the Club Restaurant had opened its windows. Men at several other tables and booths were pumping plumes of cigar smoke into its still air, pervading the room with a damp, pungent smell.

"You're too pure, Harry. You don't like Scotch, and you don't like cigar smoke."

"I'm not so pure, Edward. It's just a matter of taste."

Woo rolled his cigar between his fingers, testing it, appreciating its feel, and then snapped off its tip with a tiny silver guillotine that the waiter had left on the table. It was after he lit the cigar that his mood changed, as if he was ready now to dispense with his veneer of sociability. In a menacing tone that reminded me of movie gangsters toying with their terrified underlings, he asked, "Do you know why I invited you here?"

"Please tell us, Edward," Blair replied, calmly.

"Because you need to hear from me directly that you embarrassed me with my banker, and you impugned my integrity, with your accusations about the New China Properties Fund."

"We're very sorry if we embarrassed you," Blair said. "But as we've told you, our mandate from Mr. Shih does include reviewing your financing for the HKW bid."

"Then fuck your mandate! Fuck Shih Chai-Ming! No more reckless talk about the Fund or about me. Do you understand?" When neither of us responded, he repeated, more loudly this time, "Do - You - Understand?"

"We understand what you are saying," Blair said, "but we will do what we have been hired to do."

"Were you also hired to conspire with the *Asian Business Journal* to libel me and my family?"

I jumped in. "Mr. Shih agreed that we should collaborate with the journal so that we can provide our opinion more quickly, which is also something that you've asked for."

"In that case, your opinion will be worth shit."

"You seem anxious about the ABJ," I said. "Why is that, Edward?"

"No more fucking questions!" he said, still louder, and slammed his hand on the table.

When I started to respond, he raised his palm as if to block my words, like a school crossing guard stopping oncoming traffic.

"See my hand?"

"I do see your hand, Edward."

"It means stop talking. Just listen."

The chatter at other tables had quieted in order to hear what the fuss was about and Woo obliged them. "My investors in the Fund have shown great patience with the government's delay in approving my proposal. Until now they have tolerated libelous insinuations. But now their tolerance has reached its limit. I'm telling you this for your own good, because Mei-Ling is my sister's friend and because of the long history between our families, you must stop your provocations and you must stay clear of the *Asian Business Journal*. Otherwise, you'll be responsible for what happens."

"Are you threatening us, Edward?"

"That is my message to you," Woo said. "If you don't listen, it will be on your head."

Woo's silver Blackberry that he'd placed on the table beside his Chivas started vibrating and he picked it up to take the call. "Yes?" he said. After a moment of listening, he said, "Wait a minute." With his Blackberry held to his ear with his left hand, Woo dismissed us with a small wave of his other hand that was also holding his cigar. Its smoke rose gently to join the room's permeating murk.

Once we were back outside where the air was more breathable, I said to Blair, "We got our reaction from Edward Woo. What did we learn from it?"

"His deal may be in peril," Blair said. "The Fund may be pressuring him to make it happen before the spotlight gets too intense."

"Or he's honestly warning us about the investors in the Fund, about what they might do."

"Could be," Blair said. "In any case, we're not going to stop now."

"Did you hear anything that gets us any closer to finding evidence of money laundering?"

"Not from Edward. But at dinner last night, that list that Erin mentioned of investors in the Fund, that could be something. We should get a copy."

"I'll ask Erin for it."

"Edward is angry and he's frustrated," Blair said. "A bad combination. Let's hope that Erin and her colleagues are ready for whatever he sends their way."

"This morning I received from Erin a copy of an internal TelePhase memo which reveals that Edward has an earlier connection with the Fund. It turns out that the Fund helped to finance his purchase of the fiber optic cable to the mainland."

"From the two Australians."

"From the surviving Australian," I said. "The other one was unavailable to participate in the transaction."

"I wonder whether the Fund's 'foot soldiers' had something to do with that," Blair said.

"We're in this up to our armpits, Blair. We need to finish it."

"I'm with you on that, my friend," Blair said. "Mei-Ling wants to help. She's enlisted one of her contacts in Shanghai to follow-up on our leads concerning the Fund. She figures that the sooner we complete our work for Mr. Shih, the less likely we are to run into trouble."

When we arrived at the office, Elizabeth told me that Erin had called. "She wants you to call her back right away."

Erin answered quickly.

"Harry?"

"Yes, what's happened?"

"Things here at the office have gotten ragged. Can you come here?"

Blair saw me pass by his door and asked, "What's going on?"

"Erin said something has happened at the ABJ office. I'm on my way there."

The open outdoor plaza in front of the China Resources Building was shimmering under an intense mid-afternoon sun and by the time I'd crossed it, my face and neck were slick with sweat, my shirt was damp, and my energy was sapped.

Nevertheless, the ABJ's office was only seven blocks away so I decided to keep walking. It was located in the Federal Building on Lockhart Road not far from the intersection with Marsh Road, in a part of Wan Chai that features an eclectic mix of new and old office blocks, densely packed apartment buildings, shops, bars, and restaurants.

Shadows cast by the buildings on Lockhart Road provided some shelter from the sun, but the air was hot and heavy, stirred like steaming soup by the cars, taxis, and buses that rumbled trunk-to-tail in the crush of daily afternoon traffic.

Although usually a brisk walker, I was trudging by the time I arrived at the Federal Building. It was roughly thirty-stories high, designed for basic function rather than style, with room air-conditioners protruding from windows all the way to the top floor. An "Office To Let" sign was posted at the entrance.

Inside the lobby, which felt a little cooler than outside, a directory beside the elevators showed that the *Asian Business Journal* was on 5/F, in Room 504.

Office doors along the hallway on the 5th Floor were painted with names and business functions in Chinese and in English, "Expositions Planning," "Shipping," "Manufacturer's Representative," and "Budget Finance." The door marked *Asian Business Journal* was locked and no receptionist was on duty to buzz me in. I knocked on the door and waited. I knocked again. Inside, a woman who was walking by looked over to the door. I waved to her.

"Can I help you?" she asked, opening the door just enough so that we could talk.

"I'm looking for Erin Haig."

"Oh, sorry, are you Harry?"

"Yes, Harry West."

"I'm Cathy Chao. Erin told us to expect you. Come in." Cathy opened the door further to let me get by her and then locked it behind me. "We had a break-in last night."

She gestured vaguely towards contents of file cabinets dumped onto the floor. "They left quite a mess."

"So I see."

"The police came and took notes but said they had little to go on."

"Did you lose anything important?"

"Luckily, no. We back up everything on jump-drives and also email our back-up files every day to our Taiwan office."

"Erin didn't mention a break-in."

"We have to be careful about what we say on the phone."

Cathy led me across the office to Erin who was standing, talking with two men.

"Welcome to ABJ's office in Hong Kong," Erin said, taking my arm. "Harry, let me introduce you to Robert Leung, our Hong Kong Managing Editor." Robert Leung and I shook hands. He was middle-aged, wore round glasses, and had shoulder-length straight black hair laced with grey. "And this is Eugene Suh, one of our local reporters." Eugene Suh looked younger, in his early thirties.

"Erin told us that you are related to Tung Mei-Ling," I said.

"We are distant cousins," Eugene replied. "We travel in different circles."

"And you've already met Cathy," Erin said.

"Very glad to be formally introduced," I said.

"How do you do?" Cathy replied, smiling, as we shook hands.

Still holding onto my arm, Erin told her colleagues, "Harry and I shared the flight over from San Francisco. Harry is co-founder and principal at Blair West International which, as we know, is working on a project for the government concerning Edward Woo's proposal to buy HKW."

Robert Leung said, "As you can see, some people don't like what we're doing."

"You mean the break-in?"

"Not just the break-in. Did Cathy show you our picture gallery?"

"I left that for you, Robert," Cathy said.

Leung led us to a wall on which head-shot photographs were tacked of himself, Erin, Cathy Chao and Eugene Suh. A large red X had been slashed over each picture using a Magic Marker. Chinese characters had been written on the wall under the pictures. Leung translated, "Final Warning."

"Spooky," Cathy said.

A white cotton string was hanging loosely from the pin that attached Leung's photo to the wall. The bottom of the string looked like it had been cut.

"What's the significance of the string?" I asked,

"It was holding a box-cutter blade," Leung said. "Police took it for analysis."

"It's a triad warning," Eugene said. He added, in a gloomy voice, "They're telling us what will happen next if we don't do what they want."

"We don't know that for sure, Eugene," Leung said. "They're just trying to scare us."

"Well, it worked for me," Eugene replied.

"We won't let them stop us," Leung said.

"What do you think about all this?" I asked, looking generally at Leung's three colleagues but primarily at Erin. She said, "We're not quitting."

Leung said that he'd offered ABJ staff members an opportunity to take a leave from work until after the articles were published. No-one had accepted.

"Last year our Taiwan editor was jailed for six months after he refused to withdraw a story about a corrupt politician," Leung said. "This is what we do."

"Where is he now?"

"You're looking at him," he said. "Shit happens."

"Edward Woo knows that we're working together," I said.

"That's to be expected. You should assume that we have no secrets from him, not in Hong Kong."

"He demanded that we stay clear of you. He was quite emphatic."

"What did you tell him?"

"We're not backing off either," I said, proving that consultants, like journalists, can wear a badge of courage.

"Good."

"Last night, Erin told us that you have received a list of names of investors in the New China Properties Fund."

"That's right. We're trying to check the list now, to learn more about these names."

"What have you found out?"

"The list does appear to be authentic. It has a header showing the name New China Properties Fund and describing the file as an investor worksheet. The problem is that it's just a list of names; it tells us nothing about who they are. We're working on it."

"Robert, can you share your list with us? We have a contact in Shanghai who could do research on these names."

"No doubt it would help you with your consulting engagement."

"It would," I agreed. "It could provide the evidence that Mr. Shih needs."

"Unfortunately your Mr. Shih will be overruled by Woo's allies in the government."

"Yes, but not so easily once your articles are published," I said. "We're on the same side, Robert."

"Promise me that that you'll put this information to good use no matter what happens to us."

"We will."

"Even if Edward Woo manages to shut us down."

"Yes."

Leung instructed Eugene to copy the file onto a flash drive that he'd give to me before I left the ABJ office.

"Well, I'm glad that's settled," Erin said. "I've got some more work to do here, Harry. Can you wait for me for a half-hour or so?" I took a chair at a desk by a window. The late afternoon sun found its way into the ABJ office and Leung lowered the Venetian blinds to block the direct sunlight, which he said would make the room too bright and too hot, even with the window air conditioner cranked as high as it would go.

Cathy joined us, holding a sheet of paper. "We just received a fax."

"What's it about?" Leung asked.

"Our man in Shanghai – you know who I mean – says he wants to talk with us about his list."

"Can you get him on the phone?"

"Erin is talking to him now." And then to me, Cathy said, "He speaks English."

Erin got up from her desk and came over. "He says he is in Hong Kong. He says he wants to talk with us in person, but only with me."

"Why only with you?" I asked.

"I think he feels more comfortable talking with a *gweilo*," Cathy said. "No offense, Harry."

"None taken."

Erin said, "I don't know why. That's what he said."

"Are you comfortable with that?" Leung asked.

"Yes, I'm here to be a reporter, Robert. I want to do the job."

"Good. Then go ahead with it."

"He says that he'll meet me at the Grand Hyatt lobby in about a half-hour. I gave him my cell number in case we need to coordinate."

"I'll walk with you to the Hyatt," I said. "It's close to the Blair West International office."

Eugene handed me a flash drive. "Here it is," he said. "Be careful."

"Thanks," I said, putting the device into my pocket.

Erin and I re-traced the route I had taken earlier to get to the Federal Building, but it was much cooler now that the streets were entirely in shadow, the sun having sunk too low to clear the office buildings and apartment blocks. As we approached the China Resources Building, Erin said she would prefer that I wait at my office while she proceeded to her rendezvous at the Hyatt. I could join her at the Hyatt later, in an hour or so. If her meeting was still underway, I could make eye contact with her to let her know that I'd arrived. If her meeting ended earlier, she would call me at the office.

"Will you be OK?" I asked.

"I will."

"What do your security procedures say about going alone into meetings with strangers?"

"We're not supposed to, but we can make exceptions. He's our source, and he's risked his life to help us," Erin said. "He wants me to come alone."

"I'd prefer to stay with you. I can wait for you at the Hyatt. I can hide discreetly behind one of the columns in the lobby until you've finished your meeting."

"My gallant protector!"

"Well, if you are attacked, I'll distract the bad guys by screaming loudly while I run away."

Erin laughed and said, "I'm a pretty fast runner myself. I'll be alright, Harry."

Eleven

ELIZABETH AND BLAIR had left by the time I got up to our office, so I used the code that Elizabeth had given me for the push-button combination lock on the door.

When I inserted the ABJ's flash drive in my PC and opened the file purported to be the list of investors in the New China Properties Fund, I saw only rows of Chinese characters so I had no idea what the file actually contained. I copied it onto my PC's hard-drive and emailed it to Blair, as well as to myself for additional back-up, and then dropped the flash drive into a porcelain jar on Blair's desk where it sank out of sight amidst his pencils and ballpoint pens.

In my email to Blair, I wrote, "The attached file appears to provide the list that we discussed. Can you ask Mei-Ling to share this with her resource in Shanghai, so that he can find more information about these names, if they are names?"

I also sent a project update to Jerry, letting him know that we had obtained useful information for our client and that our report would be written and submitted during the next few days since our client was anxious to receive whatever we could tell him. I read current news articles on Yahoo. Then, I noticed that almost an hour had passed. It was time to check on Erin at the Hyatt.

The Grand Hyatt lobby featured gleaming black marble pillars, a wide staircase to the mezzanine level, and a high white ceiling dome laced by gold and silver trim and centered at its peak by a massive hanging glass crystal chandelier. Receptionists stood ready for duty behind their counters. I did not see Erin anywhere in the lobby. I checked the shops off the lobby, without success. Then I went upstairs to the mezzanine level where there were easy chairs, couches, and coffee tables for use by hotel guests and visitors, but still no Erin.

I took one of the easy chairs on the mezzanine level that had a view of the lobby below. By now, I was regretting that I hadn't insisted on staying with Erin. After five long minutes sitting and watching, the notion occurred to me to check with the registration desk in case she had left a message. I stood in line while several businessmen from Japan were assigned their rooms. Finally, I reached the counter. "I expected to meet someone who appears not to be here. Can I ask you if you saw her, an American woman, red hair, about thirty-five years old, around five feet five inches tall? Her name is Erin Haig."

The woman at the registration desk, Ms. Leng Tan, registration associate, did not recall the person I described but said that she would ask her colleagues. She dialed a number on her phone and said something mostly in Chinese but also including "Erin Haig." A man appeared from a room behind the registration desk whose badge identified him as assistant manager Andy Ho. "Are you Mr. Harry West?"

"Yes, I am. Do you have a message for me?"

"I'm very sorry, sir, may I see your identification, please?"

I handed my passport to him. Andy Ho flipped it open to the picture page, glanced at it, and handed it back. "Thank you, Mr. West. I do have a message for you." He opened a drawer under the counter and retrieved a Hyatt envelope which was sealed with a notation on the back: "For Mr. Harry West (Personal)."

The note inside read, "Contact feared he was being watched and he ran off. I will wait for you in lobby at your hotel."

To get to the Furama lobby, you first have to ride an escalator up one floor from the hotel's street level entrance. The registration desk is situated just to the left of the top of the escalator. To the right, there are the usual shops selling magazines and personal necessities, designer clothes, and H. Stern jewelry. Straight ahead, as in the Hyatt and other international hotels, there's an area for hotel guests and visitors to sit, socialize, and watch the passing scene.

Erin and Robert Leung were sitting at one of the lobby tables where they could monitor both the elevators and the escalator. "We were waiting for you," Erin said, standing to greet me with a hug, a notably lingering friendly hug, it seemed to me. "I'm glad you found us."

"Me too."

"Were you worried?"

"I was. When I didn't see you, I started imagining the worst."

"We called your office but you must've already left. There were developments with our contact."

"So I gathered from your note. How did you know that I'd ask about you at the Hyatt's registration desk?"

"I guessed that you would, being that you are such a smart, logical guy."

"What if I hadn't?"

"I figured that you would eventually return to the Furama and we would meet you here."

"Why didn't you just wait for me at the Hyatt?"

"In case I was being watched, I didn't want anyone to see us together. Robert picked me up in the alley behind the hotel so that we could elude any followers."

Leung said, "Our source was frightened because he thought someone had followed him into the Hyatt. He handed Erin a note saying they could meet again at 9 A.M. tomorrow morning at the Renaissance Hotel in Wan Chai."

"About a block from our office, close to the Hyatt," I said. "I've seen it, on the way back to the Furama."

"Right."

"How did you recognize your contact?" I asked Erin.

"He told me on the phone that he was thin and would be wearing a blue suit."

"Like a lot of men in Hong Kong."

"This guy was really thin," Erin said. "Wispy, like you could blow him over with a light breeze. He looked sickly, hunched over like he had a bad stomach ache. And he looked really scared. He was in a big hurry and he was clearly nervous and jumpy. He came right up to me when I entered the lobby. He asked, 'Are you Erin Haig?' I told him that I was. Then he said 'I'm being followed,' and put the note in my hand. As soon as I took it, he scurried right by me and out the door. The whole thing took about ten seconds."

"I'll come with you tomorrow to the Renaissance," I said. "If your source is scared, you should be scared too."

Erin was thinking about it, I could tell, and it was my impression that she was about to accept my offer when Leung said, "Thank you but there is no need."

"Robert, I was kicking myself at the Hyatt for not staying with Erin. I don't want to go through that again."

"I understand," Leung said. "But Erin's meeting with our source will not take long. We need to hear what he has to say about the list and we don't want him to be made so nervous that he'll run off again. Erin will meet him in a very public place, so she will be safe. Also we have security procedures. Right, Erin?"

"Right," she replied. And then to me, she repeated her earlier assurance, "I'll be fine, Harry."

Leung reached for his briefcase and stood up, "I have to go, Erin, I'll see you tomorrow morning after your meeting."

After he'd left, I asked Erin, "Are you sure about the Renaissance?"

"Yes. Don't worry."

"Can I get anything more for you here? Have you had dinner?" She told me no, but she wasn't hungry since she had been snacking while waiting in the Furama lobby. "How about you?" she asked. I replied that I wasn't hungry either since I had picked up a sandwich in the Hyatt lobby.

"What I'd really like is to see the view from your room," Erin said.

"That can be arranged," I said.

After my breakup with Alexandra, Jerry and Vicki Seligman tried to match me with several attractive women, but no fires were lit from their arranged encounters. I'd heard that Alexandra was lonely despite her high-profile business success and that she would welcome my call, but I opted to avoid the entanglements that would follow. While on the road for RLW, and then for Blair West International, I became familiar with business hotels,

Marriott brands where available, Radissons or Holiday Inns otherwise, and contrary to what you'd expect from movies about road warriors, I never encountered a woman on these trips who displayed any interest in knowing me better. If there were women in my vicinity who did send such signals, I missed them. If I were to visit the bars in my hotels more often, I might have a different story to tell. But not being much of a drinker, I seldom enter a hotel bar except to pick up a sandwich when I check in at my hotel after its restaurants are closed. On such occasions, I've been more interested in my sandwich than in meeting others in the bar.

In short, even if I'd had the opportunity, it hasn't been worth the trouble, it seemed to me, to get involved with anyone. But seeing Mei-Ling again awakened in me a desire for company, and into that re-opening came Erin. She was smart, and ambitious, and I was attracted to her. I liked her. I enjoyed being with her. I didn't question her interest in me. Whatever our reasons, what mattered now was that we'd found each other.

Erin and I stood together at my window overlooking the harbor. It was dark outside and we could see the lights of boats on the harbor and in Kowloon on the other side. "Can you see the Sheraton, there, just to the right of the theater?" she asked. She brought her head close so that we were looking in the same direction.

I felt Erin's hip and thigh against mine as we stood looking out. She put her arm around my lower back, and I leaned towards her, touching the hair at her temple with my lips, breathing her scent. She turned her face towards me. Her lips felt warm, and our tongues touched. Her hands roamed up and down my back. She pulled me towards her. I felt her breasts against my chest, and my hands descended down her lower back. We were pressed against each other and Erin said, "This could get serious," and edged me over to the bed. She unbuttoned her shirt, and then her bra, so that her breasts hung free, and pulled off her skirt and red panties. She straddled me on the bed, undid my shirt buttons one-by-one, and my belt, and I wriggled free of my clothes. She lay on top of me quietly for a moment, her breasts on my chest, her breathing against my cheek. Then she slowly began to grind against me, rising up so that her breasts brushed against my face and I caught the nipples in my mouth and licked and sucked them as they came into reach. I was as hard as stone. She pressed against me. We rolled over. Now I was on top and she opened her legs, so that I slid into her, smoothly, into hot wet silk, and she was moving under me, I could feel her hands on my buttocks pulling me in further, her inside muscles rippling against me.

Later, we lay on the bed with her head on my chest.

"We're good together," Erin said.

"I think so, too," I replied. "I feel good being with you. Better than I've felt in a long time."

"Me too," she said.

"I want to get to know you better."

Erin giggled. "You've got a great start on that."

"No, really. I'm serious. After you've written your articles here, and you return to the US, let's stay in touch. See what happens."

"I'd like that," Erin said. "Very much."

I drifted into light sleep. The room was still dark when I woke up a while later and found that Erin's back was towards me, and I was spooned against her. I put my arm over her and gently cupped her breast. She murmured and sighed and held my arm tightly so that we remained pressed against each other.

I awoke next to a sound in the room at 5 A.M., an hour before the clock radio was set to emit its wake-up chirp. Erin was standing at the window wearing a hotel bathrobe. "I have to get back to the Sheraton to change my clothes before my meeting," she said. "Sorry to wake you. I'm just about to take a quick shower."

"Let's be green and conserve Hong Kong's fresh water supply by sharing," I said.

The Furama had outfitted the shower with both the overhead sprayer and a second nozzle on a flexible stainless steel hose coiled on a hook just under the faucets. Guests could select either nozzle or both at the same time by swiveling a lever. The outer edge of the tub, opposite the wall, was two feet high and wide enough to accommodate indented seats that were carved into it. A light nylon shower curtain could be pulled along the outer edge to protect the rest of the bathroom from the spray. I stood by the shower, naked and still, except for a stiffening body part that Erin had gripped to pull me into the shower. She turned on a light flow of warm water from both the overhead and hand-held nozzles. "Let's soap each other," she said. Her hands were warm and slippery with soap bubbles as she laved my shoulders, my back and chest, my buttocks and my erection. Then, she turned her back to me. I slathered soap on her body from her shoulders down to between her legs and massaged her gently and insistently. Erin braced herself leaning against the front wall of the shower. I entered her and we rocked against each other until she shuddered and I jolted convulsively against her. We remained locked together for a few more moments, and then I withdrew, and we sat inside the tub, Erin's head against my shoulder, as the warm water splashed down on our heads and backs.

"Nothing like a good soak to start the day," she said. "I'd better get going. Would you like to link up again this evening?"

"Of course."

"I'll email you when I know my schedule," Erin said.

"I want to come with you to the Renaissance."

"Thank you, no. Just keep your little buddy there ready for when we see each other tonight."

"You can count on that," I said.

Twelve

FEELING RELAXED, verging on cheerful, I took my time over breakfast and walked to our office from the Furama to enjoy the fresh air of the morning.

Elizabeth greeted me by pointing to the watch on her wrist. She said that Blair was waiting for me. He looked up from his monitor screen when I knocked on his door. "You're late this morning," he said. "You feel OK?"

"Very well rested, thank you."

"We've had a last-minute meeting set up for us with Richard Fung, the chairman of Hong Kong Wireless. Mr. Shih says that Fung is heading off on a three week trip so this is our last chance. The Wireless Center is right next to the train station in Central. Let's talk on the way over."

We grabbed a taxi in front of the China Resources Building and after Blair instructed the driver on our destination, he said, "Your file from the *Asian Business Journal* could be just what Mr. Shih needs."

"So you were able to read it?"

"Not me. Elizabeth. I could only pick out a few of the characters."

"What did she say is in the file?"

"That it is a list of names, and for each of the names, it does provide an amount of money and a date. It appears to be an internal document for the manager of the Fund. And its title is quite descriptive, 'Investments – New China Properties Fund.'"

"Did you mention the list to Mr. Shih when you talked with him this morning?"

"I did, and he's very pleased. Now we need to verify that the names on the list are public officials. Mei-Ling is sending the file to her man in Shanghai. He'll collect whatever info he can on each of them, their backgrounds, official positions, and so on."

"Excellent."

"You left in rather a hurry yesterday," Blair said. "What was going on at the ABJ office that Erin couldn't tell you about on the phone?"

I told Blair about the vandalism, the defaced photos, and the hanging box-cutter blade.

"That's a triad signature," Blair said. "Not good."

"Leung has established security procedures for the ABJ staff."

"How's Erin holding up?"

"Erin's concerned, as are the rest of the staff. But she's still forging ahead. In fact, after my visit to the ABJ office, we walked to a meeting that she'd arranged at the Hyatt with their source from Shanghai, the man who gave them the list. She went ahead while I came into the office to drop off the file."

"Did you find out why they were meeting?" Blair asked. "And what happened there?"

"Their source contacted the ABJ to let them know he was in Hong Kong. Apparently he wanted to meet to discuss the list. He asked to see Erin specifically. In any case, the meeting was aborted. He was spooked because he thought he was being followed. He put a note into her hand as she was coming into the Hyatt lobby and he was heading out, in order to schedule another meeting with her for this morning at the Renaissance Hotel. It's set for a few minutes from now, at 9 A. M."

We were shown to an executive conference room on the top floor of the Wireless Center.

Richard Fung arrived five minutes later, brisk and businesslike, with his suit jacket off, the sleeves of his blue dress shirt folded up to his elbows, a perfectly knotted solid metallic red tie, and black leather suspenders.

"Shih Chai-Ming forwarded your bios to me," he said, "so I know your backgrounds and your firm and I understand your assignment. I told Shih that I wanted to meet you so that I could tell you directly, face to face, that Edward Woo must not be allowed to take control of Hong Kong Wireless."

"Why not?" Blair asked.

"Because he is a weak and impetuous man and by partnering with the New China Properties Fund, he has allied himself with miscreants. He should know better. His father warned him not to pursue his bid for my company, especially not with an equity partner like the Fund."

"So Woo Jian-Min tells you about his conversations with his son Edward?"

"About this conversation, yes. He had to tell me, since at the time he was on my Board."

"And now Mr. Woo has joined the Singapore group that's also bidding to purchase HKW," I said.

"He did so as a personal favor to me, for the good of the company," Fung said. "I opposed the first bid from the Singapore group to persuade them to raise their offer. I didn't expect them to drop out."

"Which provided an opening for Edward."

"I blame myself for that. I had to beg the Singapore group to return to the table and the only way they would was if they were joined by Woo Jian-Min."

"Mr. Fung," I said. "Do you have evidence that you can share with us that the New China Properties Fund is engaged in money laundering?"

"If I had hard evidence to back up what I believe is true, Edward's proposal would have died long ago. The Fund is very secretive about the sources of its money. Clearly, it has a lot to invest but we have no proof that it is dirty money. That's what we need."

Inadvertently I glanced at Blair and caught his eye, both of us thinking about our list of names. Fung noticed, and asked, "What evidence have you found?"

Blair replied, "We are making progress, Mr. Fung. That's all we can say now until we're more confident that we have valid information."

"Good," Fung said. "I'm glad you're making progress."

"To continue what you were telling us earlier," Blair said, "what would happen if Edward and the Fund gained control of Hong Kong Wireless?"

"By laundering money through HKW, I believe they would turn my company, one of the most important companies in Hong Kong, into a criminal enterprise. They would feed on it, using its cash for their own purposes, buying influence and protection, becoming even more dangerous and difficult to confront than they are now. We can't allow that to happen."

Fung's assistant came into the conference room and handed him a note. He told her, "Give me five minutes."

"One last thing," I said. "Are you aware of the articles coming out from the *Asian Business Journal*?"

"Yes. These articles will help."

"Do you know that the ABJ writers have been threatened?

"No, but I'm not surprised."

"Their office was vandalized yesterday."

"The ABJ staff should be protected. What they are doing is important for the future of Hong Kong."

Blair and I stopped in our lobby cafeteria for a quick lunch on our way back to our office.

We were still in the restaurant when Elizabeth called Blair on his cell, and asked for me. She said, "Harry, a Cathy Chao called. She says it's urgent. She says you know the number."

I used Blair's cell to call the ABJ office number. Cathy picked up.

"Harry, have you been in touch with Erin?"

"No, not since early this morning. What's happened?"

"When do you mean, early this morning?"

"Around 6 A.M. Why, Cathy? What's going on?"

"We have a security rule for each of us, if we're out during the day, to call the office at least once every two hours. Erin called in just before 9 A.M. to let us know that she had arrived for her meeting at the Renaissance and then she called again at 9:10 A.M. to say that our source had not shown up. We've heard nothing since then."

"What does Robert Leung say?"

"He said I should contact you and anyone else Erin might be in touch with. We have reported Erin as a missing person but the police don't get serious about looking until forty-eight hours have passed. They say people are always wandering off and then turn up later surprised that anyone was worried about them, and that there are so many tourists in Hong Kong, they don't have enough resources to look for everyone."

"Erin wouldn't just wander off."

"I know. And she's been so careful about following our security rules."

"Thank you for calling me. I wish I had a better answer."

"OK."

"I'll be in the office for the next few hours. Please let me know right away if you hear anything."

"What's going on?" Blair asked.

"Cathy Chao works at the ABJ. She says that Erin has not phoned in as required by the ABJ's security rules. She's been out of touch for about four hours. They don't know where she is."

"Do you think she's in trouble?"

"I don't like this at all," I said. "Cathy told me that Erin last called at 9:10 A.M. to report that their source didn't show at the Renaissance. They haven't heard from Erin since then."

"It's still only been a few hours."

"Blair, I should have joined Erin at that meeting. She said no when I offered but I should have insisted. I let her down."

At 2 P.M., I called Cathy Chao again. They still had not received word from Erin. Robert Leung had visited the Renaissance and couldn't find anyone there who recalled seeing her in the lobby. He'd gone to the Sheraton and accompanied a hotel customer service manager to Erin's room; she was not there. ABJ's contact whom she was supposed to meet did not answer his cellphone. Erin didn't answer the cellphone lent to her by the ABJ for her time in Hong Kong. Both Leung and Cathy had left voicemail and text messages. Cathy said that searching Hong Kong without police assistance was pointless and that they heard the same response from the police every time they called. "Wait forty eight hours."

"I have an idea for a way to change that," I told Cathy. "I'll get back to you shortly."

"Any news of Erin?" Blair asked, when I walked into his office.

"No, and the Hong Kong Police are not helping. The more time that passes, the colder the trail, and meanwhile they're doing nothing."

"What can I do?"

"Let's enlist Mei-Ling," I said. "She can make things happen in Hong Kong."

Blair called Mei-Ling and told her I was also on the call.

"Hello, Harry," Mei-Ling said, "My contact in Shanghai is looking into your list of names."

"Thanks, Mei-Ling. The reason..."

"I was very impressed with Erin. I could tell that she likes you."

"Erin is the reason we're calling," I said. "She went out this morning for an interview and has not called into her office since then, despite their rule to call in every two hours. Her colleagues have contacted everyone they can think of, including the police, but there is no trace, and the police won't get involved."

"Because of their forty-eight-hour rule?"

"Right. Blair thought you could put out some feelers."

"Of course I will, Harry. I hope she's alright. I'm sure she must be."

"I hope so too," I said.

"Tell me, who was Erin meeting this morning, and where?"

"She was supposed to meet the ABJ's source from Shanghai, the one who provided the list."

"What's his name?"

"No-one at the ABJ mentioned his name. They're protecting their source."

"Then, tell me about the meeting."

"The meeting was scheduled for 9 A.M. this morning at the Renaissance Hotel in Wan Chai. It had been re-scheduled from yesterday evening at the Grand Hyatt, when Erin first crossed paths with their source who was on his way out of the Hyatt because he thought he was being followed. Erin called her office shortly after 9 A.M. to report that their source had not shown up. They didn't hear from her after that."

"Has anyone contacted the ABJ's source?"

"They tried but he doesn't answer his mobile phone."

"Harry, do you have a picture of Erin that I can use?"

"No, I'll get one, and send it to you."

"I'll see what I can do, Harry. Don't worry."

Blair, having done his part by enlisting Mei-Ling, said he had to leave for an appointment. He would pick me up next morning for another meeting with Mr. Shih. He said he had informed Mr. Shih about Erin's disappearance.

I called Cathy Chao, told her about Mei-Ling, and asked for a picture of Erin.

"We have one that I'll email to you right now," Cathy said.

The picture of Erin that Cathy emailed to me had been taken in front of the ABJ's Federal Building. Erin was standing at the entrance, smiling, squinting a bit into the sunlight. I forwarded the picture to Mei-Ling and Blair. I also made several hard copies for myself on our color printer.

Before leaving the office, I called Erin's room again at the Sheraton; no answer. I left another message. I also called the number Cathy had given me for Erin's borrowed mobile phone. Again, no answer, and the voicemail box was full.

Outside the China Resources Building, the air was still and humid as if held in suspension and there were red and orange streaks on the clouds from the late afternoon sun.

The driver of the first taxi in the line beside the plaza was napping with his head slung back on the headrest behind his seat, his mouth hanging open. He was startled awake when I opened the rear passenger door and slid into the seat behind him. "Furama Hotel," I told him, and he jerked us away from the curb for the short ride back to my hotel.

I went directly to my room. The message light on my phone was dark. I called the ABJ office. No answer there. I tried Erin's room at the Sheraton again; no answer there, either.

My attempt to distract myself from worrying about Erin by watching an old Bruce Willis action movie on the TV met with limited success even though the story line was not complex: Bruce is up against overwhelming odds; he frustrates the bad guys; they all die deservedly violent deaths; after he emerges out of the smoking wreckage, his bosses admit they were mistaken when they ordered him to stand down.

At 11:30 P.M., I called Erin's room at the Sheraton again; no answer.

My window was lit suddenly by a bright white flash, followed by the rolling, ripping boom and crash of thunder. The window shook from gusts of wind and from the sheets of rain beating against it.

Thirteen

THE STORM WAS GONE by morning, and beams of sunlight cut through the mist streamers that swirled up from the surface of the harbor like dancing ghosts.

I called the Sheraton, hoping, believing, that Erin would pick up. She'd tell me that her absence had been only a misunderstanding. She'd apologize for letting everyone worry but it couldn't be helped, and we'd understand when we heard her incredible story. She'd report that she'd been abducted but was able to escape when her kidnappers left a door unlocked. Although she'd endured a terrifying experience, she was fine now, just needed to rest, and then she'd tell us all about it.

Still, however, no answer in Erin's room. I called Robert Leung on his cell. He said he was on his way into the ABJ office. He hadn't heard anything. We arranged that we would talk later in the morning and that we'd keep each other posted.

On our way to Mr. Shih's office, Blair reported that Mei-Ling had contacted ranking officers in the Hong Kong constabulary. The police were now taking Erin's disappearance more seriously, partly because Mei-Ling was asking but also because they finally understood that Erin was a working American journalist and not just a tourist gone missing.

Mr. Shih stood at his window, watching us park in the courtyard below. He came down to meet us and walked with us back to his office. He asked about Erin.

I said that we had nothing yet but at least the police were involved now, finally, and we were looking forward to hearing what they were doing, and what they'd learned.

Mr. Shih asked his assistant to bring us tea and to get Chief Inspector William Berriman on the phone.

Mr. Shih told us that Berriman had served with the police during the British administration and had stayed on after the transition to help train Chinese officers. As a Chief Inspector in the Hong Kong Island regional division, he would be aware of Ms. Haig's disappearance and of the status of the police investigation.

Mr. Shih's assistant buzzed on the intercom to announce that she had Chief Inspector Berriman on the line. When he took the phone, Mr. Shih said, "Chief Inspector, Stephen Blair and Harry West, our consultants from Blair West International, have joined me in my office. They know the journalist from the *Asian Business Journal* who has gone missing and who was working on a story of interest to me and to the Government. I have you on speakerphone so that they can participate in this call."

Chief Inspector Berriman said, "Good morning, gentlemen."

"Are you involved in this matter, Chief Inspector?"

"Very much so. I am in charge of the case."

"What can you tell us about it?"

Berriman said, "We've confirmed that Ms. Haig was in the Renaissance Hotel in Wan Chai before she disappeared…"

He paused. It seemed that he had nothing else to share with us, so I said, "Chief Inspector, this is Harry West. Can you tell us more? We know the context, so we can be helpful."

"Candidly, Mr. West…"

"Please call me Harry."

"Alright, Harry, I was just about to add that I've been instructed by my superiors to keep you and Mr. Blair fully informed, to consider you as our collaborators in this investigation, and I will make every effort to do so."

Apparently Mei-Ling had called the right people and had been persuasive, as always.

Blair said, "Chief Inspector, we're grateful for your understanding."

"What else have you learned?" I asked.

"Ms. Haig was seen in the Renaissance lobby by Front Desk clerks. They identified her from the picture shown to them by our officers. They recalled that she was standing near the Front Desk for almost fifteen minutes, and then left. We retrieved the hotel's security video of the lobby. It shows that Ms. Haig arrived in the lobby at 8:55 A.M., and left at 9:12 A.M., and that she was alone during that time. The video also shows her making a brief call on her mobile at 9:10 A.M."

"Her colleague Cathy Chao told me that Erin called her at that time to report that the person she was supposed to meet had not shown up," I said.

"We've requested that the mobile operator provide us with records of any calls to or from her mobile on that morning, and subsequently," Berriman said. "Ms. Haig's disappearance takes on a more worrying aspect now that we've had another incident at the office of the *Asian Business Journal*, where she worked."

"What other incident?" I asked. "Has there been another break-in?"

"Not a break-in. It was an apparent mugging of an editor there, name of Robert Leung."

"When did this happen? I was just talking with Robert earlier this morning. He said he was on his way to the ABJ office. Is he OK?"

"Mr. Leung was assaulted when he arrived at his office this morning. He was struck mostly on his arms and legs, one of his arms was broken, and his head was cut when he fell to the ground. He was patched up at a clinic and seems functional now, though shaken up, understandably."

"Have you identified his attackers?" I asked.

"Not yet. One of my officers took statements from Mr. Leung and others at the scene."

Blair asked, "Are you aware that the ABJ has been warned to stop its publication of articles on corruption in Hong Kong?"

"Yes."

Mr. Shih said, "We can't have journalists in Hong Kong being attacked."

"I agree," Berriman said.

I asked, "May we exchange our contact information with you, Chief Inspector, so that we can keep each other up to date?"

"By all means," Berriman said, and we each read off our respective phone numbers and email addresses.

We were walking towards the China Resources Building from Blair's parking garage when I told Blair to proceed without me, that I wanted to check out the Renaissance where Erin had gone for her meeting.

"Harry, Chief Inspector Berriman told us that the police have already questioned people there."

"I know. I just want to see for myself. It's nearby. I'll catch up with you later."

I went straight to the Renaissance Hotel's Front Desk, my picture of Erin in hand. I introduced myself and explained to the woman behind the desk, Ms. Lily Tau according to her name badge, that Erin Haig was a close friend who had disappeared after coming to the Renaissance to meet someone around 9 A.M. the previous morning.

I placed Erin's picture on the desk. "We've heard nothing from her and we're very concerned."

After considering the picture for a few moments, Ms. Tau said, "Police officers were here early this morning asking about this person."

"Yes, I know. They told us that hotel staff at the Front Desk recalled seeing Erin. Were you one of the staff who did?"

"Yes, I did see her and I informed the police officers. I believe that a security video confirms that your friend was here in the lobby. I don't know what I can add beyond what I told the police."

"I understand," I said. "I'm asking in case anything has occurred to you since the police were here."

"I don't know…"

"For example, about whether you noticed Erin being approached by anyone? Or where she went when she left the lobby?"

"Before she left, she asked me where the Ladies Restroom is, and I told her."

"Did you mention that to the police?"

"I don't think so. It didn't occur to me as being important."

"Where is this Ladies Restroom?"

Ms. Tau pointed in the general direction of the elevators. "It's on the other side of the elevators," she said, "but you can't go in there."

"I know. Can you send someone there to look around?"

"Our lobby area restrooms are cleaned many times each day. We would have heard by now if there was anything unusual."

"Ms. Tau," I said. "I really don't know what to ask next and would appreciate your help."

"Well, one of our restroom attendants may have seen her." She consulted her screen and then called someone on her phone. Once again, I lamented my lack of knowledge of Chinese since I had no idea what she was saying, except that towards the end of the call she appeared to be receiving information, nodding her head and taking notes.

"I spoke with our maintenance services manager," she said. "She will contact the restroom attendant who was on duty yesterday morning and get back to me shortly."

"Thank you," I said, "I'll wait here." I stood aside so that Ms. Tau could serve guests who had lined up behind me.

About five minutes later, Ms. Tau's phone rang. She listened, and then turned to me. "The restroom attendant who was on duty is a Filipina. She is reluctant to talk with police."

"Please assure her that I am not with the police and I see no need to identify her to the police. I just want to know if she saw my friend. Please tell her that my friend's life may be in danger."

Ms. Tau spoke into the phone in English, "He is not police. You will not be identified. OK. I'll tell him."

"She will meet you now outside the Ladies Restroom."

"Thank you, Ms. Tau," I said.

"I wish you good luck finding your friend," she replied.

I was standing outside the Ladies Restroom for a few minutes collecting curious glances from women entering and leaving it, when a Filipina in a light blue uniform approached me. Unlike other hotel staff, she was not wearing a name badge. I assumed that she had removed it.

She looked at me appraisingly. "You are not Hong Kong police?" she asked. Although she was short and slight, almost delicate in appearance, her manner was very direct.

"No, I'm not with the police and I'm not even from Hong Kong," I said. "I'm American. Look, here's my driver's license." I opened my wallet showing my Massachusetts license.

"You are Mr. West," she said, confirming her observation by referring to my headshot photo on the license.

"Yes."

"And you want to know if I saw your friend."

"Yes. I understand that you were working in the Ladies Restroom yesterday morning when she may have been in there."

"Do you have her picture?"

"Here it is," I said, handing it to her.

As she looked at it, I asked, "Did you see her?"

She studied Erin's picture for another moment or two. "I did see her," she said. "I complimented her on her red hair and she thanked me, and she left a gratuity in the attendant's jar."

"Did she say anything else to you? Did she give any indication where she was going next?"

"No. But before she left the Ladies, she received a call on her mobile and I heard her say, '...in your car' and 'no problem, see you shortly.'"

"When was that?"

"It had to be just before 9:15 A.M. because that is when I take my break in the morning, and I left just after your friend."

"You have been enormously helpful," I said, and pressed 160 HK dollars into her hand, equivalent to twenty US dollars.

"You're very welcome, sir," she said. "I hope you find the lady safe."

When I returned to our office, I told Blair what I'd learned at the Renaissance, and he placed a call to Chief Inspector Berriman.

Berriman's assistant picked up the phone and put us through.

"Berriman here."

Blair said, "Harry obtained information at the Renaissance Hotel that you should know."

I told Berriman about my interaction with the Ladies Restroom attendant.

"If Ms. Haig was going to see someone in a car and she expected to see that person soon, she may have been headed out to the hotel car park," Berriman said.

"I didn't know the Renaissance had a car park," I said.

"It's behind the hotel and it's monitored with a security camera. We'll check the video."

"And you'll let us know what you find out?" I said, not really asking, but just to confirm.

"Yes, of course."

"Also, Chief Inspector, when you receive the wireless operator's records of calls to Erin's cellphone, can you pay particular attention to that call she received around 9:15 A.M.?"

"Harry, I've been doing police work for a long time. It did occur to me that we'd want to identify who called Ms. Haig just before she went missing."

"Sorry," I said. "I'm new at this."

"Apology noted and accepted," Berriman said. "You did well, Harry. We'll follow up."

Berriman called us back an hour later.

144

"The call to Ms. Haig's cellphone at 9:15 A.M. came from a prepaid mobile so there is no information on the caller. We do know that this prepaid phone was purchased in a Tsim Sha Tsui electronics shop ten days ago. The records in the shop indicate it was purchased with cash. We also know that the prepaid phone was close to the Renaissance when the call was placed, I suspect in the hotel's car park."

"Were you able to retrieve a video of the car park that shows Erin was there?" I asked.

"We were, and it does show a person who appears to be Ms. Haig. I'm having a screenshot showing her image faxed to your office now so that you can confirm that it is indeed Ms. Haig. The video shows her approaching a black Mercedes and looking into an open window on the rear door on the driver's side. It shows her standing there for several minutes, talking with someone inside. Then the door is opened, she gets in, and the door is closed behind her. The car then departs the car park, driving slowly, with Ms. Haig still inside."

Elizabeth came into Blair's office holding the fax. The woman standing by the Mercedes was Erin, beyond doubt. "That's Erin Haig," I said.

"Excellent. We have that settled, at least," Berriman said.

"She looks serious, but not frightened," I said.

"That's my observation as well."

"Can you read the license plate on the car?"

"The surveillance camera caught it when the Mercedes pulled out but it's hard to read. It was partially in shadow. Although we enhanced the video, we can't yet make it out."

Blair asked, "How about the man that Erin was supposed to meet?"

"Mr. Leung has identified him as a citizen of the People's Republic of China who lives in the Shanghai area. We have put a request with Customs to find out whether he has left Hong Kong, and we've requested a watch at the airport and at border crossings into the mainland and into Macau."

"Is there anything else?" I asked.

"Mr. Leung also confirmed that the person shown in the security video is Ms. Haig. He said that his security guidelines are very specific against getting into vehicles to conduct interviews. Ms. Haig was supposed to stay in an open public place at all times. He doesn't understand why she would get into the car."

"Erin must have known the person in the car, for example the man she was supposed to meet. She must have been convinced that it would be safe."

"Evidently. And we still don't know that it wasn't safe. Ms. Haig could turn up at any moment with a perfectly good explanation."

As soon as our call ended with the Chief Inspector, Blair's phone buzzed. It was Elizabeth. Robert Leung was waiting at her desk just outside the door to Blair's office.

Fourteen

A WHITE PLASTER CAST covered Robert Leung's left forearm from his elbow down to his hand. A bandage was taped just above his forehead where his hair had been shaved. His eyes were bruised under his glasses and there was blood on his upper lip that had not yet scabbed over. One of the arms of his glasses was held together with white surgical tape.

Once we were seated in Blair's office, Blair asked, "Would you like some tea?"

"Thanks, no, Elizabeth already offered."

"Chief Inspector Berriman told us that you were attacked this morning."

"Just outside our building. Someone called my name and I turned around, and two men came up and starting hitting me; I think one of them had a hammer and the other one a wood baton; I wasn't looking too carefully, I was just trying to protect myself. I fell onto the pavement. I tried to get up but they kept beating me. They were not wearing masks so it seems they didn't care whether I could identify them. Maybe they planned to kill me. Two big fellows, both Chinese."

"How did you get away?"

"A driver in a car on Lockhard Road was honking his horn, making a lot of noise. He may have called police on his mobile. Or someone else did, I don't know, but they arrived quickly. By then the two thugs had taken off. I was lying on the sidewalk."

"How do you feel?"

"Like shit," Leung said. "My arm aches and I've got bruises all over that hurt like hell. I checked myself out of the clinic so that I could get our first article into print and onto newsstands. We were waiting for more information from our source but this now seems unlikely, so we are going ahead. We have enough. At least, when we've published, whoever is trying to intimidate us will have less incentive."

"What about their incentive to retaliate?" I asked.

"I guess we'll find out. Our printer will get our issue into the mail and on newsstands by this evening. I have the article on a flash drive which I brought with me so you can get an advance look, if you want."

Blair took the small memory device from Leung, copied the article onto his laptop, sent a copy of the article to me via email, and handed the flash memory stick back to Leung. I reached into the porcelain pencil jar on Blair's desk and retrieved the other flash drive that Leung had given me the day before with the list of names, and returned it to him as well.

"Let's talk about Erin," I said.

"That makes me feel even more like shit," Leung said. "I sent her out to that meeting. I waved you off when you offered to join her. In a way, I deserve the beating that I got from those two thugs."

Silently, I agreed. Leung did deserve a beating. I did too, for accepting "no" for an answer.

"What can you tell us about the man who Erin was meeting?" I asked.

"His name is Chen Qiwei."

"How did you recruit him?" I asked.

"We didn't. He contacted me and volunteered to send us inside information on the New China Properties Fund. He's an accountant who was hired by the manager of the Fund to review its accounts. He found an encrypted list of names that he believed to be investors in the Fund. When he broke the code, he confirmed his suspicion that the list includes names of officials who were responsible for the destruction of his village in Pudong, across the river from Shanghai. He told me quite openly that he wants revenge on these officials. He provided the list of names to us, which I shared with you."

"Have you heard from Chen since Erin's disappearance?"

"No. And I can't reach him. He doesn't answer his mobile."

Blair printed two copies of the ABJ article and handed one to me, so that we could read it at the same time.

Corruption in Hong Kong
By Erin Haig, Eugene Suh, Cathy Chao, and Robert Leung

Hong Kong has prospered because of its tradition of transparent business transactions under rule of law. This tradition is now under pressure as a result of money flooding into Hong Kong from dubious sources.

Why is this a problem so long as Hong Kong receives the money?

The answer is that illicit money requires local protection, which usually comes at a price, thereby fostering an ecosystem of extortion and bribe taking.

For example, consider the recent proposal by TelePhase, a telecoms company owned by Edward Woo, to acquire Hong Kong Wireless, the territory's largest mobile phone operator. We do not comment on the merits of the deal. That's up to others to evaluate. Rather, we focus on the financing that TelePhase has obtained for this acquisition, in particular the proposed equity investment from New China Properties Fund, a shadowy group based in Shanghai.

In its proposal document, TelePhase identifies this fund as providing 70% of the equity financing for the deal, although TelePhase provides assurance that it will retain legal control of the acquired company. Very little is known about the New China Properties Fund, except that it seems to have a lot of money to invest. Mr. Woo's lawyers have provided the name of a Fund "General Manager" but he has proven to be highly elusive and we cannot confirm that he really exists. The receptionist who answers the phone at the New China Properties Fund office in Shanghai claims that no-one is available to answer questions.

A knowledgeable source, who has requested to remain anonymous, has provided us with names of people who are believed to be investors in the New China Properties Fund. We have been expecting to learn more from our source but he has now disappeared under mysterious circumstances. We are publishing this list now on our website, www.abj-HKSeries.com, rather than waiting any longer. We are doing this to avoid rewarding those who are responsible for the disappearance of our source.

To date, we have identified several persons on this list as public officials in Shanghai, and we are working to identify more. It is unlikely that such officials could afford to participate in the Fund based on their publicly revealed compensation. Hence the following questions: Do they have sources of income that are undisclosed and therefore suspect? Or are they permitted to participate for a "discounted" level of investment as a means to pay them off for special favours?

Consider, for example, the case of Pudong District Communist Party of China (CPC) Secretary Teng Lee. He *is shown to have invested the equivalent of US$400,000, an amount far greater than a district CPC secretary could earn from his salary. Teng Lee's parents are both schoolteachers and he is an only child. He worked with the Pudong Centre for Land Reserve managing acquisitions of land in Pudong to provide space for building developers. According to public records of the Pudong Centre for Land Reserve, developers paid tens of millions of dollars for rights to build in Pudong. However, the displaced village residents claimed that they received little compensation. Evidently most of the money paid by developers failed to make it to the people directly affected by the land seizures. Given this history, how did Teng Lee obtain US$400,000 to invest in the New China Properties Fund? CPC district secretary Teng has not answered our calls to his mobile phone number nor has he responded to our email messages.*

The TelePhase bid to acquire HKW is currently under evaluation by the Communications Department in Hong Kong. One issue being reviewed is the possibility that the financing from the New China Properties Fund includes money that Fund investors obtained illegally. If so, the Fund would be engaged in money laundering, and TelePhase would be complicit in this activity. Mr. Edward Woo, who declined to comment for this article, has allies in the government who may seek to help him to circumvent the review process. One reason that we are focusing on this deal is to shine a spotlight on it so that such improper influence cannot be brought to bear, or if attempted, will no longer enjoy obscurity in the shadows.

Under current Hong Kong law, transfer of HKW control must be subject to a finding that all aspects of the transaction are legal, including the financing for the deal. We do not have conclusive evidence that the New China Properties Fund is a conduit for corrupt money. However, circumstantial evidence tends to support this suspicion. Lacking more transparency by the New China Properties Fund or by Mr. Edward Woo, a different conclusion cannot be put forward with confidence.

Mr. Woo's earlier purchase of a fiber optic cable system linking the Hong Kong to factories in China's Guangdong province was also financed by the New China Properties Fund. That transaction was allowed to proceed without objection by the government. While the fiber cable system is an important asset, it does not have the same significance as Hong Kong Wireless. Therefore, if there are questions to be answered, they should be answered for this transaction.

Next Article in this Series: The Woo Family in Hong Kong and mainland China

Editor's Note: Journalists in some countries do their jobs at risk of legal prosecution, physical harm, and even of losing their lives. Hong Kong takes justifiable pride in its record of allowing journalists to work in safety.

153

Therefore, it should alarm residents of Hong Kong that during the preparation of this series, the ABJ's office has been vandalized and its managing editor has been attacked in the street. ABJ has also been threatened with libel suits, a device that is commonly used to intimidate journalists. What is most alarming, however, is that Ms. Erin Haig, the lead writer of this article, disappeared yesterday morning while pursuing an interview with one of ABJ's sources of information, the same source who has also disappeared. Police are investigating. Photographs of Ms. Haig and of a car that she was seen entering before her disappearance have been posted on the ABJ website. Anyone who recalls seeing Ms. Haig since yesterday morning is requested to inform the police. Contact information for this purpose is available on the ABJ website.

"This should shake things up," I said.

Leung nodded. "We hope so."

Blair's cellphone, which was being re-charged on his desk, vibrated, and he picked it up. "Hi Mei-Ling," he said. He listened to Mei-Ling whose voice I also could hear, albeit indistinctly, on his cell. "Thank you, I'll call you back in a bit."

After Blair put his cellphone back on his desk, he said, "Mei-Ling says that her contact in Shanghai recognizes some of the names on the list as local officials and he is doing more background research on them."

I asked Leung, "Can we let Mei-Ling know Chen Qiwei's name so that her contact in Shanghai can check his background, and find out what he can about him?"

"Go ahead. You can tell her," Leung said.

Blair dialed Mei-Ling and gave her Chen Qiwei's name. "She's on it," Blair told us after he put his phone down.

Almost immediately, his cellphone buzzed again. Leung and I watched Blair as he listened to his caller. Then, "OK, thank you for letting me know. I'll tell the others who are here with me. Harry West and Robert Leung of the ABJ. He seems OK. We will. Thank you."

"That was Chief Inspector Berriman," Blair said. "Police have located the Mercedes that was shown in the hotel surveillance video. It was parked illegally overnight at a dock in the Yau Ma Tei district, just north of Tsim Sha Tsui in Kowloon. It was towed before daybreak this morning. It's the same car. They found one of Erin's business cards pushed into the crease of a seat where it meets the seat-back. Also a scrap of paper with Mei-Ling's name and mobile number."

"Mei-Ling gave that to Erin at our dinner," I said. "In case Erin needed help."

"Yes, I recall that."

"The fact that it was left in the car along with Erin's business card could mean she was trying to send a message, like, 'I was in this car, and whoever finds this, please call Mei-Ling.'"

155

"I agree," Blair said. "Also the Chief Inspector told me that the license plate is registered to the owner of a restaurant in Kowloon, in the Mong Kok area, but they don't know where he is. He dropped out of sight more than a year ago after his restaurant was closed due to unresolved health infractions, and his family also moved out of their apartment. Neighbors had no idea that he owned a big Mercedes; they've only seen him on a motorbike. His restaurant was very small, not much more than a stall."

Leung said, "Sounds like a phantom registration. Criminals use the names of people who are deceased so that the cars can't be traced."

The ABJ issue was printed and on the street by late afternoon. CNN's Hong Kong bureau allocated two minutes to the ABJ article and to the "battle for Hong Kong Wireless" in its cycle on "Asia Business Reports."

Hong Kong's Minister of Communications and Transport, the politically-appointed head of Mr. Shih's department, was quoted saying that Government was examining the proposed deal and would take care to ensure that it was fully vetted before it was approved.

CNN's presenter, Janice Huang, reported that Edward Woo declined to comment on tape but that his company had released a statement, "TelePhase has built a solid reputation in Hong Kong for integrity in all of its business dealings. Our proposal to acquire Hong Kong Wireless is legitimate in all respects and good for all stakeholders. We reject any insinuations that our company is involved in improper or illegal acts. We will respond vigorously to such insinuations through all legal means."

During his interview, Robert Leung answered Ms. Huang's questions with a vigorous defense of the allegations made in the ABJ article. Erin's picture appeared on the screen. It was the same photograph that Cathy had sent to me of Erin standing in front of the Federal Building on Lockhart Road. "Anyone with information about Ms. Erin Haig should call the police," Janice Huang said. She read out loud the police phone number that was scrolling along the bottom of the TV screen.

Fifteen

IT WASN'T EASY to write our report for Mr. Shih while I was calling Erin's room at the Sheraton every fifteen minutes.

But we had a job to do.

The first part of our report about Edward Woo's takeover bid for Hong Kong Wireless, which we referred to as *viability,* was mostly for show so that Mr. Shih could claim that he'd hired consultants for the usual reasons, to assess business risk for the company and for the territory that relied on its services. On these matters, we gave Woo's proposal high marks.

What really mattered to Mr. Shih was the second part of our report, called *suitability*. Given what we'd learned about the New China Properties Fund, Woo's stonewalling, the intimidation of the ABJ, and Erin's disappearance, we concluded that the issues surrounding Woo's bid warranted more formal government inquiries. We still needed more information about the names on the ABJ's list before we could point to clear evidence of money laundering, but the result was the same; Mr. Shih could cite our report as justification for withholding approval.

"Thank you," Mr. Shih said, when we met to discuss our report, "I can use this."

Blair said, "We'll keep feeding you information about the names as our source in Shanghai finds out more about them."

"Excellent, thank you, Blair." Then, turning to me, Mr. Shih said, "Well, Harry, it seems that you and Blair could do the job after all."

"Yes, but that's mostly due to the *Asian Business Journal*," I said. "And concerning that, Mr. Shih, I have a favor to ask. I'm staying over in Hong Kong to help to find Erin. Will you cover my living expenses while I'm here?"

Mr. Shih agreed to cover my expenses for another week.

True to his threat, Edward Woo's libel suit demanded full retraction of all statements in the ABJ article implying that TelePhase received illegal financing for its proposed acquisition of HKW, or that he exercised improper influence over Government policy. Woo's lawyers obtained an injunction against any further publication by ABJ in Hong Kong until the matter was resolved. The ABJ office in Hong Kong was closed pending a court decision to lift the injunction. Woo's lawyers said they held open their option to broaden the libel suit to include other parties who were found to have contributed to ABJ's publication of its libelous article, which I read as a warning directed at us. The ABJ placed its Hong Kong staff on paid leave. Robert Leung rejoined the ABJ office in Taipei and emailed me that the next article in the ABJ series would be published from there.

Hong Kong's English-language newspapers found something to write every day about Erin Haig; speculations about her disappearance; perspectives offered by her colleagues at ABJ; and highlights of her biography including her upbringing, education, and career in the US before she came to Hong Kong. Blair said her story was also being covered in Hong Kong's Chinese language press. Local TV stations ran updates on the case with teasers such as, "Day 4 on Erin Haig: Police Say No New Leads." The police claimed that they were working diligently and requested that anyone with information should contact them.

Mei-Ling's man in Shanghai confirmed that Chen Qiwei was indeed an accountant and had worked on an audit of the New China Properties Fund. His home address was in a condo tower in Pudong. Neighboring condo dwellers did not recall seeing him recently and were unsure they would recognize him if they did see him. This was understandable given that the condo building was new, most inhabitants commuted every day to their jobs, and for the most part they did not know each other.

We hadn't heard from Chief Inspector Berriman for two days, not since Leung had turned up in our office. The charm of letting the police "do their job" had long since worn off.

"This is insane," I told Blair. "Erin is locked up somewhere and every minute that passes makes it worse for her. We can't just wait around for Berriman to call us."

"What do you suggest?"

"Let's meet Berriman in person to make sure that finding Erin is his top priority. We need to remind him that we're supposed to be kept informed."

Elizabeth contacted Berriman's assistant to schedule our visit with the Chief Inspector for later that morning.

The Arsenal Street entrance into the new Police Headquarters brought us into a glass-walled, marble-floored lobby. From there, we took an escalator up one floor to the forty-story tower's reception area. A woman seated behind a futuristic desk, its top being wider than its bottom like a triangle standing on a flattened tip, directed us to a footbridge that led to the Central District Headquarters in Caine House, an older, low-rise brick and stone building that had served formerly as a police barracks, and that had none of the tower's gloss or polish.

161

Once we cleared security at the Caine House entrance, a policewoman directed us to the third floor for Chief Inspector Berriman's office.

A plastic name plaque centered on a closed office door identified the space within as belonging to "William Berriman, Chief Inspector." After knocking twice, Blair pushed the door open, and we entered a small, dusty anteroom. Blair told the uniformed constable sitting behind a desk that we were expected for a meeting with the Chief Inspector. In stumbling English, the constable replied that Chief Inspector Berriman had stepped out for a moment and would return shortly. He offered us coffee or tea while we waited. I declined, as did Blair, and I told him we would wait for the Chief Inspector in the hall where we could sit on a bench, since the anteroom had no chairs for visitors. The hall was quiet except for talking and laughter in a room several doors down. An elevator door opened and a white-haired man in a rumpled suit got out and walked towards us. "I'm William Berriman," he said. "Sorry I was away from my office. I had to respond to a call from the Superintendent."

"That's OK," I said, "We just got here. I'm Harry West, and this is my colleague Stephen Blair."

"Glad to meet you in person. Why are you sitting in the hall?"

"There are no chairs in your waiting area," Blair said.

"You could have waited in my office."

When we re-entered the anteroom, this time accompanied by the Chief Inspector, the constable jumped to his feet and stood at attention. The Chief Inspector spoke to him in Chinese in a direct and peremptory tone, but he did not raise his voice. His assistant said nothing, nodded, and exited the anteroom, and Berriman led us into his office.

"I hope he's is not in trouble," Blair said. "He did offer us refreshments."

"Just reminding him that you were on my calendar and he should have known. But he's a good constable and he'll learn."

The constable entered carrying a tray of tea and plain cookies and Berriman instructed him, in English, to leave it on a side-table.

"Chief Inspector," I said, "where do things stand with your search for Erin?"

"All I can tell you is that it is progressing," Berriman said. "Concerning Chen Qiwei, we have confirmed with Customs that he has not departed Hong Kong since Ms. Haig's disappearance. Based on his mobile number provided to us by Mr. Leung, Mr. Chen's mobile phone has not been used in Hong Kong since he spoke with Ms. Haig arranging their first meeting at the Grand Hyatt."

"So who called Erin when she was waiting for Chen at the Renaissance?"

"That's an excellent question. We don't know. Could have been Chen using a different phone, perhaps borrowing it if his was inoperable, or could have been someone else. We don't know yet."

"How about the abandoned Mercedes?"

"Its owner is still missing. No-one has claimed the car."

"Chief Inspector," I said. "I'll be frank with you. It's my impression that your investigation has stalled, that there's a lack of urgency, and it's hard to bear, as the days pass and Erin's suffering is prolonged."

"We're doing what we can, Harry."

"Why not go after Edward Woo? He threatened the ABJ. Can you at least question him? Monitor his communications? Apply some pressure?"

"Harry, the Hong Kong police cannot harass one of our most prominent citizens based only on speculation. We'll have our heads handed to us by his lawyers."

"So we all just sit on our thumbs while Erin suffers absolute hell?"

"No. As I said, my officers are looking for Chen Qiwei. We're interviewing potential witnesses who were in the vicinity of the Mercedes where it was found in Tau Ma Tei. We're following up dozens of calls that we've received from people who claim to have seen Ms. Haig."

"Blair and I could confront Edward Woo," I said. "We're not subject to your constraints."

"Sure," Berriman said. "Do it."

"I'll get Elizabeth to set up a meeting for us," Blair said. "Edward will want to chastise us for our report to Mr. Shih and once we're in there, we can talk about Erin."

While Blair was on his call with Elizabeth, Berriman said, "Look Harry, I'm well aware that time is of the essence for Ms. Haig. Trust me. We're doing what we can."

"I'm afraid that 'doing what you can' is not quite good enough from Erin's perspective."

"Obviously not, since we haven't found her yet," Berriman conceded. "It's not for lack of trying."

After completing his call, Blair said. "Elizabeth is on it."

I asked Berriman, "What's the latest on the assault on Robert Leung?"

Berriman replied, "We've identified Mr. Leung's two assailants from a video taken by a surveillance camera on a light post near where he was attacked. They're muscle for hire. They work for anyone who'll pay them, businessmen, politicians, or others who find non-violent persuasion too uncertain or tedious. They collect overdue loans, evict tenants, and extract protection money, that sort of thing. We've never linked them with murder, but I suspect they'd do anything if the price is right. We'll find them before too long. Over the years they've spent a lot of time under our care. Bad boys from an early age, you might say."

"Are they triad members?"

"Not according to our triad bureau. However, I wouldn't be surprised to learn that they take on jobs for triads, on occasion."

"Is there any connection back to Erin?"

"They did not rob Mr. Leung so apparently they were delivering a message, one might assume the same message intended by Ms. Haig's disappearance."

"You mean, stop the publication of the ABJ articles."

"That's what I think," Berriman said.

"Well, if so, they'll be disappointed. The first ABJ article has been printed and more are coming."

There was a soft knock on the door. Berriman said, "Enter," and his constable came in. He stood ramrod straight at the door and said something in Chinese and the Chief Inspector informed us that he had been called to another meeting.

"Don't give up, Harry," Berriman told me. "We'll find Ms. Haig, I promise you."

"We're counting on you to let us know as soon as you get more information."

"I will. Meanwhile, feel free to call me anytime if you come up with ideas for us to pursue."

"You can be sure that we'll do that, Chief Inspector," I said.

I asked Blair, while we were crossing the footbridge back to the Arsenal House lobby, what Berriman's assistant said when he came into the office. Blair seldom spoke Chinese in public but he could understand some of what he heard. "He said the Superintendent wanted to see Berriman again. I also picked out a phrase like, 'sensitive in top circles.'"

Blair said that we were scheduled to meet Bill Schmidt and Emily Wang for lunch at the Luk Yo Teahouse, a traditional Hong Kong *dim sum* restaurant on Stanley Street in Central. "I set this up in response to Bill's email on your first day in Hong Kong. I decided we should go ahead with it, if that's OK with you."

"Have to eat somewhere," I said. Seeing Bill and Emily again would provide a welcome, albeit temporary, diversion from my anxiety, and my guilt, about Erin.

Stanley Street is short and steep, steep enough that its sidewalks turn into steps at the higher end. It was on Stanley Street that Blair and I had found a copy shop to print our reports for our first project for Mr. Shih. That shop was gone now, replaced by "Noodles Quick."

Bill and Emily were standing in front of the Luk Yo Teahouse's dark red doorway, about halfway up Stanley Street just past the new noodles shop. Bill was stocky, with thinning light brown hair and a smooth round face. Emily also was sturdily built but shorter than Bill by about a foot or so. "Look who's here," Bill said, his hand outstretched, "all the way from Cambridge, Massachusetts, USA." Emily said, simply, "Hi Harry."

Inside, we encountered an elderly man sitting on a raised stool, a lit cigarette dangling from his mouth, with his arms resting on a lectern amidst small scraps of tan-colored paper and a ceramic bowl filled with cigarette butts. Behind him, we could see that the street-level floor of the restaurant was jammed with small round tables and booths occupied mostly by old, paunchy Chinese men who were slurping their soups and picking at the food items placed before them by servers weaving among the tables bearing trays loaded with small dishes.

The elderly man, who had a two-day grey stubble, and was wearing a stained t-shirt, baggy pants, and open scandals, asked, "You have reservation?" Blair said that we did and showed him a confirming note written by Elizabeth Li in Chinese characters. "Go upstairs," the man said, pointing behind him at stairs leading to upper floors of the restaurant.

The wooden stairs were narrow and had no handrail. When we reached the second floor, we came upon a woman with short grey hair, wearing a grey smock, who glanced at Blair's note, and then pointed to the stairs behind her, gesturing to us to go up, go up. We ascended another set of steps, similarly narrow and stifling hot, to the third floor. Like the first two, this floor was crowded with diners, noisy, and steamy. There we were met by another woman, who said, "go up, fourth floor." Finally, we reached the fourth floor.

"Glad we have a reservation," Bill said. "It might have been hard to get a table here, otherwise."

Blair nodded, and handed Elizabeth Li's note to a male greeter at the top of the steps. He said, "first floor." Blair said, "We were told to come up here." The man said, "Go back down, first floor." He scrawled some characters on Elizabeth's note, and said, "first floor, show this."

Back where we had started on the first floor, just inside the Luk Yo's entrance, the elderly man scanned the note again, and pointed us towards a vacant table at the back of the room near the swinging doors to the kitchen. If he regretted that he had sent us on a fruitless multi-floor climb, he hid it well. Once we were seated, a waiter appeared. He offered damp gray washcloths for us to clean our hands and to wipe our sweaty foreheads. For menus, he handed each of us scraps of paper like those I'd noticed at the entry-way lectern, each covered by Chinese characters. "What you want?" he asked. Blair replied, "Bring us what you think we would like."

Soon food-carriers began arriving at our table pushing trolleys and carrying trays laden with small dishes of all kinds of food, some recognizable, some not. A woman in a smock kept re-filling our water glasses with smoky green tea. I still felt greasy from our trek on the stairs and from the hot steamy room and asked whether the restaurant had paper napkins. Apparently the answer was No, but a waiter did offer us a new selection of damp washcloths from a bucket. I wiped my forehead, face, and hands with one of the washcloths, and did feel slightly cooler as a result. It was better not to think too much about where the washcloth had been earlier.

"This place is famous," Blair said. "Real old Hong Kong. We're lucky to get a table. They don't like to set aside valuable space for *gweilo* that would otherwise be used to serve their regular Chinese customers. Elizabeth's note probably helped."

"What did Elizabeth write in her note?" I asked.

"Something to the effect that a commitment had been made to welcome us and that we would be grateful if it were honored."

"Are you sure it doesn't say to make the foreign devils sweat like pigs by sending them upstairs four floors for no reason?"

Emily, who had stayed uncharacteristically quiet until that point, offered to take a look at Elizabeth's note and settle the question. Blair handed it to her. "You are both right," Emily assured us, with a deadpan expression. "The note says, 'Sweaty self-pleasuring with pigs has been promised to these foreign devils. Please send them to the fourth floor to honor this commitment.'"

It felt good to laugh, not something I'd been doing a lot of lately. Blair and Bill joined in, and Emily allowed herself a satisfied smile.

"Nothing like sweaty self-pleasuring to work up an appetite," Bill added.

"Tell that to the pigs," Blair said. "Anyone want the last of these pork meat balls?" He snared it with his chopsticks. "Yum!"

"On a more serious note," Bill said, "What's the latest on the disappearance of your friend Erin Haig?"

Blair described our meeting that morning with Chief Inspector Berriman. I told Bill and Emily how Erin was last seen getting into a Mercedes in the Renaissance Hotel car park. "I'm terrified for her," I said.

Bill asked if there was anything they could do.

"We're open to suggestions," Blair said.

Emily said, "Offer a reward for information leading to Erin. Hong Kong people respond well to money."

"We should have thought of that earlier," I said. "I'll email Robert Leung as soon as we return to our office."

Blair added, "I'll pass the idea by Mei-Ling as well."

I asked my two former colleagues, "How are things going for you at RLW?" I already knew the answer. Since I'd left RLW, I'd received an increasing flow of resumés from RLW consultants although, unfortunately, Blair West International was in no position to hire anyone, being on life support ourselves. Also I'd heard that RLW was slow-paying its vendors in order to conserve cash, again a situation that I understood all too well at our new firm. For an established company like RLW, these were ominous signs.

"Things at RLW are great," Bill said. "So, Harry, there's a story out there that Glenn Robertson had you frog-marched to the parking lot after you refused to go along with his ILP strategy. Is that true?"

"It is."

"A sensible precaution in the circumstances," Blair said.

"I wish I could have seen it," Emily said.

For the rest of our lunch, the four of us reminisced about the characters we'd met on our various consulting projects, and about our good old days at RLW.

A trolley cart, pushed by a waiter, trundled towards our table with a selection of tired-looking cookies and melting ice cream. Blair asked, "Anyone up for desert?" and hearing no takers around our table, asked for a bill.

The waiter totaled up our bill by adding the count of the dishes still on the table to that of dishes removed earlier. After Blair paid, and we were back on the sidewalk outside the restaurant, Blair claimed a taxi that had just let out its fare on Stanley Street. He told the driver, "China Resources Building, Wan Chai." This was not a legal taxi pick-up spot but seeing no policeman in his rear view mirror, the driver agreed to take us, and motioned for Blair to slide quickly into the back seat, which he did, followed by Emily, and then by Bill who squeezed in beside her. I asked the driver to remove his newspaper and a clipboard from the front passenger seat. After grumbling about the bother I was causing him, the driver shoved these items to the floor in front of the seat, and I got in and shut the door.

Elizabeth told us that we had an appointment with Edward Woo later that afternoon. She said that Woo's assistant had asked what the meeting would be about. Elizabeth had told her that we were prepared to discuss our report to the Communications Department concerning Mr. Woo's bid for HKW. Apparently this was good enough to get the meeting.

More from habit than any real hope, I dialed Erin's room at the Sheraton. When the hotel voicemail picked up, I left the same message as on my numerous earlier calls, "Erin, this is Harry. I hope you are alright. Please call me when you get this message."

I was composing my email to Robert Leung about offering a reward for help in locating Erin when Blair came to my door. His normally ruddy face had gone stony grey. "Can you join me in my office?" he asked.

I followed him in. Blair told me that Chief Inspector Berriman was on the line.

"I'm putting you on speakerphone," Blair said to Berriman, "Harry West has joined me. Please tell Harry what you've just told me."

"A woman's body was found in the harbor. We believe that it is Ms. Haig's. Please accept my sincere regrets on this news."

Sixteen

"ARE YOU SURE?" I asked. I dragged my chair closer to Blair's desk where I could rest my head on my crossed arms and try to control roiling surges of nausea. Blair was leaning back in his chair, his eyes closed.

"The person who was found is a woman of the same height as Ms. Haig, same color hair, and wearing clothes that appear to be the same as in the hotel video. The body has been brought to the mortuary in Kowloon where I am now. Could you come here to confirm that it is Ms. Haig? Robert Leung has left Hong Kong and we are unable to locate the other ABJ staff at the moment."

"Certainly," Blair said, his voice subdued, his eyes still closed.

"Can you come now?"

"Yes."

"Good. Take the MTR. My officers will meet you at the Jordan subway station on Kowloon-side and drive you from there to the mortuary."

"We're leaving now," Blair said. "We'll be there."

My head was still on Blair's desk. I didn't feel like moving. I just wanted to rest there for a while, to try to get control over the nightmare, but when Blair asked me, "Do you feel up to it?" I replied, "I'll manage."

"You look…"

"I'll do it, Blair. I'm going to help confirm the identity of Erin's body. That's the least I can do."

"Alright, let's go," Blair said.

On our way out, Blair asked Elizabeth to call Edward Woo's assistant to postpone our meeting. "Tell her something has come up and we will be back in touch," Blair said.

"What's happened?"

"Police have recovered a body. They believe it is Erin Haig's."

Hong Kong's fast, safe, clean, and easy-to-navigate MTR subway system is the best option for those who put a higher priority on speed than on scenery when crossing the harbor to Kowloon. Even so, decisions do need to be made about specific subway lines, stations, ticket purchases, turnstiles, escalators, and exits. I had used the MTR many times and had no problems with it, but I was pre-occupied with thoughts of Erin. What had happened to her? What were we up against, that had cost her life? How could I have let her down? So I trailed in Blair's wake, letting him navigate our route, buy this, put it there, turn here, speed up, slow down, stop, wait, go.

We entered the MTR's Wan Chai station on Hennessey Road two blocks from our office. I recorded mindlessly the details of our underground journey while I grappled with what we were about to see. It was like I was watching a horror movie unfold, except that I was in it, along with Erin and everyone else around me. Down an escalator, across clean and clutter-free linoleum floors, past white walls set off by colorful tile murals of Hong Kong sights and advertisement posters inside stainless steel frames, through the turnstiles, onto the platform, and then the train, a succession of well-lit scenes. Two minutes later, at the Admiralty station in Central, we changed to the Tsuen Wan Line to cross under the harbor.

On Kowloon-side, at the Jordan station, we rode an escalator up from the platform to a concourse where signs led towards seven different exits to get to street level, one exit at each corner of the concourse and three along its sides. We took the exit marked for Austin Road, as Berriman had instructed. There, by the exit stairway, we found Berriman's assistant holding a lettered sign, "Blair." He asked us to follow him out to Austin Road where a police car was waiting, with another uniformed officer sitting behind the wheel. Once we were all in and seated, our car lurched forward, siren on and red and blue lights flashing.

Cutting through traffic as vehicles in front of us pulled over, and across intersections against red lights, it took us only a few minutes to get to the Kowloon Public Mortuary, a nondescript two-story building with a flat roof and plain white stucco walls. It didn't stand out from the other low-rise buildings around it except for a white van parked beside it with the English word Mortuary written on its side in large black letters above a string of Chinese characters.

Inside, the mortuary was quiet and smelled of chlorine. The only other occupants in the window-less waiting room, an elderly Chinese couple, sat hunched over, silently staring at the floor, on a wooden bench that was backed against one of the walls. We took two of the metal chairs on the other side of the room, and waited.

The Chief Inspector came in a few minutes later. "Sorry to keep you waiting. We had to get things set up properly. Please come with me now. This mortuary has not yet been updated with video-equipped remote viewing so we'll go directly into the cold chamber. I must warn you. The body has been in the water for some time. There are significant effects of decomposition so Ms. Haig, if that is who she is, will not look like she did when she was alive. I will wear a face-mask over my mouth and nose and I advise you to do the same."

I nodded, as did Blair, and Berriman handed each of us masks which we put on, following his example.

The door to the mortuary's cold chamber was heavy, like a door into a refrigerated meat locker. After we were inside, Berriman pulled the door closed behind us to maintain the temperature seal. It was a small room, starkly lit by a large fluorescent light on a chain hanger, and cold, a shock after the warm humid air outside, cold enough to make our breath visible as white vapor as we exhaled through our masks. An exhaust fan running at full bore sounded like a boat's outboard motor. A stainless steel gurney in the middle of the room was centered under the light. Beside it stood a woman wearing light blue scrubs, latex disposable sanitary gloves, and a face-mask like ours.

On the gurney, a body was covered by a lightweight purple sheet. Berriman nodded to the woman and she lifted the end of the sheet. Berriman was right. The face was swollen horribly and discolored with dark blotches. Nevertheless, I could still see Erin there, and the red hair, still wet and combed back, was undeniably hers. It was Erin on the gurney, her body violated by the ravages of death, so quiet, and so incredibly still.

"Harry, is this Ms. Haig?" the Chief Inspector asked.

"Yes."

The Chief Inspector looked at Blair, who nodded his agreement.

I reached over and touched the purple sheet where I thought Erin's hand might be. Very quietly, I said, "Erin, I'm sorry." Then, feeling unsteady on my feet and nauseous again, I had to get out of there. "I need fresh air," I said as I shoved the heavy door open and headed down the hall, ripping off my face-mask, and walking fast, looking only ahead of me at the sunlight beckoning on the other side of the mortuary's entrance. Once outside, I sat on one of the front steps, trying to catch my breath, waiting for the dizziness to pass. Gradually the chill of the mortuary dissipated in the enveloping outdoor warmth. Blair and Berriman joined me and stood at the bottom of the steps.

"Where was she found?" I asked Berriman, when I was able to talk again.

"The body was found this morning caught in anchoring ropes of a navigation buoy about a mile offshore. It was noticed by a crew member on one of the lighters that was loading cargo onto a nearby freighter."

"How did she get there? What do you think happened?"

"There appear to be stab wounds in her side, so it looks now that Ms. Haig was killed before her body was dropped into the water. Generally a body in the harbor is carried out to sea if it is far enough out to be taken by the tidal current. Our local Hong Kong murderers are aware of this. But if Ms. Haig was killed on the same day that she was seen entering the car at the Renaissance, the wind from the storm that night may have pushed her body against the tide so that it stayed closer to land and then became tangled in the buoy's ropes. We'll know more about cause and time of death after the autopsy is completed."

"What about Chen Qiwei?" I asked.

"I'm sorry," Berriman said, "what is your question?"

"Erin was meeting Chen Qiwei. He thought he was being followed. Given what happened to Erin, most likely Chen was killed as well. So, where is Chen's body?"

"If you're right and Chen's body was dropped in the water at the same time and in the same location, we stand a reasonable chance of discovering it eventually, like we did Ms. Haig's."

"Do you have any leads on who did this?" Blair asked.

"We're still looking for the two men who attacked Mr. Leung. We have adjusted the police advisory to include suspicion of murder. We have bulletins out on Mr. Chen and on the registered owner of the Mercedes."

"What will become of Erin's body?" I asked. *Erin's body.*

"You mean, after the autopsy?"

"Yes."

"We are awaiting instructions from Ms. Haig's family," Berriman said.

"Have you been in contact with them?" I asked.

"When we called Robert Leung on his mobile about finding the body, he told us that he'd spoken with Ms. Haig's parents earlier, shortly after she disappeared. I'll call him again momentarily to confirm your identification of Ms. Haig and then he or I will contact her parents."

"Chief Inspector Berriman, what are your thoughts now about Edward Woo as a suspect?"

"He's still high on my list, Harry."

"We had an appointment to meet with him," Blair said. "We postponed it when you called us. We can set another time. Should we?"

"Yes, do that. See what you can find out. We get snared in a thicket of lawyers when we try to talk to Edward Woo."

I wasn't surprised by what we saw in the cold room of the Kowloon Public Mortuary. Horrified, broken-hearted, nauseated, but not surprised. I had expected the worst when I saw the surveillance video of Erin entering the Mercedes. But it was almost too much to imagine Erin's terror and her helplessness against her ruthless murderers. She had teased and played with me and just days earlier I had felt her lovely smooth bare skin. We were collaborators, and we were playmates. We might have had a future together after Hong Kong.

Her death had to be avenged.

Seventeen

THE FURAMA ALTERNATED the English-language papers that were dropped outside my door each morning, leaving the *South China Morning Post* one day, and the *Hong Kong Standard* the next. This morning it was the *South China Morning Post*. The picture of Erin standing outside the Federal Building was displayed above the fold on its front page, beside the day's lead story, "Reporter Found Dead in Harbor, Apparently Killed While Pursuing Story on Hong Kong Corruption."

Chief Inspector Berriman, identified as officer in charge for the police investigation, was quoted that inquiries would be pursued regardless of where they led. He declined to speculate on who might be responsible. Robert Leung, reached by the *South China Morning Post* in Taipei, was less reticent. "Our colleague was so brutally attacked and her life tragically cut short because she was working on a story for the *Asian Business Journal* which exposes corruption involving business leaders and government officials in Hong Kong and their shady financial dealings with their counterparts in mainland China." Leung compared Erin's murder to those of martyred journalists in Russia, Iraq and Iran. He said that the ABJ would not be deterred from covering the deterioration of the rule of law in Hong Kong. On its editorial page, the *South China Morning Post* described Erin's career and decried the peril faced by a society that tolerates attacks on its journalists, "An attack on a news organization's staff and property is an attack on society itself, and must not go unanswered by the Authorities."

I called Jerry. "I have very bad news," I said. "Our friend at the journal who disappeared has been found. She was murdered."

My throat choked up momentarily and I stopped there.

Jerry said, "Murdered! Jesus!"

"So I'll stay here a while longer," I said. "In case I can be useful."

"I'm so sorry about Erin," Elizabeth said, when I arrived at the office. "Is there anything I can do?"

"Blair was planning to ask you to re-schedule our appointment with Edward Woo that we had to cancel."

"He already has, and I've already called Woo's office. That's not what I mean," she said, standing in front of me and looking up at me in a motherly way. "I mean for you personally."

"No, I'm fine. Thanks."

"Well, call on me if you need anything."

"What's the story with Edward Woo?"

"His assistant told me that he will be unavailable to meet with you," Elizabeth said. She added, framing her next words with air quotes, "'due to the events reported in the news.'"

"What does Blair say about this?"

Just then Blair joined us with a cup of coffee in each hand, one apparently for Elizabeth. "I say Edward Woo hasn't heard the last from us. He has not taken into account the arts of Mei-Ling."

"Can Mei-Ling get us a meeting?"

"She can pull her strings with Cynthia Woo."

The office phone rang and Elizabeth picked it up. "Hello, Chief Inspector," she said, "Would you like to be put through to Blair and to Harry?" Apparently Berriman said that wouldn't be necessary. Elizabeth listened, wrote several lines on a notepad, said thank you, and replaced the handset.

"Erin's parents are on their way to Hong Kong. They are expected to arrive this evening and will stay at the Sheraton in Kowloon, where Erin had her room. An ABJ staff member, Cathy Chao, will meet them and accompany them in their dealings with the police. Chief Inspector Berriman said you are welcome to meet them as well, if you wish."

"What are their names?" I asked.

"Mr. and Mrs. Donald E. Haig," Elizabeth said, reading from her notes.

"I do want to meet them. I'll contact Cathy. But now," I said to Blair, "let's call Mei-Ling."

"Harry, I'm terribly sorry about Erin," Mei-Ling said. "How are you holding up?"

"I'm fine, thank you," I said. "Thank you for all of your help. We have another request."

"I only wish that I had been there for Erin when she really needed me."

"That's also how I feel. It's too late now."

Blair said, "Edward Woo is a leading suspect. He was angry about the ABJ articles and he made a lot of threats. The police can't get to him for questioning because he's too well protected behind his lawyers. But Harry and I believe that Edward might let something slip if we can talk to him and Chief Inspector Berriman agrees. Could you get us in through the back door, so to speak, through Cynthia?"

"I can try."

"For example, if Cynthia invites us to a family gathering that includes Woo Jian-Min, I believe that Edward would want to join us in order to stay on top of our interactions with his father."

"I'll call her right away."

I emailed Cathy Chao, "What's your plan for Erin's parents?" She replied, "We'll meet at the Sheraton this evening before they turn in after their trip. They'll have a hard day tomorrow." I emailed back that I would like to meet them and asked Cathy to let me know specific time and place.

That evening, when I entered The Café at the Sheraton, I found Cathy at a corner table with a couple who appeared to be in their late sixties or early seventies. The man stood when I approached. He had short grey hair brushed straight back, grey eyes behind gold wire-rimmed glasses, a grey moustache, and wore a blue button-down shirt open at the collar and tan Dockers trousers. Cathy said, "Mr. Haig, this is Harry West, Erin's friend."

The man put out his hand, and said, "Don Haig, and this is Erin's mother, Maureen." I shook his hand, and then shook hers as well. "I'm very sorry for your terrible loss," I said. "I still find it hard to believe this has happened." Maureen Haig was thin, with reddish grey hair, and grey eyes with hint of green like Erin's. She said, "Erin emailed us that she had met someone in Hong Kong whom she liked. Cathy tells us that Erin was referring to you."

"I hope so. I liked Erin very much. But I confess that she never told me much about you."

"There's not much to know," Don Haig said, "We're both retired. We used to live on Long Island where I had a

186

practice as an architect and Maureen worked in my office. Now we now live in Arizona and we play golf."

"Every day except during sandstorms," Maureen Haig said. Then, as if an afterthought, "When she was little, we used to call her Erin Rose. She told us to stop when she went to kindergarten because she thought she was grown, and double names were for babies. Erin Rose. She was our only child."

I told Erin's parents how she and I had met, and how we were collaborating to expose corrupt business practices in Hong Kong.

"Is that why she was killed?" Maureen asked.

"We don't know for sure, but we'll find out," I said. "For what it's worth, Erin loved being a journalist…"

"Yes, she was very proud of her new job."

"…and she belongs now to a select group who've sacrificed to report the truth." Even as I intoned those familiar words, I realized how empty they were for Erin's parents and for me. "It's small comfort, I know."

They looked at me, gripped by bottomless sadness, worn out from their travel and in dread of what they'd face tomorrow. I told them that I had also lost my only child, a baby girl, which helped me to understand their loss as Erin's parents.

Maureen said, "Thank you, Harry, for your understanding and for being Erin's friend." She took her husband's hand. "Don, I'm done. Our trip here, and everything, I need to go to our room." Cathy said she would handle the bill in The Café and would return in the morning to take them to meet Chief Inspector Berriman. "Try to get some rest," she said. We both watched Erin's parents walk slowly out of The Café, holding hands.

"How are you managing, Cathy, with all this?"

"It's too much." Her eyes welled and she dabbed at them angrily with a napkin from the table. Her hand trembled as she put the napkin down. "It's so messed up. They killed Erin for what? So that Edward Woo can buy a phone company?"

"There are people who don't want to be exposed and maybe the ABJ was getting too close."

"Well, fuck that too," Cathy said. "It wasn't worth Erin's life. Robert says we need to stay low, and now he's gone off to Taiwan, and Eugene is not answering his phone or responding to email. I blame Robert. He goaded these bastards even after they warned us. And now Erin…" She stopped and picked up another napkin to wipe her eyes and cheeks. "I'm leaving Hong Kong. I'm going to Vancouver where I have family. Even if I didn't need to go into hiding, there's no reason to stay around since we've been shut down here and we don't even have an office anymore. We've been evicted from our building."

"You were evicted? Why?"

"Other tenants complained. They're worried about collateral damage if there is another attack on us. We're not fighting the eviction. It doesn't matter. Robert is setting up base in Taipei. Even if we can't get printed copies of the ABJ into Hong Kong, there's always the Internet for our online publication. Whatever. I don't care. I've just got to get out."

"But you'll still be here tomorrow for Erin's parents?"

"I will. I'll bring them to the Chief Inspector's office and then I'll excuse myself."

"Thank you for doing that."

"It's nothing, Harry. I'm glad you'll stay in Hong Kong to follow Erin's case. I hope you can help to solve it. The bastards who did this should hang for it."

Eighteen

MEI-LING TURNED AROUND to face me from her front passenger seat in Blair's Mercedes when I asked how she was able to arrange a meeting with Woo Jian-Min.

"Not officially with Woo Jian-Min," she said. "We are invited by my dear friend Cynthia. It just happens that Woo Jian-Min will be there."

"Well, it's his yacht."

"That's why Cynthia thought it would be a good place to meet. She's such a clever girl."

"Did she also invite Edward?"

"No. She and Edward don't talk much these days. But she arranged that Edward would hear about it and he sent a message to a Woo family assistant that he'll come as well."

Our two-lane road to Repulse Bay featured numerous switchbacks with no opportunities to pass so our progress was slow behind a serpentine line of cars and buses. Blair said, "We're taking the slow but scenic route over the Peak and down to Aberdeen for your benefit, Harry. We usually use the Aberdeen Tunnel to commute across the Island."

I had ample time during our descent down the south side of the Peak to observe the lush green trees and shrubs alongside the road and the blue South China Sea ahead of us. The view reminded me of Route 84 as it crosses the foothills of the San Francisco Peninsula down to the San Gregorio cliffs on the Pacific coast. Both roads wind through semi-tropical vegetation down steep hillsides towards an ocean coastline, although here, unlike in California, there were Chinese characters on the signs at the side of the road, and a dense mass of high-rise apartment buildings looming ahead of us.

We turned left in Aberdeen to follow the coast road past assorted office buildings, small warehouses, and factories. Mei-Ling saw the sign for the Aberdeen Boat Club. "Go right here," she said, which Blair did, taking us down an unpaved private road.

Blair told the security guard at the gate that we were guests of Cynthia Woo and showed his Hong Kong ID card. The guard took his time. He peered into the car at Blair, Mei-Ling, and me, scanned Blair's card on a handheld remote terminal, went around to the back of the Mercedes to read its license plate which he keyed in on his handheld terminal, and then waited a minute or so until a report came back. Finally, he returned Blair's ID card and waved us into the grounds.

As we were parking in a marked visitor's space, a woman approached our car. Tall, and slender, she spoke English with an American accent, "Are you the Blairs and Mr. Harry West?"

"We are indeed," Blair said. "Here to visit Cynthia Woo."

"I'm Jia Yanwei. I help the family with social arrangements. Please follow me. We have a tender waiting to take us to the family's yacht."

She led us to a large speedboat tied to a dock in front of the Marina clubhouse. Its glistening varnished deck had ample space for benches and chairs, although it looked comparatively tiny amongst the mega-yachts moored nearby. Waiting for us in the boat was a man in his early twenties neatly attired in white trousers and a blue jacket. He extended a hand to Mei-Ling to help her on board. Then Blair stepped across the gap, and I followed. Ms. Jia cast off the ropes connecting us to the dock and jumped on board. After we'd pulled slowly away from the dock, the young man gradually pushed more power to our three outboard motors, ratcheting their noise up to an ear-piercing scream as we raced towards a massive multistory white yacht that sat motionless at the outer rim of the harbor. Shouting to be heard over the outboard motors, Ms. Jia told us that the yacht was anchored there because it was too big to fit in any of the dockside berths.

When we arrived at the yacht, a set of steps was swung out and lowered to our boat. A plump woman appeared at the top of the steps. "Mei-Ling!" she shouted, laughing. "Welcome! Welcome! It's wonderful to see you."

Mei-Ling waved to her and started up the steps. Blair glanced at me and said in a low voice, "You'd never know that Mei-Ling and Cynthia went shopping together just last week."

Blair ascended next, and I followed him. He was being hugged by Cynthia Woo when I reached the deck, her face sideways against his chest as if she were hugging a tree. "And this must be Harry; I've heard so much about you," she said, releasing Blair and taking my extended hand in both of hers. She held on, looking up at me, locking her brown eyes onto mine, "I was very sad to hear about your friend."

"Yes. It's hard to believe what happened."

"Such an attractive woman. So much promise."

"I know."

We were both silent for a moment while Blair and Mei-Ling looked on, and then Cynthia said, "Let me show you around." She put her arm through Mei-Ling's. "Follow me."

The two of them arm-in-arm, one slender and elegant and the other short and plump, walked ahead of Blair and me as we visited the yacht's five open decks, taking an elevator to the top deck and then descending on stairs to each deck below. On the top deck, a helipad doubled as a sun-bathing terrace, adjacent to a Jacuzzi and a bar. Lower decks offered outdoor areas for seating, dining and drinking, a swimming pool, and a badminton court; and indoors, a movie theatre that doubled as a library, a health center with exercise machines and a sauna, a TV room, and a children's play area. "For the grandchildren," Cynthia said.

Everywhere we went, I saw crew members, both men and women, wearing the same outfit of blue jackets and white trousers, walking about purposefully, carrying things, doing tasks, or hovering nearby for instructions. We returned to the top deck next to the helipad where Cynthia selected a seating area. A crew member approached and asked what we would like for refreshments. "We have anything you could want," Cynthia told us, "just ask." Mei-Ling requested a gin & tonic, Blair a beer, and I a bottle of fizzy water. Cynthia said that if we'd like to use the pool, there were bathing suits available that would fit us. "Don't worry; they're new, never used!"

Mei-Ling said, "Let's just sit and talk for a while so that you can tell us what you've planned for this evening."

"Well," Cynthia said, "Daddy's on board. He's taking his afternoon nap now and will appear when we collect for dinner. He says he is looking forward to seeing his Mei-Ling again. My dear husband Andy is still at the office and will join us later. As will Edward."

Blair said, "Cynthia, about Edward, we must tell you that he is a suspect in Erin Haig's death."

"I know," Cynthia said.

"So, just to be clear with you, we plan to ask Edward questions about her murder when he's here away from his lawyers."

"Mei-Ling told me. It's alright with me. You do what you have to do. My brother is capable of anything. If he has blood on his hands, he should pay."

"We wouldn't want…"

"It will be better for our family if the truth comes out," Cynthia said. Turning towards me, she continued, "Edward and I are not close. He used to say that I was stupid, ugly, and fat, and would never get married. He mocked me in front of his friends and my friends. Do you remember, Mei-Ling?"

"I do," Mei-Ling said.

"He was surprised when Andy appeared and liked me enough to want to marry me."

"Andy didn't appear just by accident," Mei-Ling said, with a flash of the wicked smile that I recalled so well.

"Mei-Ling introduced us," Cynthia said, reaching over to clutch Mei-Ling's hand.

"But you took it from there by being so adorable."

"And so rich!" Cynthia exclaimed, saying out loud what I was thinking. "But Andy's family has money too, so he didn't marry me just for Daddy's money. When Andy and I got married, I told Edward he had to retract what he said about me. He refused. He was drinking a lot then which might be an excuse. But now that he drinks less, he's meaner than ever."

"Then we'll proceed as planned," Blair said.

"I had heard that you and Mei-Ling were good friends," I said, "but I didn't realize that she had played such a big role in your life."

"Friends! We are like sisters! Our two families, the Tungs and the Woos, have always been like one extended family. Daddy spends more time with Mei-Ling's uncle than with anyone else. Our two families lived in the same village before they migrated to Shanghai. And when life in China became impossible, the Tungs and Woos fled together to Hong Kong. Anyway we are as close as two beetles in springtime."

"Two horny beetles," Mei-Ling said, and she and Cynthia laughed like schoolgirls.

It was getting cool, with a breeze off the water now that the sun was setting, and Cynthia, after glancing at her watch, suggested that we go inside. She said we could leave our drinks and get new ones, if we wanted. Shortly after we had assembled around an inside table, I heard the whup-whup-whup of a helicopter approaching. The noise got closer and louder, and then stopped. A few minutes later, Edward Woo and Cynthia's husband Andy entered from the deck outside. Cynthia introduced Andy to me and to Blair and after we shook hands he leaned down to give Mei-Ling a hug.

Edward stood back with his hands clasped behind him and acknowledged us with a curt nod.

Andy said, "Edward kindly offered me a lift."

"I took the helicopter to avoid traffic," Edward said. "Anyway, I need to return later to my office and it will save a lot of time."

Just then, Woo Jian-Min entered from an interior doorway. He was short, with thinning wispy straight hair, quick bright eyes, and a wide smile, like an elderly Chinese elf. He wore a more formal version of the crew's uniform, a striped button-down shirt with a blue polka-dotted bow tie, a blue blazer with gold buttons, and white trousers. "Ah, here is my dear Mei-Ling!" he exclaimed. She stood with her arms outstretched and he came over to give her a hug. I could see where Cynthia got the warmth that had eluded her older brother Edward. On the other hand, anyone with a beating heart would want to hug Mei-Ling, given the opportunity.

Mei-Ling said, "It's wonderful to see you, uncle. Of course you know my husband Blair." He did, and they shook hands. "And we've brought our colleague and very good friend from the United States, Dr. Harry West." Woo Jian-Min approached me and like Cynthia had done, took my outstretched hand in both of his. "You are most welcome. Please accept my condolences for the loss of your friend."

"Thank you, Mr. Woo," I said. "I am very glad to meet you and to see your beautiful yacht."

"It's an indulgence," he said. "But I am an old man and I can afford it, so why not?"

197

Jia Yanwei appeared in the doorway to announce that dinner would soon be served, if we wished to come to the dining room. Woo Jian-Min took Mei-Ling's arm and together they led the rest of us to a wood-paneled room that was dominated by a large round table in its center. Woo Jian-Min took the chair closest to the door that led to the kitchen, which he referred to as the galley. Mei-Ling was seated on his right and Cynthia on his left. Andy, Blair, Edward and I took the other chairs with Edward seated across from his father. Each place had already been set with soup bowls and cups for tea.

A crew member rolled a trolley into the room bearing a large soup tureen. He circled our table and ladled soup into each of our bowls, beginning with Mei-Ling. Another crew member's trolley offered tea, glasses of ice water, a selection of wine, and beer. Then came numerous dishes of meats, rice, vegetables, dumplings, pastries, and other delicacies, all placed on a Lazy Susan at the center of the table that allowed each of us to serve ourselves.

Woo Jian-Min asked Mei-Ling about her interior decorating business. She replied that it was doing well. He said that some of the Woo buildings needed to update their furnishings on their executive floors, and would she be interested? Yes, of course, she replied. He advised her to call Jia Yanwei to schedule meetings with the appropriate building managers.

Woo Jian-Min turned to Edward, who was sitting glumly silent. "Why didn't you bring Jessie and my two grandchildren?"

"They've gone to our place in Bali during school break."

"How are they?"

"They're doing well, Father."

"They should visit more often. They're always welcome here."

"I'll pass that along, Father."

Cynthia reported that her Andy was now managing the Hong Kong office for JPMorgan Chase, replacing the former manager who had been re-assigned to Beijing. "If the bank asks you also to re-locate to Beijing, will you agree to go?" Woo Jian-Min asked.

"I'd have to consider it," Andy said. "We need more presence on the mainland." Cynthia did not react visibly to this hint of an impending family discussion about re-locating out of Hong Kong.

Mei-Ling said, looking at me, "My uncles Tung Kwan-ha and Woo Jian-Min still play golf every week."

"This is true," Woo Jian-Min said. "He insists that he will continue playing until he is able to win a game, or until I die, but I am trying very hard to forestall both outcomes." Then he added a remark in Chinese that caused Mei-Ling to laugh. "Just an old saying," he said, without elaborating.

199

As the Lazy Susan turned, chopsticks clicked, and tea-cups were refreshed, Andy and Blair talked about business trends in Hong Kong and in China, and Mei-Ling and Woo Jian-Min chatted about members of their respective families. Edward sat silently, watching and listening.

Cynthia, who was sitting beside me, leaned in my direction. Realizing that she had something to impart, I leaned towards her as well. She whispered, "Mei-Ling told me about you when she returned from London. She was very taken with you. Very."

"And I was with her," I said, also whispering.

"I can see why she talked so much about you. You're so handsome."

"Thank you," I said.

"She told me that sometimes she wished she had stayed in London or else brought you back to Hong Kong."

"It was a long time ago."

"She said she should have kept you instead of returning with her first husband, that she made a big mistake. She said if she could do things over, she would not make that mistake again. She would never let you go."

Since Cynthia and I were both looking down as we leaned towards each other, whispering, I didn't know whether our colloquy was being observed by anyone else at the table. I doubted that Mei-Ling or Blair would be comfortable hearing Cynthia's confidences.

"We were a lot younger then," I observed. Cynthia responded with an enigmatic smile.

My *sotto voce* exchange with Cynthia was brought to a merciful end when Woo Jian-Min demanded, "Blair, tell me about your new consulting business."

"Gladly, Mr. Woo. Our firm, Blair West International, has two offices, one in Hong Kong which I manage, and one in Cambridge, in the US, which Harry leads."

"Are you busy?"

"We are getting busy," Blair said. "The reason that Harry is here now is that we have an engagement with the government in Hong Kong."

"I have heard about your engagement," Woo Jian-Min said. "You are reviewing Edward's bid to acquire Hong Kong Wireless. What have you concluded?"

Edward Woo protested, "Father, is this the right time?"

"Why not?"

"At a family dinner?"

"I'm interested in what Blair and Harry have to say."

"They have collaborated with people who libeled me and my business partner despite my clear demands that they stop."

I caught Blair's eye. This was our cue.

"Edward," I said. "One of these *people*, as you call them, was our good friend Erin Haig, and she has just been found murdered."

"Nothing to do with me."

"Or, alternatively, it has everything to do with you."

"What are you…"

Woo Jian-Min interrupted, "Let's hear what they have to say, Edward. We'll both learn something. Blair, tell us, what have you and Harry concluded about Edward's proposal?"

Edward shook his head but did not protest further.

Blair said, "We concluded that there is an issue that requires attention."

"What is this issue?"

"It concerns Edward's financing from the New China Properties Fund. We obtained evidence that the Fund is engaged in money laundering."

Woo Jian-Min leaned back in his chair. He looked inquiringly at Edward like a judge in his courtroom inviting a response from opposing counsel.

"All lies," Edward said. "Their so-called evidence is fraudulent. It means nothing."

"I hope that's true, Edward," Woo Jian-Min said. And then, to Blair, "Are you aware that another group also has bid to acquire Hong Kong Wireless? A group based in Singapore. And that I am part of that other group?"

Blair said, "Yes, and we did find it curious that you would compete against Edward's bid."

"It's just business. Sometimes Edward and I are on different sides. But as you can see, we can still meet as a family for dinner." Edward's sullen expression didn't serve as an advertisement for family harmony. To the contrary, it suggested that Woo Jian-Min would be well-advised to bring a food taster when invited to Edward's place for dinner.

I asked, "May I speak again, sir, about Erin Haig, the journalist who was working at the *Asian Business Journal*?"

"Of course," Woo Jian-Min said.

"We believe that Erin was attempting to interview a source for their story when she was killed. Her source also has disappeared. And the registered owner of a Mercedes that she was seen entering, and that later was found abandoned in Yau Ma Tei, is also missing, along with his family."

"Where are you going with this?" Edward demanded. "What is your point?"

I turned to face him. "Where I'm going with this is that the managing editor of the ABJ was attacked and beaten on the same day that Erin disappeared. The day before, the ABJ office was vandalized. When the first installment of the ABJ series was published, you, Edward, sued the journal for libel and your lawyers obtained an injunction to stop its publication in Hong Kong."

"So what? What are you accusing me of, here in front of my family, on my father's boat?"

"You were embarrassed by the journal's reporting. You took it personally. You threatened the ABJ and you threatened us..."

"That's enough!" Edward's face was flushed. "This kind of talk will not end well for you."

"What exactly do you mean by 'not end well,' Edward?" I asked, pushing back, getting angry myself. The man might be Erin's murderer and now he was threatening us?

Woo Jian-Min interceded, "Edward, you should go outside to cool off. You are making unwise comments."

At this, Edward shoved his chair away from the table, stood up and left for the deck, without another word and without looking back.

"I apologize for my son," Woo Jian-Min said.

Blair said, "No need. We wanted to hear what Edward would say."

"Do the police consider him to be a suspect?"

"Yes, but you would already know that."

Woo Jian-Min winced to confirm this.

"Blair," I said, "let's join Edward on the deck to try to talk with him some more."

Blair turned to Woo Jian-Min, "May we be excused, sir?"

"Yes, certainly," Woo Jian-Min said. "I apologize again for my son's bad temper."

It had gotten dark. The moon was still hidden behind the hill that rose above Aberdeen, but we could see the stars, and lights were shining in Aberdeen and on the yachts and houseboats moored in the harbor. I could smell Edward Woo's cigar as we approached him where he stood in shadows at a railing. "Have you come to hurl more accusations?" he asked.

"We are just trying to learn what happened," I said. "Erin Haig was our friend."

"So you've said." Edward drew on his cigar, flaring its tip deep red.

"One thing we don't understand, Edward," I said, "is why you need financing from the New China Properties Fund. Surely the Woo family has enough capital to buy anything you want."

"When it comes to capital, the Woo family is Woo Jian-Min," Edward said.

"So you don't have access to your family's money?"

"Not unless Woo Jian-Min changes his mind. Or until he dies. As you can see, he is in good health." *Reminder to Woo Jian-Min, don't forget the food taster.* "He chose not to join my bid for Hong Kong Wireless. And then he signs up with a competitor. As he said, to him it's all just business."

"Did you see the list of names that we provided to our client?"

"The document that was stolen?"

"Yes."

"I saw it. Your client Shih Chai-Ming actually believes that this so-called list implicates the Fund."

"Doesn't it? It shows names of investors who couldn't have earned their wealth honestly. Doesn't this suggest to you that the Fund is engaged in money laundering?"

Woo smiled coldly as if he pitied my stupidity. "Someone used a computer to type in names of people he didn't like. Shih Chai-Ming will discover soon enough that others in Government don't respond well to such obvious frauds. He will be called to account."

I asked, "Edward, did you murder Erin Haig?"

"Don't be stupid."

"Yes or no?"

He didn't answer, and I added, "Can you persuade us that you had nothing to do with Erin's murder?"

"Why should I persuade you? Who the fuck are you?"

"Erin was our friend," I repeated.

"Are you asking for yourselves, or for the Chief Inspector?"

"Both."

"You need to ask, 'who benefits?' Do you think I'm better off because the reporter was killed? My project is placed at risk. CNN broadcasts insinuations about my financial partner. All of this could be easily predicted."

He flicked the glowing stub of his cigar over the railing and in the quiet of the evening I could hear it hiss when it hit the water.

"The police should look elsewhere," he said.

"Where, for example?"

"They say that the reporter was meeting a person who was a source for their articles. What if that other person was the real target and she was just unlucky, being in the wrong place when he was killed? You should ask yourselves who would gain from killing that other person."

"We've already thought of that," Blair said, "It seems to us that the answer to that question is quite clear: You, Edward."

"You're missing the point. Everything they had to say about me was going to be published, even if I did get an injunction, and even if their so-called source disappeared. I knew that. So their source could not harm me anymore. Killing him would make no difference to me. There must be others who wanted to silence him."

"Like who?" I asked.

"Others who would want to prevent their reputations from being dragged through the mud."

"Like who, for example?"

"That's for you to figure out."

Mei-Ling, who had quietly stepped onto the deck and was standing behind us in a shadow, said, "Edward, sorry to interrupt, but your father is about to retire and we need to head back. Blair and Harry, can you come in for a moment to say good-bye?"

We re-entered the dining area, followed by Edward. Woo Jian-Min stood near a doorway exchanging hugs with Cynthia and Mei-Ling, and then shaking Andy's hand. I told him that I appreciated his hospitality and Blair similarly expressed his thanks. "You are most welcome," he said. Then he glanced in Edward's direction and Edward bowed his head to his father, briefly.

Jia Yanwei entered the room to let us know that the launch was ready to take us ashore. More hugs followed with Cynthia and then we started towards the steps that would bring us down to the launch.

Andy said, "Actually, Edward, I won't be riding back with you to Central. I decided to stay here tonight with Cynthia."

"If you have space available on your helicopter," Blair said to Edward, "perhaps you could give Harry a lift."

Edward replied, "I don't owe him any favors."

"It would be a favor to me," Mei-Ling said. "Blair and I are planning to drive Harry back to his hotel but if you take him with you, we could avoid the round trip." Without waiting for Edward's response, apparently taking his agreement for granted, she asked me, "Harry, would it be OK with you to go with Edward?"

"So long as everyone here bears witness, in case I disappear, that you last saw me leaving with Edward in his helicopter," I said. An image had flashed through my mind of falling from the helicopter and my drowned body being swept by the tidal current out to sea to be devoured by sharks and crabs. Blair emitted a mirthless chuckle. Edward said, "If you don't want a lift, that's fine with me."

"Just joking," I said. "I'd appreciate a lift."

By the time Edward and I had climbed the steps to the helipad on the upper deck, I could see that the launch carrying Blair and Mei-Ling was already half-way to shore, its lights flickering like fireflies on the black water. We ducked under the slowly rotating helicopter blade and entered the craft through an open door, taking passenger seats behind the pilot, who was checking instruments. Edward said that the Plexiglas partition that separated our passenger area from the pilot had been installed to cut the noise and also enabled him to carry on conversations without being overheard. It was slid open now as the pilot prepared for our departure; Edward said something to him in Chinese and the pilot responded, also in Chinese.

To me, Edward said, "We'll arrive at my building in ten minutes. We'll fly over water around the tip of the island." We lifted off from the helipad. From my window overlooking this portion of the coastline of Hong Kong Island, which was rocky and unpopulated, the view was mostly inky darkness. But when we turned the corner, isolated multistory buildings came into view and in the distance, I could see the bright lights of Central and Wan Chai.

"How much longer will you stay in Hong Kong?" Edward asked.

"That depends on how useful I can be in helping the police find Erin's killer."

"Very noble of you. Here's some advice: Leave as soon as you can."

"Why?"

"Whoever murdered the reporter will dispose of you as well if you're seen as a threat."

"By 'whoever,' do you mean yourself?"

Edward stared at me like I was a cockroach about to experience a close encounter with the bottom of his shoe.

Apart from driving on Boston streets, I've never knowingly confronted mortal danger. I don't get a thrill from thumbing my nose at death which I expect will come soon enough on its own. But now I could almost grasp what soldiers mean when they explain why they advance towards hostile fire, overcoming their every rational instinct to flee. They say they don't want to let their buddies down. I didn't want to let Erin down. I had no choice; I had to do everything I could to bring her justice, no matter where that led.

"You won't scare me off, Edward, if that's what you are trying to do."

"Suit yourself."

"On the boat, you implied that others could be involved, and that you have ideas about who they are."

"Are you asking for my opinion?"

"Yes."

"Then, once again, ask who benefits? Who is harmed? Think about it. Whose bid for Hong Kong Wireless will win if mine fails?"

"You mean the Singapore group? Your father, Woo Jian-Min?"

"If the reporter's source was about to reveal something that would embarrass Woo Jian-Min, he would never stand for that."

"But, he's your father…"

"You weren't listening when he said, 'it's just business.' He's not sentimental when it comes to business."

We started to descend. I could see below us the floodlit rooftop helipad on Woo Jian-Min's office tower.

"Anybody else we should think about?"

"Other families that do business both in Shanghai and in Hong Kong. Families close to Woo Jian-Min. If you were paying attention this evening, you wouldn't have to look far."

"Are you referring to the Tung family?"

Edward Woo did a thing with his eyebrows and shoulders as if to say, Why not? "If my father has anything to do with this, he would have consulted with Tung Kwan-ha, his oldest and closest friend."

"So you'd point your finger at two old men as more likely suspects than yourself?"

"Are you being stupid intentionally? They get others to serve their interests."

"Who, for example?"

"For example, they are both dear 'uncles' of someone my father believes can do no wrong, who is as close to him as his own daughter and certainly closer than his only son, who always gets what she wants, and who is perfect in every way. His perfect princess."

"Surely you don't mean Mei-Ling?"

He shrugged.

211

"You expect me to believe that Mei-Ling would have anything to do with Erin's murder?"

He shrugged again.

We touched down on the rooftop helipad. I followed Edward out of the helicopter and walked silently with him across the roof towards the elevator. While we were waiting for the elevator – he would get off at his floor and I was heading towards the lobby – I said, "Erin's murder will be solved, I'm sure of it. If you had nothing to do with it, this will come out, and I apologize to you for my suspicions. If it turns out that you are responsible, then..."

"Yes, yes, you will make me suffer, and my life will turn to shit. Don't flatter yourself. You'd just become one more among my enemies who are trying to bring me down. I'm still here. I always win. Take my advice to leave Hong Kong."

"That won't happen."

"Then tell your Chief Inspector what I told you if you're serious about finding who killed the reporter."

"I am serious about it, Edward," I said. "So if you do have Erin's blood on your hands, don't get too comfortable."

"Do you have any idea why you are standing here with me on the rooftop of my father's building?"

Another riddle. "No, tell me."

"Because, even though you tried your puny best to provoke me, I chose not to dump you out of my helicopter. Don't make me regret my self-restraint."

THE TRAIL OF MONEY

Neither on Edward Woo's face nor in his dead black eyes was there the slightest trace of a smile.

"Thanks for the ride," I said.

Nineteen

WE CALLED Chief Inspector Berriman to report on our interactions with Edward Woo.

"Did he confess?" Berriman asked.

Blair replied, "No, but he did offer theories to pursue."

"I'm curious to hear them," Berriman said. "I also have news. Last night, we arrested the two thugs who attacked Robert Leung. They were identified after being taken in earlier last night for disturbing the peace outside a bar on Mody Road in Tsim Sha Tsui. We interrogated one of them last night."

Blair asked, "Chief Inspector, do you video record your interrogations?"

"Yes."

"Then we'd like to watch the video of one you did last night."

"Sorry, privacy of suspects, and so on. But I'll tell you what we learned."

The clock was running on my time in Hong Kong, and if this thug was Erin's murderer, or could lead us to him, I wasn't overly concerned about his privacy. I needed to hear for myself what he said, not just Berriman's summary. "Excuse my French, Chief Inspector, but that's bullshit," I said. "You promised that you would share everything with us about the case. We want to see this video. This is important. Your suspect may have said something relating to Erin that we'll pick up, something that you missed."

Blair asked, "Chief Inspector, if the prisoner waives his privacy rights, can you show it to us?

"Why would he do that?"

"You could tell him that it will be taken into account at his sentencing."

"I'll consult with his lawyer and get back to you." Berriman said.

An hour later, Berriman called to tell us that the prisoner, Chu Y.Y., did consent to our seeing the video.

"This is by way of a trade," Berriman said. "After you watch the video, you can tell me about Edward Woo's theories."

Berriman's assistant met us at the Caine House entrance after we'd cleared security, and escorted us to the Chief Inspector's office.

Berriman adjusted the monitor on his desk so that it faced us directly. "I'll give you a bit of an intro before we watch the video," he said. "I was in a viewing room watching the interrogation through one-way glass; I communicated with the police interrogator via a microphone. You'll hear a Chinese-to-English translator who was with me in the room. We use her for interrogations concerning serious offenses and to help those of us still on the police force for whom Chinese is not our first language."

The Chief Inspector started the video player. On the monitor, a large man with a chubby face was seated in a wooden chair at a plain wooden table. His shiny clean-shaved head appeared to rest directly on a bulked up back and chest, with no neck discernible between head and body. Beside this big fellow was a slender man wearing a suit and tie. Berriman identified him as a government-paid lawyer, one of the territory's law student interns who represented indigent defendants as part of their law training. The interrogator was a woman in a police uniform standing across the table from the two men, her hands resting on the back of a chair. Wiry, like she worked out regularly, with an angular face etched by sharp cheekbones, she watched the suspect silently while he stared down at his thick-fingered hands clasped on the table.

The action started on the video with an instruction in English from Chief Inspector Berriman to the police interrogator, "Please indicate that you hear me and then start the interrogation." She touched her ear in which she was wearing an ear-bud, and then spoke in Chinese, her words being repeated almost simultaneously in English by the translator, "I am Interrogator Lin and I am now starting an interrogation of Chu Y.Y. in the presence of his lawyer, Mr. Stanley Cheng. These proceedings are being audio and video recorded. Mr. Chu Y.Y., please tell me your address and occupation."

He said he was a laborer and lived in different boarding houses with no fixed address.

"Mr. Chu Y.Y.," she said, "You have been arrested for assaulting Mr. Robert Leung on Lockhart Road, in Wan Chai, on Friday, May 20th. This event was captured on a video surveillance camera on a light-post at the intersection of Lockhart Road and Marsh Road. You and your accomplice in this assault were seen to be beating Mr. Leung with a steel hammer and with a wood baton. These are both potentially lethal weapons and their use in this assault could support an additional charge of attempted murder. A photograph of you has been identified by Mr. Leung. Do you admit the charges for which you are arrested?"

Chu Y.Y. looked at his lawyer, who said, "Please show us the surveillance image." After a photograph was passed across the table and reviewed by the lawyer and suspect, there was muttering between them, and then the lawyer said, "Mr. Chu Y.Y. agrees to the charge of assaulting the victim but states he was not using a hammer, that he was only carrying a wood baton." Berriman paused the video and told us that this apparently was correct. The surveillance video showed that the other suspect held the hammer.

Interrogator Lin asked, "Will he testify that his partner in this attack beat Mr. Leung with a steel hammer?" Then, addressing the suspect directly, "Let me remind you that the entire episode was captured on cameras overlooking the street."

"He will. He will cooperate in the expectation of leniency."

"His cooperation will be taken into account. Tell us who ordered this attack, when, where, and by what means." The lawyer told the suspect that he should answer.

"We receive instructions on notes left in a message box at one of our rooming houses. We also receive cash payments in envelopes in the same message box. We do not know who writes the messages, only that we are paid after we do the jobs."

"What were your instructions?"

"Rough up the guy, Leung, on his way to his office. Bang him around. Teach him a lesson."

"How were you to identify Mr. Leung?"

"There was a picture with the note. Also we were supposed to call him by name, to make sure."

"You weren't instructed to kill him?"

"No, never, just to give him something to remember."

"Why did you not wear masks? Were you not concerned about being identified?"

"Usually when we bang someone around, they don't want more trouble. Identifying us to the police brings more trouble for them. They keep their mouths shut."

"Can you give us the note and the picture of Mr. Leung that you received?"

"We destroyed them before we did the job, like we always do."

"What about the payment and the envelope it came in?"

"One thousand HK dollars each, in cash. The envelopes also are destroyed. We were paid the same day."

"Who recruited you and made the arrangements to communicate through these messages?"

"One of the times we were in jail, another prisoner told us we could make money by doing jobs for people he knew. He said if we agreed, he would let other people know who would tell us what to do."

"What is this prisoner's name?"

"I don't think he told us and we didn't ask."

"Would you recognize him if you saw him or his picture?"

"I don't know. This was three or four years ago and I've never seen him since."

"So you don't know who he is?"

"No. We just check the message box every few days and when there is something for us, we do it, and get the money."

"Was he a member of a triad?"

"Based on his tattoos, maybe."

"Are you?"

"No."

"Do you work for triads?"

"I told you, we don't know who hires us."

"What is the address of the rooming house where these messages and payments are left?"

After Chu Y.Y. provided an address, Berriman paused the video again and told us that he had arranged to have non-uniformed police watch the rooming house. He said he needed to coordinate this surveillance with the Kowloon West Police district. "We'll monitor the place for a while, look for people dropping off or picking up messages, and then try to follow the chain, see how far up we can get."

"Did he just say this rooming house is in Yau Ma Tei?" I asked.

"He did," Berriman said.

"How far is it from the location where the Mercedes was found?"

"Not too far, a few blocks. Interrogator Lin will get to that."

He re-started the video.

"You have no fixed address but you live mostly in the Yau Ma Tei area, is that correct?" the interrogator asked.

"Yes, rooming houses, apartments, depends on how much money I have, and what's vacant."

"Did you stay at the rooming house where the messages were left?"

"Sometimes."

"How about during the night before the assault on Mr. Leung?"

"Yes."

"Do you ever hire out to work on the lighters that moor in the harbor at Yau Ma Tei?"

"Sometimes, if they need help loading or unloading, they offer cash money and we go out."

"So you know the people who work on the boats?"

"Some of them."

The lawyer said, "I don't see what this has to do with the assault on Mr. Leung."

The police interrogator replied, "Police will interview people at the docks to check on what your client tells us about his movements in the Yau Ma Tei area preceding the attack on Mr. Leung. Will you instruct him to answer, please?" The lawyer complied, telling Chu Y.Y. to answer.

"And they know you?" she asked, continuing her line of questioning.

"Some do. Mostly when they see me and others near the dock, they can tell that we look strong enough, and they say here's the job, if you want some cash."

"Where were you and your partner on Thursday, May 19th, the day before the assault on Mr. Leung?"

"I'm not sure."

"It was only a week ago," the interrogator said. "If your memory is going to fail you now, when I am asking you questions, we will have no choice but to proceed with a charge of attempted murder."

"We were drinking at places nearby our rooming house."

"Were you near the dock at Yau Ma Tei anytime that day or evening?"

"Occasionally. We kept moving around."

"Did you notice a large black Mercedes that was parked there?"

"I don't remember."

"You don't remember seeing a large black Mercedes parked at the dock at Yau Ma Tei?"

"No."

"The car was parked there overnight on May 19th so it must have arrived during that day or evening. You say you were nearby the dock occasionally on that day. Do I need to remind you again about your memory?" Chu Y.Y. leaned over and whispered in his lawyer's ear. The lawyer responded by nodding his head affirmatively.

The lawyer said, "May my client have some water?"

"Certainly," the police interrogator said. About a minute later, the door to the interrogation room opened and the Chief Inspector's assistant appeared with a glass of water which he placed on the table in front of the suspect.

"Now, do you remember the Mercedes?"

"We saw it in the afternoon. It wasn't there in the morning. We talked about it. We figured it was somebody important who was not worried about parking."

"What time in the afternoon?"

"It was after lunch because we had noodles at a place near the dock and the Mercedes wasn't there then."

"Can you give me a time?"

"After 2 P.M."

"Did you see who was driving the car or any passengers?"

"No."

The police interrogator handed a photograph across the table to Chu Y.Y., and asked, "On the same day, May 19th, did you see this woman in the vicinity of the Mercedes in Yu Ma Tei, in a boat in the harbor, or anywhere else?"

Berriman stopped the video. "As you've probably guessed, that's a photograph of Ms. Haig." Then he pressed Play again.

Chu Y.Y. took the picture and looked at it briefly. "No, never," he said. "The Mercedes was empty and no-one was around. I've never seen this woman."

"Are you sure?"

"Yes." Chu Y.Y. had squirmed earlier when asked about the Mercedes. In his response about Erin, confirming that he had not seen her, he revealed no uneasiness. If he was feigning indifference to her picture, he was doing a good job of it

"Why were you reluctant to tell me that you saw the Mercedes?"

"If an important person left it there, I don't want to be the one who identifies his car."

"You mean, someone who might do you harm if he found out?"

"I don't need that kind of trouble."

The interrogator stopped at that point and looked towards the viewing room. We heard Berriman's voice, telling the interrogator, "Ask him about the break-in at the ABJ office."

Interrogator Lin said, "On the night of Tuesday May 17th the office in which Mr. Leung works was vandalized. Were you involved in that?"

The lawyer asked, "Are you also charging Mr. Chu with that crime?"

"We are asking him for information that will help us in our inquiries."

"Then he is not obligated to respond," the lawyer said.

"Doesn't matter," Chu Y.Y. interrupted. "It wasn't me. I wasn't there. Don't know anything about it."

"When did you last see Mr. Chen Qiwei, who has been visiting Hong Kong from Shanghai?"

"Never heard of him." Chu's reply was quick but, it seemed to me, delivered with less confidence than his denial about the vandalism.

We again heard Berriman's voice, "Please inform Chu Y.Y. that we will seek to confirm his statements and that we will talk with him again. Tell him that we are also interrogating his partner and will surely discover any lies which will go very badly for him as a multiple offender. Tell him that we will prosecute him for attempted murder if we discover that he has lied to us. If he needs to change his statements, he should do that now and not wait until police discover he has lied. Get a detailed accounting of where he and his partner were during the days and evenings from May 17th to 20th, every location, no matter how briefly they were there."

When asked by Interrogator Lin if he wanted to modify his statements, Chu Y.Y. said no. Interrogator Lin then walked Chu Y.Y. through a step-by-step accounting of his whereabouts on each of the days in question, after each of his answers following up with, "What did you do there?" "Who were you with?" "How long were you there?" "Who saw you there?" and, "And then where did you go?"

According to Chu Y.Y., except for the attack on Robert Leung on the morning of May 20th, he spent this entire time harmlessly drinking in bars, eating at food stalls, sitting on benches, walking around, and then checking in at the rooming house, and he could not say whether anyone saw him in any of those places. With that, the interrogation ended and a policeman entered the room to escort Chu Y.Y. back to his holding cell.

After he stopped the video, Chief Inspector Berriman asked us, "Any comments?"

225

"Yes, I have a comment," I said. "I think it's suspicious that the Mercedes was left out in the open in Yau Ma Tei where it surely would be found with Erin's business card in the back seat."

"Why would they do that?"

"So that police would look for witnesses in the wrong place. I assume you still haven't located anyone in Yau Ma Tei who saw Erin and Chen Qiwei being taken from the Mercedes and placed in a boat."

"You're right about that. No-one admits to seeing them."

"What if Erin and Chen were put in a boat somewhere else, and then the car were driven that afternoon to Yau Ma Tei and left there to throw you off? It would be less noticeable if there were just a driver with no passengers, especially with no passengers who might struggle or shout for help. The driver could slip out of the car when there was a crowd around so that no-one would remember seeing him."

"Harry has a point," Blair said. "During the day the dock area in Tau Ma Tei is always packed with workers and with vehicles making short stops to unload, so people wouldn't notice a car being parked there until later."

Berriman said, "Unfortunately, we don't have a video showing the arrival of the car and who got out of it. The video surveillance camera nearby was not working. Seems to have been knocked out."

226

I asked, "Does the Mercedes have a record of other parking tickets or traffic violations?"

"No."

"So, again, as I said before, if this was the first violation involving this car and it was flagrantly parked in a zero-tolerance zone, I'd guess that the police were intended to find it there whereas Erin and Chen Qiwei were actually loaded onto a boat somewhere else."

"Do you have any ideas about where that 'somewhere else' might be?"

I recalled the Woo family yacht moored in the Aberdeen marina and the speedboat we'd taken to get to it. If Edward Woo were involved, he'd have access to other boats there as well. "What about the Aberdeen area?"

"Unlikely. If the boat departed from Aberdeen, they would have just headed out to sea and Erin's body would not have been found where it was."

Blair said, "On this, Harry, I agree with the Chief Inspector. Erin's body would have been carried westward by tidal currents so it most likely entered the water east of the buoy where she was found, in other words somewhere in the vicinity of Yau Ma Tei, outside the typhoon shelter there."

"So," I asked Blair, "what's your best guess?"

"That Erin was on a boat that departed from one of the docks north of Yau Ma Tei, because the area to the south, in Tsim Sha Tsui, is too crowded and always well lit."

Berriman said, "We'll look into it. I'll assign officers to look for witnesses near the docks north of Yau Ma Tei."

"What's the next step with your interrogations?" I asked.

"We'll try again to put the same questions to Chu's partner. He wouldn't say anything last night. But he may decide to be more cooperative now that Chu has talked to us."

"What do you think of Chu Y.Y. and Erin?"

"I doubt that he was involved unless he is a much cleverer liar than he looks. These may in fact be separate events."

"Could still have been ordered by the same person," I said.

"Indeed. And that's why I want to hear about your conversation with Edward Woo."

We told Berriman about Woo's claim that he would not have wanted Erin murdered because that obviously would create problems for his bid to acquire HKW.

"That doesn't hold water," Berriman said. "The consequences of committing a crime are always much more obvious in retrospect."

Berriman agreed with Edward's other supposition that Chen Qiwei was most likely the primary target. "Once we find Mr. Chen's body, assuming that we do, we can verify time of death," Berriman said. "You had the same idea right from the beginning, Harry, that Erin was just an unlucky bystander, and I think it makes sense."

"Edward had more to say during our helicopter ride back to Central," I said. "For example, that we should consider his father Woo Jian-Min as a suspect, since he would want to prevent the release of harmful information about Woo family interests."

"A loyal and loving son," Berriman said.

"He also speculated that other families with business activities on the mainland and in Hong Kong might be involved. He implied that he had in mind the Tung family and in particular Tung Kwan-ha, given that he and Woo Jian-Min are very close."

"It's a big stretch but I accept that we shouldn't entirely rule out Woo Jian-Min," Berriman said. "Nor Tung Kwan-ha, for that matter. Both families have a lot to protect. But we'd need to be very, very sure before taking any steps in that direction. You can't aim much higher on the Hong Kong social ladder. My superiors would need a lot of persuading before I'd be unleashed."

"There's more," I said. "I haven't mentioned this to Blair because I'm sure that Edward was just playing me, but he implied that if Tung Kwan-ha had a role, then so might Mei-Ling, helping him and Woo Jian-Min."

"What total rubbish," Blair said. "He *was* playing you, Harry."

"I don't buy it, Blair, don't worry," I said.

Berriman said, "Blair, your wife is not a suspect, no matter what Edward Woo says, so you and Harry need not be concerned about that."

He rubbed his eyes and ran his fingers back through his hair. "I'll put a notice out to the cable TV news channels and the newspapers with Ms. Haig's picture and a picture of the Mercedes. We'll advise that anyone who saw Ms. Haig on Thursday May 19th anywhere nearby to Yau Ma Tei, in or around the Mercedes, or getting into a boat, should notify the police. We'll say that police are pursuing certain leads and are seeking to establish a timeline. Maybe we'll get lucky."

After we left Caine House, I said to Blair, "Sorry about introducing Mei-Ling's name back there."

"Berriman made it clear that there's no need to be concerned about Mei-Ling, no matter what Edward says. Not a problem."

And yet, for me, it *was* a problem. Berriman hadn't ruled out the possibility that Tung Kwan-ha played a role in Erin's murder, on his own or allied with Woo Jian-Min. Thus, as Edward hinted while dripping his poison into my ear, how could we discount totally the possibility of Mei-Ling's involvement? Mei-Ling for whom the Tung and Woo family patriarchs were beloved "uncles?" Mei-Ling the sophisticated woman of means and influence in Hong Kong, and frequent traveler to Shanghai, who knew everyone who was anyone? For me to think of Mei-Ling in this way, even to consider her objectively as a suspect in Erin's murder, was outrageous, traitorous, unimaginable. It violated everything that I'd ever known and felt about her. And yet, my luminous, beautiful, unobtainable Mei-Ling, how well did I know her now, really?

Elizabeth stopped us before I opened the door to my office. She whispered, "A man is in there to see you. He wouldn't give his name. He says he wishes to meet you in connection with Erin Haig. I put him in your office, Harry, and told him you both would be back soon."

"How long has he been waiting?" Blair asked.

"About twenty minutes. I gave him tea. He said he would wait as long as necessary. He demanded that I close the door to the office."

We entered my office. A man was sitting in one of my visitors' chairs. He rose to greet us, appearing relieved that we'd arrived, like someone who's been waiting for hours in a hospital Emergency Room to be seen by a doctor, but also wary, and tentative, watching us closely. He was emaciated. There were dark, damp shadows underneath his baggy, watery eyes. His plain blue suit jacket hung loosely on his bony shoulders, and his shabby suit trousers had long since lost their press.

"My name is Stephen Blair, and this is my colleague Harry West," Blair said. "How can we help you?"

"My name is Chen Qiwei," the man said.

Twenty

"WE THOUGHT YOU WERE DEAD," I said.

"Please help me," Chen Qiwei said, pursing and licking his thin chapped lips.

"Do you need a doctor?" Blair asked.

"No. I need protection."

"Mr. Chen," I said. "Before we talk about anything else, you must tell us, did you meet Erin Haig at the Renaissance Hotel in Wan Chai?"

"No."

"No? She went there at your request."

"I didn't meet her."

"While she was there, she was called on her cellphone to go to the Renaissance car park, where she was seen getting into a Mercedes. What can you tell us about that?"

"I can't tell you anything," Chen replied. Although heavily accented, his English was serviceable.

He sat down stiffly using the arms of his chair for support. "I saw on TV that the reporter was killed. I have been in hiding. They will kill me too if they find me."

"Who will kill you?" I asked,

"Assassins hired by the New China Properties Fund."

"Let's be very clear about this," I said, speaking slowly, emphasizing each word. "Again, Mr. Chen, you are telling us that you were not inside the Mercedes at the Renaissance Hotel in Wan Chai, the car that Erin Haig was seen to enter?"

"No, I wasn't there. I told you. I did not even go to the Renaissance. It was too dangerous for me. I was hiding."

"Where?"

"In my room at the Holiday Mansions in Tsim Sha Tsui."

"Where's that?"

"On an alley off of Nathan Road, close to Salisbury Road."

"Near the Sheraton Kowloon," I said.

"Yes."

Blair said, "The Holiday Mansions is a hostel for transients."

"That's correct. I stayed the whole time in my room except to pick up food at night from street vendors, until I came here. Before I say more, promise me that you'll help me."

"Sorry, Mr. Chen," I said. "First, you'll have to answer our questions."

When he just looked at me without replying, I continued, "Why did you come to our office and not go directly to the police?"

"After I saw the news report that the reporter's body had been found, I just hid in my room. I received an email from Robert Leung that police were searching for me, and that they believed I also was killed, so this morning I emailed back to Leung that I was still alive. He replied that I should contact Chief Inspector Berriman."

"Why haven't you done that?"

"I responded to Robert Leung that I can't trust the police."

"So you came here?"

"He told me to contact you immediately instead, or he'd call the Chief Inspector himself. That's why I'm here."

Blair said, "Leung was right. We have to let Chief Inspector Berriman know that you are alive and with us here. He is a senior police officer who is working to solve this crime."

Chen thumped the arm of his chair. "No! No!" he pleaded. "You must not do that. He might be working for the criminals."

"We've met the Chief Inspector," Blair said. "We would be very surprised if he were."

"But you can't be sure," Chen insisted.

"My wife, Mei-Ling, knows everyone in Hong Kong," Blair said. "She would have told me if she'd heard any rumors about the Chief Inspector. If you like, we can call her now so that you can hear that from her directly."

"Your wife is Chinese?"

"Yes, so what?"

"What is her family name?"

"Tung Mei-Ling," Blair said.

"She is a member of the Tung family? From Shanghai?"

"The Tungs are a highly respected family, both here and in Shanghai."

"I know about the Tung family," Chen said. "I've changed my mind. Please do not call Tung Mei-Ling. Please just contact the Chief Inspector. If you hand me over to the police and inform them that you are interested in my fate, it will not be so easy just to make me disappear."

"What's your problem with Mei-Ling?" I asked.

"She is a member of the Tung family."

"Why does that concern you?"

"I don't want to talk about it here. Not now. I will tell everything to the police."

Blair said, "We're getting nowhere, Harry. Let's call Berriman."

When Chief Inspector Berriman's assistant picked up the phone, I said, "The Chief Inspector please, tell him it is important." A moment later, he came on the line. "Berriman here."

"Chief Inspector, this is Harry West. You are on speakerphone in my office and there are several others here with me."

"Hello, Harry."

"Information has come to our attention that is highly relevant to the Erin Haig matter. Can you visit us in our offices – you know the address – as soon as possible?"

"Yes, I can do that."

"Can you bring officers with you but have them wait for you in the lobby of our building, and not join you in coming directly to our office? Will that be alright?"

"I'll be there shortly," Chief Inspector Berriman said.

Blair left us, saying that he could use the time to do some work in his own office but would return when the Chief Inspector arrived.

For the next fifteen minutes, Chen sat and gazed morosely out of my window. He declined to answer any more questions. He refused Elizabeth's offer to refresh his tea.

Finally, Elizabeth opened the door to my office and said, "Harry, Chief Inspector Berriman is here." Blair entered first, followed by Berriman and a large uniformed policeman.

When I glanced at the uniformed policeman who was standing impassively beside him, Berriman said, "When I am advised that I should bring officers, I conclude that I may need to take someone into custody. It is my policy always to have an officer present to assist. I trust that is acceptable to you."

It was not a question, but I answered anyway, "Yes, certainly."

Blair said, "Chief Inspector Berriman, may we introduce Chen Qiwei, whose name you know. Mr. Chen has requested protection. He believes that he is in danger from assassins hired by the New China Properties Fund."

The Chief Inspector stared at Chen as if examining a lab specimen, a seasoned policeman's stare. "Are you the Chen Qiwei who met with Ms. Erin Haig at the Renaissance Hotel in Wan Chai?"

Chen rose, grimacing, back to his feet. "Yes, I am Chen Qiwei but I did not meet with her at the Renaissance."

"Were you inside the Mercedes that Ms. Haig was seen to enter at that hotel?"

"No, I told these others, I was not there. I was in hiding in Tsim Sha Tsui, at the Holiday Mansions, near Nathan Road. I was being followed."

"You did not see Ms. Haig at all that morning?"

"No. I only met her only once the day before, very briefly at the Hyatt, but I did not meet her at the Renaissance as I had planned."

"Why not?"

"I was afraid. So as I told you, I went into hiding."

"Did you send a message to Ms. Haig that you would fail to meet her as arranged?"

"No, I did not want to leave a note at the Renaissance in case someone would see me. If I used my mobile, it could be traced."

"Mr. Chen, please give over your passport."

Chen retrieved a red People's Republic of China passport from an inside jacket pocket. The Chief Inspector opened it, scanned the identification page, and said, "I am addressing you formally in my capacity as a senior officer of the Hong Kong police. If you withhold information or misrepresent any facts, you will commit an infraction. Do you understand?"

Chen confirmed that he did understand.

"Before we take you into custody, I will once again verify your identity as shown on your passport from the People's Republic of China. Are you Chen Qiwei, resident of the Harmony Flats in the Pudong district of Shanghai, born 21 May 1968?"

Chen confirmed that he was.

"Then," Berriman said, "Mr. Chen Qiwei, I am taking you into custody as a material witness to the murder of Ms. Erin Haig. We will ask you questions formally once you are in custody. You may have the services of a lawyer, if that is your wish. Do you understand?"

Chen affirmed that he understood.

Berriman and his uniformed policeman were about to escort Chen out of Blair's office when I spoke up. "Mr. Chen said he would talk to us after he was assured of protection. We want to hear what he has to say. May we listen in when you interview him?"

Berriman replied, "Unfortunately, we must limit attendance at police interviews. But if Mr. Chen consents, I'll arrange for you to see the video."

"I do not consent!" Chen said, glaring defiantly at the Chief Inspector.

"Why not?" I asked. "You promised that you would answer our questions once we arranged for your protection."

Berriman said, "So, Mr. Chen, you do not consent to the video of your interview being shown to Mr. Blair or Mr. West?"

"No video! I want them to be present."

"There is no need for that," Berriman said. "If you give your consent, they can watch the video."

"No. Videos can be altered. It's better for me if outsiders are present. I will feel safer."

"I can assure you that we do not alter our video recordings of interrogations."

"I want them to be present," Chen repeated. "When I answer your questions, I must know that what I tell you will be heard. If you do not allow them to watch, then I will tell you nothing."

"Very well. Do you hereby request the presence of Mr. Stephen Blair and his associate, Mr. Harry West, at your police interview?" the Chief Inspector asked.

"Yes."

"We will obtain your signature to that effect," Berriman said. He turned towards Blair and me, "I will schedule Mr. Chen's interview to start at 2 P.M. this afternoon in the Caine House interrogation room. You are invited to observe. My assistant will meet you at the building entrance and bring you to the viewing room."

"We'll be there," Blair said.

Chen shuffled out of Blair's office, a small, drab figure between the much taller Chief Inspector and his even larger uniformed policeman.

As promised, Berriman's assistant met us at the Caine House entrance, as he had on our visit earlier that day. This time, however, he led us down a flight of stairs to a sub-ground-floor level. We stopped at a door with a blackened window on which there were Chinese characters, as well as lettering in English, *View Room Interrogation 1*. He knocked twice and opened the door.

Berriman was standing inside with another man, whom he introduced as Superintendent Peng. The Superintendent looked younger than Berriman and much neater. Every hair on his head was in place, his eyebrows were trimmed and his cheeks and chin were closely shaved, as smooth as a proverbial baby's bottom. Whereas Berriman wore a lived-in suit and his shirt collar was unbuttoned, Peng's suit was sharp, well-fitted, and obviously expensive, made of the finest light-weight wool. His blue-striped dress shirt was accented by a crisp white collar and a deep purple silk tie knotted with perfect symmetry at his throat. Superintendent Peng welcomed us politely. When I got close enough to shake his manicured hand, I could smell the rich scent of his after-shave. He did not look like one for tromping through crime scenes in his tasseled loafers of soft black leather, or for clamping handcuffs on the thick wrists of heavy-set thugs like Chu Y.Y. His was indoor work.

Berriman told Superintendent Peng that Chen Qiwei had requested our presence at his police interview and had formally waived his privacy rights. He added that we were helpful in apprehending Mr. Chen and were knowledgeable about the investigation, that we came recommended by Mr. Shih Chai-Ming in the Communications Department, and were friends of the murder victim, Ms. Erin Haig. Then he informed us that Superintendent Peng commanded the Hong Kong Island police division in which Chief Inspector Berriman worked and that he had taken a personal interest in the case. Finally, for his part, Superintendent Peng added that he would be grateful for any insights that we were able to provide. All very polite.

Chen was seated at the same interrogation table that had accommodated Chu Y.Y. for the interview we had watched earlier that day on Berriman's monitor. The harsh light in the room reflected off his skull under his comb-over. He was alone on his side of the table. Berriman told us that Chen had declined legal representation, that he claimed he had nothing to hide and would answer all questions without reservation. The interview would be conducted in English at Chen's request so that Blair and I would hear his words directly rather than through a translator. Interrogator Lin, the same interrogator whom we had seen that morning on the video, was seated across from Chen at the plain wooden table.

Below the one-way glass in our viewing room, a control panel was equipped with a video monitor, speakers, a microphone, and some buttons. Berriman spoke into the microphone, "let's begin now."

Interrogator Lin told Chen that the session was being recorded, that anything that was said would be available for evidence. She asked him to confirm his identity ("Chen Qiwei of Pudong district, Shanghai, China") and to confirm that he had declined to be represented by a lawyer during this interrogation session. She said he could change his mind on this matter at any time. Did he agree with this? Yes. She said that in addition to police officers, several interested parties – Mr. Blair and Mr. West – were observing the interview from the viewing room, as he had requested. Did he still wish for their presence in the viewing room? Yes.

Chen poured tea into his cup from a teapot that was on the table. "I am sorry. I am thirsty." He sipped his tea holding his cup in two hands like a soup bowl.

He told Interrogator Lin that he had entered Hong Kong alone and had not met anyone in Hong Kong except for his brief meeting with Erin Haig at the Hyatt Hotel in Wan Chai.

"Where were you staying in Hong Kong?"

"Until I went to the Hyatt to meet the reporter, I was staying at a Chinese businessman's hotel next to the Mong Kok MTR station. Then I moved to a hostel."

"Tell me more about your meeting with Ms. Erin Haig at the Hyatt. How was it arranged?"

"I sent a fax to the editor of the *Asian Business Journal* to let him know I was in Hong Kong. Then she called me on my mobile and I asked her to meet with me."

"Why?"

"I had more information for the *Asian Business Journal*. I wanted to give her my information in person because I assumed that my mobile phone and email were being monitored."

"Why did you assume that?"

"When I was in Shanghai, I noticed people following me. They were not trying to hide."

"You have said you also noticed that you were being followed at the Hyatt where you were supposed to meet Ms. Haig. Did you see who was following you?"

"Two men were pretending to read newspapers but I knew they were watching me. It was obvious they did not belong in the Hyatt. They were not tourists, and not businessmen, more like laborers. One was fat, the other not so fat, but scruffy, rough looking. They were not far away, only two or three tables from mine in the lobby."

243

Interrogator Lin said, "I have ten pictures that I will lay out on the table, numbered from one to ten. Please tell me if any of these pictures are of the men that you saw." She retrieved an envelope from her attaché case, and placed the ten pictures in a row on the table.

In our viewing room, Berriman told us that the pictures had been ordered randomly and then numbered. They were all of men who had been arrested recently for assault and included the pictures of the two men who attacked Robert Leung.

Without any hesitation, Chen put his finger on one of the pictures, and pushed it towards Interrogator Lin, and then did the same for a second picture. "These two," he said. "I am certain of it. I saw them clearly."

Interrogator Lin picked up the two pictures, one in each hand, and pressed them to the viewing glass so that we could see them. "Mr. Chen has selected Number Four and Number Seven."

Number Four was Chu Y.Y., and Berriman told us the man in the other picture was Chu Y.Y.'s partner. I recalled Chu's quick denial that he knew Chen Qiwei. But why would he have lied, given that Chen was alive and unharmed?

"So you left the Hyatt and on your way out you informed Ms. Haig that you would meet her instead the next day at a different hotel."

Chen said, "When I saw the reporter enter the lobby, looking for me, I got up to leave. I passed by her, getting close enough to put a note in her hand, which I had written and folded while I was waiting. In my note, I said I was being followed, that it was too dangerous to meet at the Hyatt, but that we should meet instead the next morning at the Renaissance. I took a taxi to the Wan Chai MTR station, where I caught a train to Tsim Sha Tsui. I was watching for the two men but did not see them. I took a room at the Holiday Mansions. I left my suitcase at my hotel in Mong Kok so they would think I was still at the hotel."

"Did the two men at the Hyatt see you pass your note to Ms. Haig?"

"I didn't look back to check."

If Chen was right that Chu Y.Y. and his partner were watching him in the Hyatt, they would have seen him leave, and they must therefore have seen Erin as well. Chu Y.Y. claimed not to recognize her picture. Could he have been so focused on Chen Qiwei that he didn't notice Erin? Was that plausible?

"What happened next?"

"I decided not to go to the Renaissance. Then, when I saw the news that the reporter had disappeared, I decided to stay in my room except to go out at night to get food. After I saw the report that her body was found, I contacted Robert Leung of the *Asian Business Journal* and he told me to go to the office of Mr. Blair. That is what I did."

"Ms. Haig was seen entering a Mercedes at the Renaissance, and this car was later found parked illegally in Yau Ma Tei. Were you in that car at any time?"

"I was never in any car. I was in my room at Holiday Mansions the entire time."

"Did anyone see you at Holiday Mansions on the morning that Ms. Haig disappeared?"

"People at that hostel do not look at each other. I doubt that anyone will remember seeing me."

"You said you paid your hotel bill in cash every day. How about the hotel manager to whom you gave the money?"

"I inserted a payment envelope in a one-way slot under a glass partition at the reception desk. The payment envelope goes in there and is collected later. I was trying not to be noticed so I waited each time until no-one was watching."

"Tell me more about the high officials and businessmen who you believe were having you followed."

"The following started after I sent information to the *Asian Business Journal* that I obtained from an investment fund in Shanghai. Someone there must have suspected me."

"What is the name of the investment fund?"

"The New China Properties Fund."

Until now, Superintendent Peng had seemingly devoted his attention to his BlackBerry, his thumbs tap-dancing purposefully on its QWERTY keypad.

Apparently, however, he'd been listening. He shoved his BlackBerry back into its belt holster and spoke into the viewing room microphone, "Stop the interview now and join us here." Putting her hand on the earbud in her left ear, Interrogator Lin said to Chen Qiwei, "I have been asked to pause our interview. I'll return soon." She exited the interrogation room, leaving Chen alone at the table, and a moment later entered our small viewing area.

Superintendent Peng said, "You are heading down the wrong track. We are not investigating an investment fund in Shanghai. We are trying to solve a murder in Hong Kong. Focus your interrogation on questions that bear upon the murder."

"Sir," she said, "surely if Mr. Chen was being tracked by people he was planning to expose and Ms. Haig was writing about those same people, they would be persons of interest in this crime."

Berriman stepped in, "That is also my opinion, Superintendent Peng."

"Asking questions that do not relate directly to the murder are a waste of time."

"Later, we can sort out what he tells us," Berriman said. "We don't know in advance what will be helpful."

Peng insisted, "The Interrogator shall focus on Chen's interactions with Ms. Haig. Ask what he saw at the Hyatt that frightened him. Check his story out. Leave the corruption matter for the newspapers. That's not our job in this case."

I could not let this pass unchallenged. "I agree with the Chief Inspector," I said. "We should find out more about the people Mr. Chen was seeking to expose."

Instead of replying to me, Peng told Berriman, "I have not objected to the presence of these gentlemen but they must be advised of their limited status here. This is an internal police matter."

Berriman said to Blair and me, "Superintendent Peng is correct that you are invited here only as observers. I thank you for your opinion. However, we can resolve this matter ourselves."

"Would you like us to leave the viewing room while you discuss it?" Blair asked.

"That won't be necessary," Berriman said. Then he turned back to Superintendent Peng. "Mr. Chen is telling us about people he was seeking to expose as being corrupt. I agree with Interrogator Lin that therefore they are persons of interest in the murder of Ms. Erin Haig. I believe that the interrogation should be allowed to proceed and I would so instruct Interrogator Lin."

"I see the matter differently."

"If you wish to overrule me, Superintendent Peng, I will step down from this investigation, file my report on progress to date including my reasons for stepping down, and you may assign someone else."

After considering this for a moment, Peng backed down. "That will not be necessary." He advised the Interrogator, "Try to stay on point."

Chen was still seated at the table, his hands on his tea-cup, when Interrogator Lin re-entered the interview room.

"Some information needed to be reviewed," she said. "Let's proceed. You were going to tell me about the officials and businessmen who you were exposing to the *Asian Business Journal*."

Chen said, "They are party cadres and other officials in Shanghai who take bribes and they are businessmen who pay them for their special favors. They use the New China Properties Fund as a front to transfer their dirty money into legitimate businesses. They eliminate anyone who gets in their way."

"Tell us their names."

"In Shanghai and Hong Kong, two of the leading business families are the Woos and the Tungs," he said. I could feel Blair going quieter than quiet, like he had stopped breathing, as I had, and I saw Berriman glance at him before turning back to the viewing glass.

"Who else?"

"Officials who did the bidding of the property developers in Pudong and are therefore responsible for the calamities there. I have already provided many of their names."

"How many are you talking about?"

"About sixty. Or more. I don't know, because others work for them, as I said before."

"Why did you contact the *Asian Business Journal*?"

249

"I discovered that the destroyers of my village in Pudong are among the criminals who invested in the New China Properties Fund. When I read that the *Asian Business Journal* was investigating the New China Properties Fund, I sent a fax to the editor, Robert Leung. He promised that he would protect my identity if I gave him information about the Fund."

His voice quavering now with indignation, Chen said, "Despite his promise, I was being followed, so they must have found out. You say I will be protected while I am in your custody. But no-one will do anything about the criminals because they have bribed the police and other Government officials. Meanwhile here I hide for my life. They are the criminals but I am the one in jail."

Berriman clicked on the microphone to Interrogator Lin. "He said earlier that he was going to provide more information to the ABJ. Ask him about that."

She did so, without missing a beat. "You said that you were going to give the *Asian Business Journal* more information. What information are you referring to?"

"I have documents that prove that the Fund is a conduit for dirty money."

"Earlier you provided a list of names to the Journal that you said are names of investors in the Fund."

"Yes."

"Are you aware that questions have been raised about the validity of this list?"

"What questions?"

THE TRAIL OF MONEY

"Whether the list is a forgery, since anyone could print up a list of names and claim they are investors of certain amounts of money."

"It's not a forgery. Authorities should investigate the names on the list. That's all I ask."

"What about your additional documents?"

"They'll prove what I've said."

Once again Superintendent Peng addressed the Interrogator through the viewing room microphone, "Stop for a moment and await further instruction."

Then he turned to Berriman, "Where is this taking us? Are we building a case to harass the leading families and officials in Shanghai and in Hong Kong?"

Berriman replied, "In his sworn testimony, our material witness has now referred to documents that may shed light on the crime we are investigating."

"I don't see the relevance."

"Sir, he was planning to give these documents to the reporter who was murdered. If we don't request the documents, we will have to explain why we failed in a capital case to pursue all leads that are made known to us, why we held back apparently because of the high rank of some who may be implicated. Are you prepared to face such questions?"

Superintendent Peng said, "You should have coordinated the interview topics with me beforehand."

"Yes, sir."

"You will bear full responsibility for any repercussions."

"Yes, sir."

Backing down again, Peng said, "Then you may proceed, but you are on notice."

Berriman instructed Interrogator Lin to continue.

She asked Chen, "What is the nature of your proof?"

For an instant, Chen seemed to smile, the first time I'd seen an expression on his face that wasn't stubborn, fearful, or resentful. It was a fleeting smile of satisfaction, not much more than a twitch in his lips, as if he'd planned for this moment. I wondered whether the others had caught it.

"Xie Sien, the manager of the New China Properties Fund, was afraid that the Fund investors would accuse him of stealing their money; that because they were thieves themselves, they assumed others would steal from them too."

"Was that true? That the investors didn't trust Xie Sien?"

"They trusted nobody. Xie Sien realized that their suspicion would be dangerous for him. That's why he hired me to make sure that his accounting of each of the investments was completely correct. Also that's why, earlier, he asked each investor to verify his investment with the Fund by signing a receipt showing the amount and the date, which Xie Sien also signed, and which was witnessed with a third signature by Xie Sien's wife. All of

252

the investment receipts were kept in a locked file. I told Xie Sien that I couldn't approve the accounting unless I saw the original investment documents. Initially he said they were too secret but then he agreed if I promised that I would not copy them."

"And you gave him that promise."

Chen's thin lips creased in another quick smile. "Yes, I did. Xie Sien and I had gone drinking together and he thought I was his friend as well as his accountant. He handed me the file just before leaving for his lunch. He asked whether I wanted to join him. I said I wasn't feeling well and would prefer to stay in the office to do my work. Xie Sien always ate in the same restaurant, always the same noodles, pork, and beer, always for the same amount of time, just over an hour. I brought the file to a copying machine in a supply room down the hallway from Xie Sien's office. To be sure that I wouldn't be caught if Xie Sien returned early, I gave myself only forty minutes. During that time, I copied more than fifty receipts, and hid the copies, each on a sheet of paper, underneath my shirt. Although it was hot, I wore my suit jacket to make sure that Xie Sien wouldn't notice the bulge. That night, I made additional copies for safe-keeping in a copying center near where I live in Pudong."

"So these receipts are your proof?"

"Each receipt shows three signatures, of Xie Sien, the investor, and Xie Sien's wife. They show large amounts of money that the officials could not have earned from their salaries alone. Once the Authorities obtain these receipts, they'll have evidence that the investors in the Fund will not be able to deny. Their signatures are on the receipts."

"Do you have other documents apart from the signed investor receipts?"

"The Fund paid government officials and police for protection. I found records of these payments that Xie Sien kept so that he could prove that he didn't steal the money. I copied them as well."

The Interrogator asked, "Where are these documents now?"

"I prepared a package for the *Asian Business Journal* which I planned to give to the reporter when we met. I left instructions with a friend to mail other packages of these documents if I were to disappear."

"Mail to whom?"

"To CNN, to newspapers, and to the Hong Kong police."

"Since the outside world believes that you did disappear," the Interrogator said, "have these documents already been mailed?"

"Not yet. My friend will mail the documents if he does not hear from me."

"Can you give us the package that you planned to hand to Ms. Haig, the *Asian Business Journal* reporter?"

"I did not keep it with me. I gave it to my friend for safekeeping before I went to Mr. Blair's office."

"Can your friend provide these documents to us?" Interrogator Lin asked.

"Yes. I will make a call to my friend to arrange it."

"I will pause now for additional instructions from the Chief Inspector," Interrogator Lin said.

Berriman said, into the mic, "Hold on for a moment." He turned to Blair, Superintendent Peng, and myself. "Any other questions we should ask?"

The Superintendent shook his head.

"I have one," I said. "Earlier in his interview, Chen said he was in Hong Kong alone and met no-one here except for Erin. Now he is talking about a friend who seems also to be in Hong Kong. He should clarify that."

"Good catch," Berriman said. He told Interrogator Lin, "Ask him whether his friend is in Hong Kong and if so, whether Chen wishes to revise his earlier statement that he was alone in Hong Kong."

When this question was put to him, Chen seemed unconcerned by the evident discrepancy in his testimony. "Until I knew that you were interested in my documents, I saw no reason to reveal the existence of my friend."

"Do you understand that you're obligated to give us truthful answers?"

"And I have, except about my friend. I just wanted to protect him. I'm sorry." Once again, Chen's lips twitched in what seemed like a smile.

Berriman leaned towards his mic. "I think we've got enough for now."

255

Interrogator Lin ended the interview by thanking Chen for his assistance. She said that he would be held in custody pending additional investigation. He would be allowed to contact the person who would send the documents. A uniformed policeman entered the interview room and stood at the door, holding it open. Chen preceded the officer out of the door, and Interrogator Lin rejoined us in the viewing room.

Superintendent Peng asked Berriman, "How long do you intend to hold this man in your custody?"

Berriman replied, "He is a material witness. We have no basis yet to charge him. Depending on our investigation, once we conclude he has not committed any crime, we would then release him."

Peng said, "If he is not charged, and if he has told us everything he knows, he should be removed from our custody. We have no reason to believe that he really is in danger. Just because a man is afraid doesn't mean he can demand police protection."

"We can hold him while we check his story," Berriman said.

"No. Either you charge him, or release him. We are not running a hotel. We cannot afford to keep in custody everyone who says that he is afraid. I have to leave now for another meeting. I'll discuss this case with you again later."

After Peng left, Berriman turned towards Blair and me. "Any thoughts?"

"Chen's copies of the receipts will cause serious trouble for investors in the Fund," Blair said. "You can see why they'd want to stop him."

"Or to kill him for revenge once the documents are released," I said.

"I don't know whether we can hold him here based on that supposition," Berriman said.

I asked, "Did you notice that Chen smiled when he described how he copied the Fund's documents, like he'd been waiting for that moment in the interview?"

"I did see that," Blair said. "It was quite startling on such an otherwise miserable face, almost like he was gloating."

"He's been through a lot," Berriman said. "And what he did took courage. It's understandable that he'd be pleased to tell us about it."

I said, "His identification of the pictures of Chu Y.Y. and of his partner indicates that they were at the Hyatt and contradicts Chu's statements last night that he didn't know Chen Qiwei and hadn't seen Erin."

"We'll talk again with Mr. Chu," Berriman said.

"Chief Inspector," I said, "now that we know Chen is still alive, we need a new theory for Erin. Obviously she was not killed because she was a bystander to Chen's murder. Where does this leave us?"

"Right now, to be honest, I don't have any good theories, Harry."

"What will you do, then, to find her murderer?"

"We'll check on Mr. Chen's story that he stayed at the businessman's hotel in Mong Kok and then at the Holiday Mansions. When was he there? Did he meet with anyone? That sort of thing. We'll review his documents when we receive them. We'll have another chat with Chu Y.Y. As for theories of the case, we'll rule out no-one as Ms. Haig's killer, until we learn otherwise."

"Did you check whether the cellphone Chen was carrying was the same as the prepaid phone used to call Erin?" I asked.

"We did, and it wasn't."

"So, who called Erin's cellphone while she was in the ladies restroom at the Renaissance? What was said on that call that got Erin to go to the car park? Who was in the Mercedes? And why did Erin get into the car?"

"All good questions," Berriman said. "Once we answer them, we'll have Ms. Haig's killer."

Interrogator Lin asked, "What if she approached the car expecting to see Chen and when she got there, a person was pointing a gun at her, telling her to get in?"

Berriman said, "The surveillance video shows Ms. Haig talking with someone inside the car for a few minutes and then she seemed to get in willingly. She gave no indication of alarm. It appears that the person in the Mercedes was someone she trusted, which narrows the possibilities somewhat."

Blair added, "Also most likely someone who Erin believed would provide information for the ABJ articles."

"Now that we know Chen Qiwei wasn't in the car," I said, "we should re-consider other assumptions as well."

"Like what, for example?" Berriman asked.

I replied, "For one thing, we've assumed that it was a man in the car. What if it were a woman? Erin's guard would be lower, even more so if the person were someone she knew, someone who, as Blair just said, offered information for Erin's article."

Someone like Mei-Ling, I couldn't help thinking. It wasn't until I heard my own words to Berriman that I realized what I was implying, as if my subconscious had decided for me, get this vexing scenario out in the open, and if it's wrong-headed, let others knock it down. I wondered whether Blair had made the same connection. I kept my eyes on Berriman.

Berriman said, "Whoever was in the Mercedes, he or she would have to know about the appointment with Chen at 9 A.M. at the Renaissance and that Chen was not going to show up for it. Assuming Chen did not share this information with anyone – we'll ask him but I would doubt it in view of his story today – then who else knew? Both about the 9 A.M. appointment, and that Chen would not show?"

Interrogator Lin asked, "Couldn't the person in the Mercedes have followed Ms. Haig to the Renaissance without knowing anything about the meeting with Mr. Chen?"

259

"I don't see how," I said. "Erin would have taken the MTR from Kowloon. Someone in a car could not have followed her."

Berriman said, "If she were followed on foot into the MTR, her follower could have contacted the driver of the Mercedes once she arrived at the Renaissance. But, for now, let's assume that she wasn't followed, but that the person or persons in the Mercedes knew beforehand about Ms. Haig's appointment with Mr. Chen. Where does that take us?"

"I knew about the appointment," I said. "But I did not tell anyone about it until just before 9 A.M. when I told Blair. Robert Leung also knew and he may have told someone. We should check on this with Leung."

"We'll ask him," Berriman said.

"What do you plan to do with Chen after you receive his documents?" I asked. "Will you push him out the door, as Superintendent Peng seems to want?"

"The Superintendent is correct on the law. We must release Chen unless we are able to place charges or there is good reason to believe that holding him will be material to prosecution of charges against others."

"What if he disappears after he's let go?"

"We'll have to take that chance. For now, however, Chen will stay in our custody."

During our taxi ride back to our office, Blair offered none of his customary quips or wry observations. He grunted when I remarked that Superintendent Peng appeared to be pursuing his own agenda in trying to stop Chen's interrogation. He maintained a glum silence when we arrived back at our office and were greeted by Elizabeth. I told her that Chen Qiwei had a lot to say but the case was still not solved. She said Blair had several phone messages which she had left on his desk.

Blair said, "Good, thanks. Harry, can you come with me into in my office?"

"Sure."

"And shut the door after you, please."

I did so.

After we were both seated, he said, "There was a lot of talk about the Tung family."

"I noticed that."

Blair said, "I'll see if Mei-Ling can make sense of what Chen said about her family."

I didn't say anything, and Blair continued, "I heard where your comments to Berriman were leading, about who was in the Mercedes. About that person being a woman whom Erin trusted."

"Seems to me that's at least a possibility."

Blair's good nature has always amazed me. Where others take umbrage, he's amused. When confronting setbacks, Blair remains calm, even cheerful, a voice of reason, and blithely confident that everything will work out for the best. Not now, however.

Blair erupted, "What I want to know is, Harry, what in hell are you thinking? That it was Mei-Ling in that Mercedes? For Christ's sake! Get a grip!"

"Blair, trust me, the very idea makes me sick. I can't believe that we're even talking about Mei-Ling in this way. But I'm trying to keep an open mind. If Chen Qiwei is telling the truth, we can't rule out that the Tungs are in this along with the Woos."

"If," Blair said. "If. If. If. You and I need to stop talking now. I'll discuss this with Mei-Ling."

"Blair, you know how fond I am of Mei-Ling."

"So I've heard."

"But, let's face it, could the Tungs in Shanghai and in Hong Kong be involved while Mei-Ling was completely unaware of it?"

"Harry, I can't listen to any more of this. I'll connect with you later."

I concluded that it would be best to leave while Blair was still asking nicely. "Call me at the Furama when you are ready to talk some more," I said.

He did not respond, instead focusing on placing the papers on his desk in neat piles, and I left, shutting his door quietly behind me.

Elizabeth was at her desk. "Harry, I heard shouting in there. What's going on?"

"Erin's case is taking unexpected turns," I said. "Blair needs time to work things out."

"Well, if you won't tell me, I'll ask Blair," Elizabeth said.

I was checking email in my room at the Furama, mostly deleting spam messages that promised better sex, cheap Canadian drugs, and money that was being held for me in Nigeria if I wished to claim it, when the phone rang.

"Harry, do you really, honestly, seriously believe I had anything to do with Erin's murder?"

"Mei-Ling, I'm sorry..."

"A suspect in a horrible crime points his grubby dirty finger at my family and you believe him?"

"Mei-Ling, we've known each other a long time. I've always loved you from the first moment that we met..."

"So why the suspicion? You're avoiding my question. I'm so disappointed, Harry. How could you?"

I thought that if I laid everything out for Mei-Ling honestly and frankly, and we could discuss it, then I could put aside the maddening doubt that festered in my brain. "Mei-Ling, please, just give me a few minutes to explain." She was breathing harshly into the phone but she didn't say anything, so I kept talking. "We need to find out who was inside the Mercedes in the Renaissance's car park. Who knew Erin's cellphone number and called her? Who was trusted enough by Erin such that she was willing to open the car door and get in, disregarding the ABJ's security rules?"

Hearing no response from Mei-Ling, I continued, "We were told today that both Woo and Tung family members in Shanghai are involved in the New China Properties Fund. If this is true, would they have a stake in stopping the ABJ story? This is what…"

The phone went dead. Mei-Ling had hung up.

Five minutes later it rang again. I picked it up.

"Harry West."

"This is Blair. Mei-Ling can't stop crying. She says that you believe she is a murderer. She wants nothing more to do with you. And she has ordered me to end our partnership."

"Blair, I'm just trying to lay out the questions that need to be addressed, just as the police are probably doing right now."

"That's not how it sounds to Mei-Ling, nor to me."

"Let's meet to talk about it."

"The more you talk, the deeper the hole," Blair said, hanging up.

I lay on my bed thinking about Mei-Ling, and Erin, and the imminent and abrupt end of my partnership with Blair, wondering whether I could have done anything differently. I'd assumed that Mei-Ling and I would always share a special bond, that we'd never be less than loving friends, and now that was gone. But what choice did I have? To do what I could to discover who was responsible for Erin's murder, I had to consider every possibility, however

264

remote, no matter how distasteful, without ruling anything out in advance. Anyway, as I'd told Blair, if facts emerged that implicated Mei-Ling, it wouldn't be long before police would be asking the same questions as I had.

My phone rang, again. And, again it was Blair, but this time he was not calling about Mei-Ling; he had just heard from Chief Inspector Berriman.

"Berriman says they've checked Chen's story. They have confirmed that he stayed at the hotel in Mong Kok and also in the hostel. The hotel didn't have the information earlier because their reservation system was down and the hotel was late in entering guests' passport information. No-one can confirm Chen's whereabouts on the day that Erin went missing. There is no information that what he said is untrue but also nothing to back it up. Apparently no-one saw him."

"Because he was in hiding, trying to stay out of sight," I said.

Blair said, "Berriman has other news as well, about the Mercedes. Seems a witness has told the police that on the day that Erin disappeared, around lunchtime, he saw the car at a dock a bit less than a kilometer north of Yau Ma Tei."

"Where you suggested the police look for witnesses."

"Yes, well..."

"And?"

"The witness said he saw people standing near the car but only for a moment, since he kept walking and did not stop to look, and he was not near enough to see them clearly. But he did notice that one of them was a woman who had short reddish color hair."

"Erin."

"It would seem so. There was a man beside her who was Chinese. She didn't seem to be struggling but she was standing close to him so she might have been under restraint in some fashion."

"Who was the man?"

"His back was to the witness. Average height, average build, like millions of others in Hong Kong. There was one other person standing beside Erin. Again the witness did not get a good look but he thinks this other person was a woman who was Chinese."

"What did she look like?"

"He thought she stood like a younger person would, very slender and casual, although he wasn't sure. In other words, not Mei-Ling, if that's what you're thinking."

This was not a good time for me to observe that Mei-Ling "looks much younger than her age."

"Now that the police have another location for the Mercedes, they are going door to door in the area to find other witnesses," Blair said. "They're also looking for witnesses who saw Erin in a boat near the dock, or who noticed anything unusual in any boats in the vicinity of the dock plus or minus two hours around lunchtime. There are always fishermen out there working on their boats. If someone looked up from doing whatever it is they do, he may have noticed something unusual. That's Berriman's hope, anyway."

"Also," Blair added, "Chen's documents were dropped off at Caine House by a bike messenger. The messenger says he picked them up, wrapped in plastic, under a bench on the Tsim Sha Tsui promenade. He doesn't know who left the package for him, only that he was paid his delivery fee in cash left in an envelope with the package. Berriman is reviewing the contents now. He says he will decide based on his reading of the documents whether to open new lines of inquiry."

After a light dinner in the Furama's rooftop restaurant, I returned to my room and found an email from Blair, "Be in the office at 9 A.M. tomorrow for a conference call requested by Mr. Shih."

Twenty One

BLAIR SCARCELY LOOKED UP when at 9 A.M. sharp I walked into his office and took a seat in front of his desk. Instead he punched in Mr. Shih's number on his phone. When Mr. Shih came on the line, Blair told him that we were both present for the call.

"There have been important developments," Mr. Shih said. "The Authorities received documents last night that indicate the New China Properties Fund has indeed been involved in money laundering for its investors, as we suspected. Edward Woo has withdrawn his proposal to acquire Hong Kong Wireless, and an investigation has been launched by Hong Kong's Securities and Futures Commission into other transactions involving the New China Properties Fund. The documents also specifically identify certain officials in Hong Kong as having received money from the Fund. One of the officials identified in the documents is my Minister, who has now been put on leave. He was one of Edward Woo's allies inside my Department."

"What about others identified in the documents?' Blair asked.

"A prosecutor in Shanghai has ordered the arrest of an investor in the Fund, an official in the Pudong Centre for Land Reserve. The prosecutor says she may also order additional arrests. Authorities also have launched an investigation concerning several business groups and leading families in Hong Kong and in China, including the Woos and also, Blair, the Tung family, since they were named."

"OK."

After our call ended with Mr. Shih, I said to Blair, "Seems that Chen's documents were persuasive."

"Seems so."

"I hope that the investigation concerning the Tung family doesn't cause a problem for Mei-Ling."

"Strange that you would say that, Harry, in the circumstances. But it shouldn't. She has nothing to worry about."

"I gather that Mei-Ling is still upset with me."

"'Upset' doesn't cover it. She can't believe that you would actually suspect her as complicit in Erin Haig's murder. I have to dissolve Blair West International. Mei-Ling gave me an ultimatum, 'Pick Harry or me.' You can guess my decision on that."

"Blair, I have to pursue the open questions wherever they lead. I owe that to Erin."

"And what do you owe to Mei-Ling? Or to me?"

"To find out what happened."

"Well, that's it then," Blair said. "Pursue your open questions."

There was nothing more to say.

Elizabeth was sitting at her desk, looking sad. She got up and followed me into my office.

"I don't like what I'm hearing between you and Blair," she said.

"I don't like what you're hearing either."

"I'm serious."

"Eavesdropping is against company policy. We'll have to dock your pay."

"Harry, you and Blair are a great team. And you're good friends. Don't let it end this way."

"How much do you know?"

"Blair told me everything when I asked him directly."

"So you know about Mei-Ling."

"Yes. Are you surprised that she's unhappy with you?"

"Am I wrong to consider the possibility that the Tung family is involved in all this, given what we've heard?"

"No. But Mei-Ling? That's too much, Harry."

"What am I supposed to do, Elizabeth? Mei-Ling and I…"

"I know."

"…but when I think of what Erin must have suffered, I can't stop. I can't ignore a possible explanation for what happened, even if it contradicts everything that I believed, even if it turns my life upside down."

"Not just your life, Harry."

"I know, but Erin deserves justice."

"Why don't you and Blair try to solve this case like consultants? Review the data. Do your rankings and ratings and scorings and whatever it is that you do to come up with the most probable solution."

"What if that solution turns out to involve Mei-Ling after all?"

"I think Blair will take that chance," Elizabeth said.

"Then do us all a favor, Elizabeth. Persuade Blair to join me in reviewing the data so that we can solve the case like consultants."

"I'll try," Elizabeth said. "If he won't come willingly, I'll drag him in here."

"And then I want you to stay in the room with us as a referee, instead of listening through the door."

"Will do, Boss."

Blair followed Elizabeth into my office. "Elizabeth informs me that we're going to work this out whether I like it or not," he said.

"We've come this far. It's worth a try."

Elizabeth said, "Just forget that I'm here. Do your consultant thing."

"Blair, thank you for doing this," I said. "I know that it's hard for you. It is for me too."

"Well, if it gets you to drop your insulting speculations about Mei-Ling…"

"I'd love to do that, Blair."

"Focus," Elizabeth warned.

"Right," I said. "Let's discuss each person's motives and means."

"You have the floor," Blair said.

"Can we start with Mei-Ling?"

"Fine."

"We need to be objective, to think about Mei-Ling the way that the police would do."

"Fine, Harry. Let's just get started."

"To be clear…"

"Fuck, Harry, let's see what you've got, and we'll deal with it!"

"OK, first, Mei-Ling's motive. She reveres her uncle Tung Kwan-ha. She is close with her Tung family members in Shanghai, and also close to the Woo family. Chen Qiwei was trying to get documents to the ABJ that show involvement by the Tungs as well as the Woos in the New China Properties Fund. This information would embarrass Mei-Ling's family members. It would likely have dire consequences for some of them, especially in Shanghai. So, Mei-Ling might – so the police might think – have tried to prevent this from happening. We've learned that Chen had other ways to get his information out but Mei-Ling would not have known this and anyway people

272

who are under stress do not always act rationally. OK so far?"

"Keep talking," Blair said.

"Good. So, let's now consider means. Let's assume that Mei-Ling could have found out about Erin's meeting at the Renaissance and that she and people helping her expected to find both Erin and Chen Qiwei there."

"Why should we assume that?" Blair asked. "Even I didn't hear about the Renaissance meeting until that morning, when you told me. The only ones who knew about it ahead of time were Robert Leung, Erin, you, and Chen Qiwei."

"Someone could have learned about the meeting from Robert Leung and passed that along to Mei-Ling."

"Like who?"

"Like Mei-Ling's cousin Eugene Suh who works at the ABJ and who might not be as distant a cousin as we were led to believe. We need to find out whether Leung told Eugene about Erin's meeting at the Renaissance."

"The Chief Inspector was going to check that."

"Let's call Leung and ask him ourselves."

Elizabeth found Leung's cell number, which presumably would work in Taiwan, and I placed the call. Leung picked up, "Hello, Blair," he said, evidently reading Caller ID from our office phone line.

"Robert, this is Harry West. Blair and Elizabeth are here with me."

"OK, Harry. Do you have news for me from Hong Kong? Is Chen Qiwei OK? I haven't heard anything from him since your email that he turned up at your office."

"Mr. Chen is fine. He's in police custody now as a material witness, I think mostly for his own protection, as he requested."

"I'm glad to hear it. I believe him when he says he's in danger."

"At Chen's request, Blair and I were invited to watch his interrogation. He told the police that he had additional documents that he'd planned to hand over to Erin, and he arranged for these documents to be provided to the police. They include receipts for money invested in the New China Properties Fund, each signed by the investor, by the Fund manager, and by the Fund manager's wife as a witness."

"That should do it," Leung said. "Hard for the Fund investors to deny their own signatures."

"It would seem so. Government here has begun a formal inquiry and apparently things are afoot as well on the mainland, and Edward Woo has withdrawn his proposal to acquire HKW."

"When did all of this happen?"

"Last night, after the police obtained the documents. Someone in Government must have called Edward to let him know."

"Great, Harry, thanks. We'll put together an article to explain how the pieces fit together. Have there been any more developments about Erin?"

"A witness came forward who says that he saw the Mercedes that picked Erin up at the Renaissance, at a dock north of Yau Ma Tei, and that one of the people he saw standing next to the car was a woman who fit Erin's description. Police are now searching for other witnesses in that area. We are trying to figure all of this out, Robert, and in that connection we have a question for you."

"Shoot."

"Concerning the meeting scheduled between Erin and Chen Qiwei at 9 A.M. at the Renaissance, did you let anyone know beforehand?"

"Yes, I sent a text message to Cathy and Eugene about it the evening before, just after I left you and Erin at the Furama."

Elizabeth shot me a curious look. Blair was studying his hands on the table and didn't react visibly.

"You texted Eugene Suh?"

"Yes, both Cathy and Eugene, as I said. Why? It's one of our security procedures, to keep everyone informed about our meetings; who, where, when."

"Do you know where Eugene is now? Cathy says he's disappeared."

"He's not responding to my emails or voicemails, nor to Cathy's. So I don't know where he is. I assume that he's staying out of sight until he feels that the danger has

275

passed, which may be soon, given your news about Chen's documents."

"Thanks, Robert, that's what we wanted to know. Blair, do you have any other questions for Robert?"

He shook his head. I thanked Leung again and we ended the call.

"Shit," Blair said.

"So Mei-Ling could have learned about the meeting in time to do something about it," I said. "Let's dig deeper."

"Fine."

"Then here, unfortunately, comes the easy part. As we both know, Mei-Ling is one of the few people who could induce Erin to open the door of that Mercedes and to get in without first calling her office. Mei-Ling could have organized the Mercedes on short notice. She could have hired people to drive the vehicle and to control Erin once she was in the car. Actually, she would not have needed to hire anyone if other Tung family members helped out, such as Eugene Suh, for example. Too bad he's not available to tell us where he was on the morning of May 19th."

"Wait a moment," Blair said. "How could Mei-Ling have 'organized' the Mercedes? It was phantom registered, probably being used by criminals."

"The Tung family must have connections in Hong Kong that could put them into contact with whoever had the car, and from that point on it would just be a matter of money to acquire it."

276

Blair said, "If the Tungs wanted to prevent disclosure of Chen's documents, surely they'd go after Chen and leave Erin alone unless she happened to be with Chen at the time that he was taken, and we know now that he wasn't taken and she wasn't with him."

"Yes, but maybe they planned to hold Erin until Chen turned up at the Renaissance and when Chen didn't show, things got out of hand with Erin. Actually, by that point, they might have been unable to let her go anyway."

Blair said, "You're forgetting Mei-Ling's help in getting the police to look for Erin."

"I did think of that. Mei-Ling did cause the police to take Erin's disappearance seriously and to establish that we should be kept informed. It's also true that as a result, Mei-Ling herself was fully briefed on progress made by the police, and on what they were thinking, since I assume that you shared that with her."

"Of course I did," Blair replied. "Why wouldn't I? Mei-Ling has always been our most valuable ally. She did more than help us with the Hong Kong police. She recruited her man in Shanghai to research the ABJ's list of names and to confirm Chen's address in Pudong. At our dinner together, she shared sensitive information about the New China Properties Fund. These are not the actions of someone trying to hide anything. Precisely the opposite."

"There's one more item to consider," I said. "The scrap of paper found in the Mercedes on which Mei-Ling had written her mobile number."

"What about it?"

"What if Erin left it there to identify Mei-Ling as her captor?"

"Or she left it so that whoever found it would know to call Mei-Ling, as you surmised earlier. Do you have anything else on Mei-Ling, Harry?"

"No. I'm done."

"So now let's move on," Blair said. "Your points about Mei-Ling are duly noted. Who's our next candidate villain?"

"We should review the pluses and minuses for Edward Woo, our prime suspect from the beginning. He claims that Erin's murder was counter-productive for him, but would he have figured that out in advance? He had a motive, to protect his deal and his reputation. He was angry about the ABJ. He may already be implicated in the killing of the Australian who wouldn't sell the fiber cable system to him."

Blair asked, "Why wouldn't Edward go after Chen instead of Erin? It was Chen who had the documents."

"Suppose Edward believed that Erin had already obtained them. Or he figured that Chen would bring the documents with him to the Renaissance. So when Chen didn't show, he decided that he had no choice but to kill Erin, and then planned to find Chen later."

"So you're assuming that Edward knew about the meeting," Blair said.

"Yes, I don't know how, but he has a good network in Hong Kong, as we know. The people following Chen could have found out that information, somehow. Edward also could have had Erin followed from Kowloon to the Renaissance, so he decided to start with Erin, and wait for Chen to turn up. If Edward were in the Mercedes and told Erin that he was willing to talk to her, face-to-face, Erin would figure that she had a chance to get a new angle on the story. Edward could have told her that he would only talk if she got into the car and didn't call anyone first. Her ambition to get the story would have led her to ignore Leung's security rules."

Blair said, "The major problem with the Edward Woo scenario is that his lawyers were already geared to manage the situation and he was successfully raising doubts about the list of names, so why risk blowing things up by abducting and murdering a journalist who happens also to be a US citizen and thus catnip for CNN and other international media? I think the logical thing for Edward would have been to watch Erin, consider her as bait, and wait for Chen to show up."

"Alright, setting Edward aside for the moment, how about Woo Jian-Min, in order to protect the Woo family interests?"

Blair replied, "But if Woo Jian-Min wanted to muzzle the ABJ, why go after Erin? It would be more effective to eliminate the journal's managing editor, Robert Leung, and not just by having him beaten up on a public street, but

279

killed, and then also dispose of Chen when he re-surfaced. Also, concerning the question of why Erin got into the Mercedes, it's unlikely that Woo Jian-Min would have been in the car himself, and no-one else he hired would be trusted by Erin, hence she would not have gotten into the car. Next!"

"Obviously Chen's documents are a disaster for the investors in the New China Properties Fund. Perhaps, as Chen said, the investors hired assassins to kill him and anyone else who received the documents, such as Erin. So they settled for Erin when Chen went into hiding, and they assumed, as we've said for the others, that they could get Chen later."

Blair shook his head. "I don't like the Fund investors as the principal villains. Villains, yes. But not for this crime. Who would have been inside the Mercedes? Some random thug? Erin would never have gotten in. It wouldn't happen. Also, again, why bother with Erin? Like Woo Jian-Min, they would have gone directly to the top and eliminated Robert Leung. If the Fund investors are behind this, all they achieved by murdering Erin was a lot of unwelcome publicity that hardly serves their purposes; just the opposite, in fact."

Elizabeth, who had been watching and listening intently, her eyes flicking between Blair and me when each of us spoke like she was tracking a ping-pong ball as it was smacked back and forth across the net, said, "Can I make a suggestion?"

"Please do," I said.

"You've assumed that Chen and not Erin was the murderer's primary target and that whoever committed the crime ended up worse off."

"Right."

"What if the opposite were true? What if Erin were the primary target and her killer benefited? What if he wanted the publicity that resulted from Erin's murder?"

"Let's play with it," Blair said. "Who do we have that would fit?"

"Robert Leung," I said.

"What's his motivation?"

"Fame for himself and for the *Asian Business Journal*. He'll be a big deal when he returns to Hong Kong, having exposed the corruption here despite all the threats and the real dangers as demonstrated by Erin's murder."

"I don't think so," Blair said. "Erin would have been puzzled to see Leung in the Mercedes. In fact, she would have been amazed. It would be totally out of character, and creepy."

I said, "Leung could have turned up at the Renaissance and told Erin, 'there've been some developments, hop in and let's talk about them.'"

"But Leung didn't have a car in Hong Kong," Blair said. "Erin would ask him where he got the Mercedes and why, and it's hard to think of any answers he could give that would be persuasive. Anyway, Leung had many other opportunities to meet alone with Erin, so why pick this time and place to abduct her, out in the open in the Renaissance car park with its video surveillance? Who else do we have?"

It was then that I recalled Chen Qiwei's quick secret smiles during his police interrogation, like he was pleased with how things were playing out.

"We have Chen Qiwei," I said.

"You mean, despite all his denials about meeting Erin at the Renaissance when he was asked by us, by Berriman, and again by Interrogator Lin?"

"If he's the one, he'd lie. Let's run down what we know about him. Obviously he knew about the meeting at the Renaissance. He knew Erin's cell number since his contact with her to arrange their first meeting at the Hyatt. So he could have made the call to Erin, telling her that he was waiting for her in the Mercedes in the Renaissance car park. Since Erin expected to meet him and believed that he was frightened of being followed, it would seem plausible to her to change the meeting location to the car, rather than in the lobby."

Elizabeth said, "Having seen Mr. Chen, I could understand why Erin would not have feared him."

"Exactly right, Elizabeth. Chen looks frail. From Erin's perspective, he's one of the good guys. If Chen told her that they needed to drive somewhere where they would not be observed, I could understand how she might willingly get in the car."

282

"But this requires that Chen was not hiding out in the Holiday Mansions as he claims," Blair said.

"Berriman told us that police have not found anyone who saw Chen at the Holiday Mansions that morning," I said. "We've assumed that this was because Chen was in hiding. But he could have left the Holiday Mansions when no-one was around to see him go."

Blair began pacing back and forth in front of my office window. "You are on to something, Harry. Chen needed publicity to ensure that his information would not be suppressed or dismissed. To avenge the destruction of his village in Pudong, his story had to be taken up by the Authorities in Hong Kong and in China. What gave his story more juice was Erin's murder. And during Chen's interrogation by the police, we all jumped on his revelations about the New China Properties Fund and its investors. We all agreed – that is, all of us except for Superintendent Peng, who may have had his own reasons – that it was relevant to identify the sources of influence peddling and money laundering. Chen dangled his documents in front of us during his police interrogation, an interrogation that was witnessed by us as external observers, and you'll recall his vehement demand to have us there. The police had no choice but to request the documents. They were investigating a capital crime and the documents might have evidentiary value. And of course, Chen was happy to provide them. Once the police received the documents, they were compelled to share them with the Authorities which, as we now have learned, led to official inquiries that otherwise might have been suppressed."

"If that was Chen's plan, it worked brilliantly," I said. "And Erin's murder was key to making it work."

"What about Chu Y.Y. and his partner hoodlum?" Blair asked. "Who hired them to attack Leung? And who was the Chinese woman the witness saw near the car?"

"One at a time," I said. "First, Chu says he doesn't know who hired them. Also if Chen Qiwei were pulling the strings, he'd be able to select their pictures from the set shown to him by Interrogator Lin, as he did."

"And the witness who saw the Mercedes and the woman standing beside Erin?" Blair asked.

"Is it so unlikely that Chen would have a woman accomplice? Or that the witness is fake and working with Chen to mislead the police, so the car was never actually at that other dock north of Yau Ma Tei, but somewhere else where there were no witnesses?"

"How did Chen get the Mercedes?" Blair asked.

"His friend in Hong Kong could have obtained it."

"You're both so clever," Elizabeth said. "Are you ready now to kiss and make up?"

Of all the narratives that we'd considered, I found Chen's the most compelling. But it was still only a theory.

We needed evidence. Lacking evidence, we needed witnesses. As of now we lacked both, so to confirm that

Chen was Erin's murderer, we needed him to confess. Either that, or to convince us that he was innocent.

Twenty Two

"CHIEF INSPECTOR, we've developed a theory about Erin Haig's murder," Blair said, once we had Berriman on the phone.

Berriman asked us to hold on while he gave instructions to his assistant that he should not be disturbed. "You gentlemen now have my full attention," he said.

"Let me start by asking you an important question," I said.

"Go ahead, Harry."

"What's the current status of Chen Qiwei?"

"We released Chen from custody an hour ago. It was Superintendent Peng's judgment that he has told us everything he knows, including providing the documents that he promised, so we have no more to learn from him about Ms. Haig's case."

"Is that also your opinion?"

"It is. Otherwise he would still be in custody. I had no specific reason to hold him."

"Was he anxious about being put back onto the street?" Blair asked.

"In fact, he left quietly. He did not insist on staying. He did agree to contact us before he left Hong Kong. Why do you ask?"

"We believe that the facts of the case point to Chen as Erin's killer," I said.

I walked Chief Inspector Berriman through our reasoning, suspect by suspect, leaving out no-one.

About Mei-Ling, Blair said, "Sorry to interrupt, but Harry mentions Mei-Ling only because there are Tung family investors in the New China Properties Fund. Obviously we never seriously considered her as a suspect."

Berriman replied, Brit-to-Brit, "Quite so."

"What do you plan to do about Chen Qiwei?" I asked.

"Too bad you didn't call me with your theory before we showed him the door."

"It would be conclusive if you could find anything connecting him with the Mercedes."

"Until now we have not found a match with Chen's prints, nor with his hair or his clothing."

"What about the witness who says he saw the Mercedes. What do you know of his background?"

"He works mostly in restaurants and with the fishermen when they need extra hands. Came down from the mainland about ten years ago. Why?"

"We suggest that you find out more about him, in case he's working with Chen."

"Can you get Chen back?" Blair asked. "If we're right about him, he might run now that he has accomplished what he set out to do."

"I don't have enough evidence to hold him in custody. We'd just have to release him again."

I asked Berriman, "How did you get Superintendent Peng to agree to open an investigation of the transactions involving the New China Properties Fund?"

"He had little choice once we received Chen's documents."

"Couldn't he still have put the documents aside as being irrelevant to Erin's murder? This is what he was arguing during Chen's interview."

"He could have, but given the attention being focused on this case, the Superintendent agreed that we had to move on it."

"Exactly," I said. "We think Chen's motivation to murder Erin was to ensure that you would have to act on his information. And it worked, just as he planned."

"We'll keep an eye on Chen to make sure he doesn't slip away," Berriman said. "We'll haul him in as soon as we find evidence for your theory. If he's responsible for Ms. Haig's death, he won't get out of our hands again, I assure you."

I told Blair, "I need to clear the air with Mei-Ling."

"I'll see what I can arrange," he said.

The three of us met that evening for an early dinner at Nikko, a Japanese restaurant on the third level of a shopping center near the Furama. Mei-Ling and Blair were waiting at a table when I entered the restaurant through a red hanging curtain. Mei-Ling greeted me with a cool arms-length handshake. No air-kisses or hugs, but she did seem to have calmed down, somewhat.

"You've decided that I am not Erin's murderer after all," she said, giving me a frosty look.

"I understand why you were upset. I'm sorry."

"Do you have any idea what that little man has unleashed?" Mei-Ling asked.

"Do you mean the investigations of your family and the Woos?"

"Of course I do, don't be cute. Investigators are poking into my Uncle Tung Kwan-ha's personal and business affairs. They're even demanding that I explain some of my interior decorating contracts. In Shanghai, the Tung and Woo families are under suspicion, and their old friends are afraid to talk to them for fear of guilt by association. No-one wants to attract the attention of the new prosecutor there, a very arbitrary and harsh woman. Here in Hong Kong, Woo Jian-Min is being asked pushy questions from people who just a week ago would have trembled at the chance to shine his shoes."

"But you are not blaming me for these investigations, I hope."

"No, the investigations are not your fault."

"Thank you."

"But Harry, how could you believe that I would be capable of harming Erin? I would want Chen to be killed, if I'd had the chance, but poor Erin!" Mei-Ling started to tear up and I could barely restrain myself from taking her in my arms, notwithstanding the fact that Blair was sitting right there with us.

"Mei-Ling, I humbly beg your forgiveness," I said. "I prostrate myself before you, on bended knees right here, in this restaurant."

I shoved my chair back, and knelt in front of her. I heard some women in the restaurant laugh as I went down on my knees. Blair gaped, "Don't be an ass, Harry."

"No, I like it. This is what he should do," Mei-Ling said. Then she placed her hand on my shoulder, the Mei-Ling of old. Perhaps she just needed to be approached with the proper deference. "Harry West, I will forgive you," she said. "I'll also allow Blair to keep working with you."

"Both I and Blair West International are grateful for your forgiveness."

"And one more thing," Mei-Ling said, "did you really mean what you told me on the phone, that you've always loved me since the first day we met?" She had listened to what I said, after all, even while stripping the skin off my back.

"I did mean it. Every word. How could it be otherwise?"

"Should I dump Blair and move in with you?"

"If Blair doesn't object, nothing could make me happier." Said in a joking tone but absolutely true. If Mei-Ling were available, at that moment I would have dropped everything to have her with me, with details to be worked out later. For an instant it seemed that all of our futures hung in the balance, until Blair, having observed these proceedings with a bemused expression, finally jumped in, "Sorry to play the skunk at the picnic, but I do object, since I too am besotted with Mei-Ling."

"Well that settles it," Mei-Ling said. "I'll stay with Blair. Harry, you can still love me from a distance, and we will be good friends. You may rise now, off your knees, and retake your seat."

"And perchance to dream, at times, of what might have been," I said.

After dinner, I took the Star Ferry to Kowloon to explore the Tsim Sha Tsui area where Chen had said the Holiday Mansions was located, supposedly on an alley off Nathan Road, just up from the Sheraton. I thought that Chen might conceivably have returned there after his release from police custody. If so, I would confront him. I'd demand that he respond to the facts that implicated him as Erin's murderer.

This part of Nathan Road featured scruffy stores hawking plastic-wrapped digital cameras, cellphones, and other electronic devices, assorted knick-knacks, tee-shirts, post cards, and Chinese fans; grungy hostels that rented rooms by the hour; and touts beckoning the curious to try out what was on offer behind their night clubs' doors. "We have beautiful women! Take a look!"

The alleyway was just where Chen had said. It was narrow, jammed with merchant stalls perched like hairy barnacles on both sides, offering "gold" necklaces, "pure silk" scarves, and other treasures. Past the stalls, I saw a red neon sign with Chinese lettering and also in English, "Holiday Mansions."

The dank air inside the hostel's lobby was not freshened much by a ceiling fan rotating slowly overhead. I found the registration booth at the back under a fluorescent light fixture, next to an elevator door. The booth was protected by a three-foot high Plexiglas shield which had a space underneath it to slide keys, money or messages. Although yellowed with age, the shield was still transparent enough to reveal a young woman in the booth who was engrossed in a magazine with a cover that displayed large bright red Chinese characters, exclamation marks, and unflattering photographs of people who were up to no good.

Tapping gently on the Plexiglas and speaking through a circle of holes, I said, "Hello? Excuse me. Hello?" The woman looked up, openly annoyed by the disturbance I was causing.

"I am looking for someone. Can you tell me if Mr. Chen Qiwei is in the hostel?"

She shook her head and her eyes drifted back to her magazine.

"Do you mean you can't tell me, or he is not here?"

She said, "You want room? HK$500, one night."

"No, I am looking for someone, a Mr. Chen Qiwei. Is he here?"

She shook her head again. "No English. Come back later."

"Is there someone else at the hostel who speaks English?"

She shook her head again, "Come back later."

"When?"

"Tomorrow."

She returned her attention to her magazine. I heard the rumble of the elevator. Its inner solid door slid open, followed by the clanking of the outer accordion steel gate, and two backpackers stepped out, a young man and young woman. I asked them, "Do you speak English?"

"Some people think so," the man replied, with an Australian accent.

"I am trying to find someone who may be registered here. The woman in the cubicle doesn't speak English. Do you know if there are others who work here who could be more helpful?"

"I doubt it," he said. "It's pretty basic here. They're not much on service."

"You get what you pay for," the girl said. "Cheap and cheerful."

"More like cheap and sourpuss and you should see the hall bathrooms," he said. "And the bed sheets aren't exactly crispy. But it does for us. No point in wasting money."

"Also," she said, "this place is cash for keys and mind your own business. It's not much on record-keeping. When you meet the other guests, you can see why."

"Lots of thumping and bumping, kept us awake all bloody night," he said.

"Well, it gave you some ideas of your own," she said, with a smirk. "It wasn't so bad."

With this, the man apologized for not offering more help and said they had to shove off. He slid a key under the Plexiglas, evidently having paid in advance for their room, and they exited the lobby into the alleyway.

On my way out, I held the door for a couple coming in, a Chinese woman stuffed into skin-tight shorts and body-hugging tank-top, braless underneath and nipples prominently showing, holding the arm of a man who looked Russian, and who said "spasiba" as he passed by me. He stumbled as she pulled him into the elevator. I could hear laughter inside as they ascended towards the joys of sex and commerce.

I had started on my way back towards Nathan Road when, on a whim, I took a final look behind me, and saw Chen and another man approaching the hostel entrance from the other end of the alley. In contrast to Chen's frailty, his companion was sturdy and had a full head of bristly short black hair.

They were about to enter the hostel when I called out, "Mr. Chen, please wait!"

They stopped and I walked towards them. "What do you want?" Chen asked. Unlike our first meeting at our office, he didn't seem frightened or nervous. "What are you doing here?"

"I was looking for you," I said. "I heard that you were released from custody and I wanted to talk with you."

"I was not released. I was pushed out into the street where my life is at risk. The criminals will kill me if they find me." I looked at Chen's companion, who was staring at me blank-faced, and Chen added, "This is a friend who is staying with me." He did not introduce us. "What do you want to talk about?"

"I want to talk about your meeting with Erin Haig."

"I have already told the police everything."

"I don't think so."

"What do you mean?"

"I think you lied. Your story was a complete lie."

If our theory was correct, this man standing before me in the alley had terrorized Erin. He hurt her, and he took her life. Her suffering meant nothing to him. It meant nothing that she had talent, ambition, and plans; that there were people who cared about her. Rage boiled up in me against this murderer. I wanted to smash his head against the pavement until it split like a watermelon. But I didn't. I held back. I had to hear Chen confess his crime. His friend took a step forward and put his hand on my arm. I shook it off.

"You lied," I repeated. "You're a murderer. You murdered my friend."

If Chen was surprised by my accusation, he didn't show it. He just looked at me, appraisingly. He started to respond, "You have no…"

I interrupted him, "Save your breath. We know that you murdered Erin Haig. The police will charge you and you will be convicted and spend the rest of your rotten life in prison. I'm here to tell you this myself before they take you away."

What I said about the police seemed to catch his attention. Also my loud voice was attracting the attention of others in the alley who were looking our way. "We should discuss why you have this idea," Chen said. His voice was calm, as if this "idea" that he was a murderer had nothing to do with him. "Join us in my room. Let's discuss it. We'll have privacy there." He pulled open the door to the hostel lobby and motioned his companion to enter, and for me to follow.

"I don't think so," I said. I was not about to accompany a cold-blooded murderer and his bulky friend to a room in a low-rent hostel where no-one knew anyone's name. But I still needed to hear Chen admit his guilt. At the alley's far end away from Nathan Road, thirty yards from where we stood under the sign of the Holiday Mansions, there was a small garden and a bench under an overhead light. "Let's talk there," I said, pointing at the bench.

Chen shrugged and the three of us walked towards the bench, with me leading the way. I sat on one end, Chen in the middle, and his friend on the other end. Chen said, "Now you can tell me why you believe that I killed the reporter."

"Do you deny it?"

"First, tell me why."

"You knew that Erin would be waiting for you at the Renaissance. Erin would only have entered the Mercedes if she trusted the person who was inside the car. You were her highly valued source, the person she had met at the Hyatt the day before, a person who she believed was courageous but also afraid and frail and therefore not a threat; a person who could help her complete the story she was writing. No-one else fits as well. It had to be you."

"But why would I want to harm the reporter?"

"You wanted more attention for the documents you had taken from the New China Properties Fund. You figured the death of an American journalist covering the story would be newsworthy, and the Authorities would have to pay attention."

"And the police believe this story?"

"Yes," I said. "Do you deny it?"

Chen did not respond, and I continued, "And when I tell the police where to find you..."

Chen's friend came around to my side of the bench. Chen said, "No, you will not tell them anything."

"Do you deny it?"

Chen closed his eyes. Then he started talking. His voice was flat, toneless, like he was re-telling a story that he'd told many times before. "People in my small village in Pudong struggled to live as true communists guided by the teachings of Chairman Mao. To protect our village against corrupt officials, they paid for my education so there would be someone they trusted who could read numbers. As they had feared, officials doing the bidding of property developers came to destroy our village and surrounding farms. Those in my village who resisted were attacked by the police. I was asked to deliver our protest to party leaders in Shanghai where I worked as an accountant. My neighbors and family believed that the Communist Party would save our village once it knew what was happening. I waited outside the party leaders' office for two days before anyone would receive me. I delivered a petition on behalf of my village and told the cadre who met me that we did not want to move. I told him that we worked hard and were self-reliant, following the ideals of our party. I reported on the conspiracy by officials to rob my family and other residents of my village. The cadre made a big show of taking a cigarette from his pack without offering me one as a common courtesy, and then blowing cigarette smoke in my face. He replied that the Pudong Centre for Land Reserve was fulfilling its mandate so that Shanghai could expand into a new city across the Huangpu. He said my village stood in the way of progress. He said that jobs would be available in factories opening up in Guangdong and also to erect the new buildings on the land currently occupied by our village and farms. He rejected my accusations of corruption as being reckless and unproven. When I tried to respond, I was arrested for fostering disunity, and sent to a labor camp where I was beaten and almost starved."

"After twelve months, I was allowed to return to my village. I found that it was gone, all of it. My parents had killed themselves rather than leaving with the others. They hung themselves in the kitchen of our family restaurant. Where my village had been, where I grew up, everyone I had known was gone, and now there were trucks, and earth movers, and piles of pipes, and steel, and bamboo scaffolding, and work crews."

"You can't blame Erin Haig for what happened to your village," I said. "You haven't answered my question: Do you deny murdering Erin?"

Chen sat with his eyes still closed, not responding.

"So you don't deny it," I said. "Since you have nothing more to tell me, Mr. Chen, I'll just leave you to the police."

I started to get up from the bench. Chen's friend put his hand on my shoulder, pushing me back down, and then Chen spoke, "I am not ready for you to leave."

"I have a cancer in my stomach," he said. "My pain is getting worse. Soon, my body will be found in my room in the hostel, killed by the knife that my friend is carrying and that he is now holding against your side. Everyone will believe that I was murdered like the reporter was, and by the same criminals. They will recall my protest that I would be killed if I was released from custody. The Authorities will be forced even more urgently to prosecute, and these criminals in Shanghai and in Hong Kong finally will pay for what they have done."

"So you admit that you killed Erin."

"My friend obtained the car in return for a favor. He drove me to the Renaissance Hotel, I called the reporter, and she came to the car. I told her I would show her my documents once we drove to a safe place, away from the people who were following me. She said she had to call her editor but I told her I would drive away if she did because her mobile call could be traced. My friend drove us to a garage where I had rented a storage room. We left her there. Then we drove the car to Yau Ma Tei. We parked at the dock where the video surveillance camera was broken. I knew the car would eventually be found. I expected the police would be looking for it since we made sure it was seen by the video camera in the Renaissance car park."

"What about Erin?"

"We waited in the hostel until after dark, after it started to rain, and then took a taxi back to the warehouse. She tried to fight my friend. He knocked her unconscious. We borrowed a truck to drive to Aberdeen where my friend keeps a boat for fishing and for visits to the islands. When we got into the boat, she tried to fight again and my friend used his knife. We drove the boat towards Yau Ma Tei where a lot of cargo ships are moored. We dropped her body in the harbor near the ships."

"You wanted her to be found."

"Of course."

"She was trying to publish your information, to help you get your story out. Did that mean nothing to you?"

"And she did help me, more than she planned. Her death served a larger purpose, just like mine will. She died so that my information about the criminals could not be ignored. You want me to say that I'm sorry? I am sorry for what the criminals did to my family and to my village and all the other villages in Pudong."

"You killed my friend. You will pay for that."

"I have already paid. Now I am collecting what is owed."

"You are planning to murder me as well," I said. Strangely, I was not afraid. I was too angry for fear. But I was very *very* alert.

"You will not be harmed if you come with us quietly back to the hostel. But if you resist in any way, then you are right, we will have to kill you."

The knife in his friend's right hand was partially visible under a jacket slung over his arm. I thought it better to go with them back to the hostel entrance where there were people nearby, rather than giving Chen's friend an excuse to use his knife while we were alone at the park bench.

"I'll go with you. Tell your friend not to get too excited."

I walked between them up the alley towards the hostel. Chen's hand gripped my left arm like a claw, his long fingernails like sharp talons biting into my skin. Evidently he was not as weak as he looked. His friend was on my other side, holding my right arm. His knife touched me as we walked, several times pricking my skin through my shirt. I resolved not to enter the hostel. If Chen wanted to deliver a message by having his body found there, he had to believe that he would get even more attention by providing my body as well, also stabbed to death, apparently the third murder of someone who asked too many questions about the New China Properties Fund. Clearly I was worth much more to him dead than alive.

Chen's friend was digging his meaty hand into my right bicep, holding it rigid, but I was able move my right forearm. I flexed it slightly from where it was resting against my stomach as if to relieve stiffness. He tightened his hold on my bicep. As gradually and naturally as I could, I shifted my right hand upwards, not far, just a few inches, but enough to reach my left shirt pocket where, since my first days as a consultant, I've carried a Cross pen and retractable pencil, each gold-plated, elegant, and virtually indestructible. I couldn't tell by feel which was the ballpoint pen and which the pencil but it didn't matter since each had a sharp metallic point. I took hold of one of the pair and held it in my palm with my thumb over the top.

I saw my chance when we arrived at the hostel doorway and Chen's friend reached to open the door. I jerked my arm free of his grasp and jabbed down into Chen's hand with my Cross writing instrument, the pencil as I found out later. I smashed it hard enough to pierce his hand all the way through. Any further and it would have pinned his hand to my arm. He screamed, clutching his hand from which the Cross pencil still protruded. I started towards the stalls and Nathan Road, trying frantically to get to safety. My shouts of "Help! Murderer!" added to the commotion produced by Chen's continuing howls of pain. I felt a sharp burning jolt in my upper right arm. I looked to see what had happened and saw blood soaking my shirt-sleeve and the blade of the knife held by Chen's friend, now bright red instead of silver. Then a second jolt against my ribs, like I'd been hit by a hammer.

There was shouting. A rush of people. I felt dizzy. Suddenly all I wanted more than anything else was to rest and to close my eyes. My legs gave way and I sank down, and my head weighed a thousand pounds as I lay with my cheek pressed against the cool asphalt.

Next I knew, a bright light burned through my eyelids. My head throbbed, and there was a dull ache in my arm and my chest. Was I dead? If so, and if the gods smiled upon me, would I meet Erin as she had appeared on the waterfront promenade, her dress pressed against her legs by the breeze? Would I join together with her again, both of us slippery-skinned, like we were in our shared shower at the Furama?

It was with mixed emotions that I opened my eyes to see Blair's round face hanging over me.

"So you're alive, you bloody idiot," he said.

"I guess so. Where am I?" My right side and right arm were bandaged, and I was lying in a bed on coarse cotton sheets. A tube was connected to my left forearm.

"You're in Queen Mary Hospital on Pok Fu Lam Road, on the southern side of Hong Kong Island," he said. "And you're bloody lucky to be here, so no bloody complaining."

"Last I remember I was outside the Holiday Mansions hostel in Kowloon. How did I get here?"

"Berriman's men were monitoring Chen Qiwei when you blundered onto the scene," Blair said. "They stood back when they saw you talking to Chen and his friend on the park bench. They followed you when you walked towards the hostel. When you shouted and tried to get away, they moved in. It was Berriman's constable who jumped on the guy with the knife so he couldn't stab you again."

"I owe him my life."

"You do bloody owe him. He saved your foolish skin."

"Was he hurt?"

"He was bruised but is alright."

"Why all the bloody insults, Blair? Did I do something bloody wrong?"

"Well, yes. When you come upon two men in a dark alley and one of them is a suspected killer, you don't waltz up to confront them. You turn around, walk the other way, call the police, that sort of thing."

"I had to hear Chen confess."

"So you admit you are a bloody idiot."

I closed my eyes for a moment. Then an obvious question occurred to me, "Where is Chen now?"

"He is back in jail along with his friend. And with only one usable hand, thanks to you."

"We were right. He murdered Erin. He and his friend did it together. There is no doubt about it. He told me everything."

"Police are testing the knife that was used on you for traces of Erin's blood. They are also comparing the new guy's fingerprints to those found on the Mercedes. Berriman expects that he'll have enough evidence to place charges for murder among other offenses."

"I'll give him more to work with when we talk," I said, grimacing from a sharp pain in my side as I took a deeper breath against the bandages.

I had a private room with a window. On a shelf under the window, there was a glass vase with red and yellow flowers, and a potted plant in a container wrapped by silver foil. In addition to the machines and intravenous drip to which I was hooked up, there was a small video screen on a pedestal above my bed. Behind a slightly opened door, I could see that my room included a bathroom.

"Nice place," I said.

Blair said that he had just arrived home with Mei-Ling when Berriman phoned to report that I was attacked in Tsim Sha Tsui and was unconscious from stab wounds, and that Chen and another man had been taken into custody. Mei-Ling insisted that I be transported to the Queen Mary Hospital which was noted for a high level of care and also offered private as well as semi-private rooms. "Once again, you're lucky that Mei-Ling got involved," Blair said. "Our other hospitals are less comfortable."

"How am I paying for this?" I asked.

"Elizabeth took care of that. You're covered by medical travel insurance that she purchased for you before you came out here." Actually I did remember an email from Elizabeth asking whether I had purchased travel insurance and I replied that I hadn't since I was generally healthy, Hong Kong was a safe city, and anyway I didn't have time to shop for it.

"Elizabeth is handling the paperwork," Blair said. "She also sent you those flowers, as a gesture from our company. And the potted plant is from Mr. Shih."

"I'll have to thank them both," I said. "And Mei-Ling. And Berriman's guys for turning up just in time. And you, of course."

"You're very welcome," Blair said, adding, "you bloody idiot."

The door to my room opened and a man with a stethoscope slung around his neck came in. "I'm Doctor Yuen," he said. "How are we doing this morning?"

"We are doing OK," I said. "Was it you who bandaged us up?"

"Yes, with help from the nurses who were on duty last night."

"How long will I need to stay here?"

Turning to Blair, Doctor Yuen said, "He just got here, and already he wants to leave."

"Seriously, Doctor Yuen," I said. "I have a flight scheduled back to the US in a couple of days. Will I need to postpone it?"

"I don't see why you would," Doctor Yuen said, while reading notes on a clipboard at the foot of my bed. "You were knocked out from shock rather than as a direct result of your wounds. You didn't lose much blood. No internal organs were injured. Your cuts have been stitched."

"So my diagnosis is that I fainted, not that I suffered a near mortal wound?"

"You were lucky," Dr. Yuen said. "A few inches right or left, and the knife would have done serious damage. You can take antibiotics which I'll prescribe now. You'll be given breakfast. You need to eat to verify that you can take food by mouth rather than through the drip. Also we'll verify that your bowels are working."

"I'll be sure to call you with the good news," I said.

"If everything goes well, as I expect, we can check you out within the next couple of hours. Just take it easy for a while. No heavy lifting. No knife fights."

Twenty Three

I WAS DISCHARGED from the hospital shortly after noon. After being pushed by an orderly to the hospital door in a wheelchair, as required by hospital policy, I walked the rest of the way to Blair's car. My chest and arm were stiff where I was bandaged, and the glare of the midday sunlight contributed to a lingering headache, but otherwise I felt surprisingly functional.

"Welcome back to the world," Blair said, as he held the passenger door open for me to ease myself in.

At the Furama, I treated myself to a sponge bath, protecting my bandages as instructed by a nurse at the hospital. I took a ninety-minute nap. Then, after a late lunch snack at the hotel, I ventured out to find a taxi to take me to our office.

"Harry, how are you?" Elizabeth asked. "We were very worried."

"All things considered, I'm doing well," I said. "Thanks for dealing with the hospital."

"Of course," she said.

I opened Blair's office door after two short knocks. He beckoned me into his office and told me that Berriman was eager to hear my story. I said that I was ready to talk to him and Blair placed the call.

"How are you doing, Harry?" Berriman asked, after coming onto the line.

"Fine, thanks. But that reminds me. I understand that the officer who saved my life is your assistant, the constable whom we met at your office. Please thank him for me."

Berriman said that he would. "He'll be glad to know that you are alright. I need your testimony concerning the assault. Are you up to that?"

"Absolutely."

"Good. I can take your testimony at your office rather than dragging you in here. Will you be available in about a half hour?"

"I'll look forward to seeing you then, Chief Inspector. We have a lot to talk about."

Pending Berriman's arrival, I retreated to my temporary office to catch up on email.

I'd received one from Jerry Seligman reporting that his first project had finally come in, which was also the first for the Cambridge office of Blair West International. He'd already started work on it and would need my help. He closed by asking, "What's going on at your end, Harry? Any leads on Erin Haig? Will you be back soon?"

In my reply email, I congratulated Jerry on his win and brought him up to date. "You may see a story online or on CNN about suspects being charged for Erin's murder, and that mentions that I was assaulted by these same suspects; however, my injuries are not too serious and I'll return to Boston on Monday, as planned."

I emailed a thank-you note to Mr. Shih for the plant in my hospital room.

Blair entered my office accompanied by Chief Inspector Berriman.

"You didn't bring a uniformed officer this time," I said.

"I didn't expect that I would need to take someone into custody. However, if the need arises, you're looking wounded enough with all your bandages that I could probably handle you on my own."

Berriman placed a small tape recorder on my visitor's table. He established on tape the time and place of the interview, and the identities of those present in the room, himself, Blair and me. He said a transcript of the interview would be sent to me for my signature to confirm that it was an accurate record and that Blair also would need to sign it. Following these introductory formalities, Berriman asked me to describe what happened, beginning with my first sighting of Chen Qiwei and his friend in the alleyway outside the Holiday Mansions. I did so, leaving nothing out, until the time that I was stabbed and lost consciousness.

"Did you see who stabbed you?" Berriman asked.

"Chen's friend was holding a knife in his hand when we were on the park bench and he pressed it against my side when we walked to the hostel. When the stabbing happened, I didn't see who did it, although I assumed it was Chen's friend. I was just trying to get away."

Berriman said that he would assign constables to look for the warehouse where Chen told me that Erin was held and for the boat that was kept in the harbor at Aberdeen on which she was killed. He said that the "witness" who claimed to have seen the Mercedes at the dock north of Yau Ma Tei had gone missing but that police were looking for him and when he was apprehended, Berriman expected that he would provide useful information. He said I might be requested to return to Hong Kong, travel expenses paid, to give my testimony in court.

"I'll be glad to come back," I said. "What will happen to Chen and his friend?"

"If convicted, both will spend the rest of their lives in a Hong Kong prison, except that the prosecutor in Shanghai plans to ask for Chen to serve as a witness in her corruption investigations. If she does, we'll ship him up there and then when he's done testifying, he'll return to his prison cell here."

"He might not survive the trip because of enemies he's made in Shanghai," I said.

312

"Would you be sorry if he didn't survive?"

"After he's revealed all that he knows, I don't care what happens to him, no more than he cared about Erin."

"Given that he planned his own death to look like he was murdered, it would be ironic if that actually happened," Blair said. "Another example of Lady Justice's special brand of humor."

"One more thing," Berriman said. "Superintendent Peng has scheduled a press conference this afternoon to announce that we have made arrests in connection with the murder of Ms. Haig. When you are contacted by reporters, I'd like you to decline to comment on any specifics on grounds that you do not want to compromise an ongoing criminal investigation."

"Fine with me."

"Before I leave," Berriman said, "I need to return your Cross pencil. We had it cleaned and sterilized to remove the bloody bits from Chen's hand."

It was elegant and functional and I'd used it happily for a long time, but I almost gagged at the sight of it as Berriman held it out to me.

"Chief Inspector," I said, "I don't want it back. I don't want to think of Chen Qiwei every time I reach for it. Please give it to your constable with my compliments, along with my Cross pen to make it a matched set."

"Are you sure?"

"Very sure," I said, handing my pen to Berriman. "I'll replace them with a new set when I get home."

"Excellent. He'll be delighted."

As predicted by Chief Inspector Berriman, after the Peng press conference, Elizabeth began receiving calls from reporters asking for my statement. I agreed to be interviewed by phone by CNN and by reporters from the *South China Morning Post* and the *Hong Kong Standard.*

Elizabeth sent each reporter a head-shot of me looking suitably distinguished.

I responded to newspaper reporters' questions in general terms. I explained that our firm, Blair West International, had been engaged by the government in Hong Kong to evaluate a proposed acquisition of Hong Kong Wireless. That we became aware of allegations concerning the financing for this acquisition as had recently been reported in the *Asian Business Journal.* That we had discussed these allegations with reporters from the ABJ including Ms. Erin Haig, who had been tragically killed while pursuing this story. That we had met Chen Qiwei who provided information concerning the corruption allegations and who also, as revealed today by the police, was now a prime suspect in Ms. Haig's murder. And that I had encountered Chen and his friend in Kowloon, where I was attacked, and where I believe that my life was saved by the prompt action of Hong Kong police officers.

The CNN presenter, Janice Huang, led her story with the Superintendent Peng news conference, followed by background on the Erin Haig murder, once again showing Erin's picture in which she was smiling into the sun. Ms. Huang summarized the allegations in the *Asian Business Journal* and mentioned that Edward Woo's bid to purchase HKW was now withdrawn. Then, at the end of her piece, with my head-shot on the screen, she stated that two suspects in Erin's murder had been arrested after they attacked me in an alleyway in Tsim Sha Tsui, where I had gone to look for them. She also reported that I was visiting Hong Kong on a consulting engagement for the government on behalf of my firm, Blair West International.

A blogger who commented on business events in Hong Kong and China posted a blog which she titled "Hero Consultant Confronts Murderers."

Her blog went viral.

Jerry emailed me that the phone in our Cambridge office was ringing nonstop, both from reporters and from potential clients who were eager to talk to the Hero Consultant.

I also received an email from Alexandra, the first since we'd exchanged congratulatory messages when we were informed that Harrington's request for parole had been denied. "Have a safe flight back," Alexandra's email read, "whether you're flying in a plane or outside it. Let's get together for coffee or dinner. No agenda. Just to talk."

After a restless night because of my bandages, and having Sunday to myself to attempt to clear my mind, I decided to indulge in a ride to the top of Victoria Peak on Hong Kong's Peak Tram. Its funicular tram cars operate in pairs, each with wooden seats and drop-down windows to allow a breeze to flow through. To start the ride up the steep hill, the cars latch to a cable running underneath, between the tracks, similar to the mechanics of the cable car system in San Francisco. Once we reached the top, I began the two-mile walk along Harlech and Lugard Roads, the narrow roads that encircle the Peak.

It was like walking through a semi-tropical forest. The road was overhung with pine, broadleaf, and palm trees. On each side there were flowering vines wrapped around the tree trunks and on high fences that shielded Victoria Peak's lush gardens and its mansions from plebian passers-by like me. It was quiet up there except for the birds and the light breeze rustling the leaves, and I stopped frequently to breathe the air which was fresh, damp, and scented of flowers. Only after I completed the circle and once again approached the Victoria Peak Station, did Hong Kong's office and apartment towers and harbor come back into view, far below.

That afternoon, Blair called me at the Furama, rousing me from a deep nap.

"You OK?"

"Just a bit drowsy. What's up?"

"I've just talked with Chief Inspector Berriman. Things are happening."

"Tell me."

"Police have located the warehouse where Erin was held and the boat on which she was killed. Evidence on the boat, including blood, is quite definitive. They also searched Chen's room in the Holiday Mansions and among other things found the passport of his colleague in crime."

"Who is the charming fellow?"

"His name is Zhu Xiaoyu; he's from the mainland, and not surprisingly, he was born in Shanghai's Pudong district, in a village close to Chen's. According to Berriman's police counterpart in Shanghai, Zhu is a common criminal who has spent much of his adult life in

317

prison in Shanghai for robberies, muggings, and assaults of various kinds. He was released most recently about two years ago and has lived since then in Hong Kong. Both Chen and Zhu have been charged with Erin's kidnapping and murder, and with your attempted murder. In addition, police were able to match Zhu's fingerprints with prints that were left on the pictures of the ABJ staff that were defaced when the ABJ's office was vandalized, so they are planning also to charge him with malicious vandalism."

"Are Chen or Zhu confessing what they did?"

"Zhu refuses to say anything whatsoever. Chen has been advised by his lawyer not to make any admissions so he refuses to answer any what, how, or why questions."

"So he's clamming up as well?"

"Not entirely. He insists that he had nothing to do the attack on Robert Leung. Interrogator Lin asked how Chen was able to recognize Chu Y.Y. and his partner from the photographs that she showed to him during his first interrogation. He said that they really were in the Grand Hyatt lobby just a few tables away from him and he believes they were following him. Berriman retrieved the security video from the Hyatt lobby for the time that Chen was there. In the video, Chu and his partner are sitting near to Chen just as he said. Also they left shortly after he did."

"Another explanation is that Chen hired them. Part of his scheme to keep everyone guessing. What does Berriman think?"

"Berriman is open to the idea that they were indeed following Chen and that someone other than Chen was behind the attack on Robert Leung. He still sees Edward Woo as a likely suspect for that, as well as others who wanted to clamp down on the ABJ."

"Did he tell you what's happening with Edward?"

"Police searched Edward's office and his home, apparently looking for documents related to the Fund. Berriman didn't tell me what they found. But as you can imagine this is embarrassing for Edward and for the Woo family. Mei-Ling has learned from Cynthia that once Edward is allowed to leave Hong Kong, he will move to South Africa to manage the Woo real estate assets there. Edward's company, TelePhase, will be folded back into other Woo holdings in Hong Kong."

For my return flight to the US, I had the same window seat on the Boeing 747-400's upper deck as on my flight to Hong Kong. When I boarded, the aisle seat, Erin's seat, was already occupied by a man with short grey hair and glasses who was reading one of the airline magazines. He looked up briefly to acknowledge my arrival and then returned to his reading.

We took off over the water towards the south but soon wheeled left and I could see below us the office towers in the Central and Wan Chai districts of Hong Kong Island. Soon, however, my view was obscured by mist and clouds as our plane headed eastward.

By my fourth birthday, I was suffering grave doubts about Santa Claus and had given up on the tooth fairy. Subsequently I also lost my ability to believe in an afterlife. But even with a rational secular view of the world, it is hard to deny the magic of email. Tap on a keyboard and your words appear on a screen at the instant they are conceived in your mind; hit the Send button and these same words re-appear within seconds to be read by your addressee anywhere on Earth.

I composed an email message to Erin at her ABJ email address, "Erin; you are on my mind at this moment and to that extent, at least, you still exist. We caught the bastards that hurt you. I loved our time together and I will never forget you. Farewell, Your good and permanent friend, Harry."

Send.

Postscript

THE FORMER Director of Pudong Centre for Land Reserve sits on the plain wooden bench with his head down, his elbows on his knees, staring at his bare feet on the filthy cement floor.

Not long ago, he was lauded as the Father of New Shanghai. He did what he had to do, evicting obstructive villagers and farmers to provide space for the gleaming new city across the Huangpu. Property developers paid him his fair share, money that he was invited to invest in the New China Properties Fund. "No-one will find out about your money," he was promised. "It will grow for you in the dark in Hong Kong, in Macao, in Taiwan, and in Singapore. The top people are doing it. You don't want to be left out. You can be rich like them."

In her television interview after his arrest, the ugly hard-nosed prosecutor boasted that she "turned over a rock" and found him wriggling underneath. But she did not find him under a rock. She found him in records stolen from the Fund, records that were supposed to be kept secret, that were handed to her in a tidy package.

Although he'd confessed, hoping for leniency, he was sentenced to death. Hoping for mercy, he appealed twice to the higher Courts. His appeals were rejected. He would be made an Example for the others.

He nurses bitter thoughts. What about my ever-ambitious Deputy Director who replaced me and now piously curses my name; he also collected plenty. And his most generous good friend, property developer Woo Junyi, whose sentence was suspended? Woo must have paid the judges well.

Boots in the corridor approach his cell. His steel door is unlatched and opened with a bang that echoes inside the cement walls. Policemen bind his hands behind him with a nylon rope and curl the rope around his neck. They push him forward down the corridor, a hand on each of his shoulders, to an outdoor courtyard.

One of the policemen snarls, "Keep your eyes down." A hand presses down on the top of his head, tightening the rope curled around his neck, chafing his skin, making him choke. A police photographer who is taking his picture positions the camera to capture the writing on the placard that hangs under his chin like a baby's bib, "Thief."

They shove him to the far end of the courtyard where hay bales are stacked against the outer wall. A policeman reads a statement with scorn dripping from each word, "You have betrayed the trust of the people and therefore have been sentenced to death for your crimes. Through two appeals allowed by law, your sentence has been upheld as just and well deserved. It will now be carried out. You will now be put to death."

His knees press painfully against the courtyard's cobblestones. His heart hammers wildly in his chest, and he has trouble catching his breath. His cheeks are wet. The smell of hay fills his nostrils. A policeman standing behind him raises a rifle towards his head, and fires.

About The Author

Peter David Shapiro lives in the Boston area. His debut novel *Ghosts on the Red Line* was published in 2011 to rave reader reviews. He invites readers to contact him through www.peterdshapiro.com.

Also by Peter David Shapiro

Another suspenseful novel featuring Harry West

Readers' praise for this debut novel:

Wonderful unlike anything I've read before

An imaginative, strange account

Paperback ISBN 978-0-9839244-0-1
eBook ISBN 978-0-9839244-1-8
www.ghostsontheredline.com

327

PETER DAVID SHAPIRO

GHOSTS ON THE RED LINE

Commuters see their Departed on Boston's Red Line trains.
Consultant Harry West is hired by the Massachusetts Bay
Transportation Authority to investigate. His project turns personal
when his ex-wife Alexandra Ben-Tov meets their beloved daughter on
the Red Line, who looks like the teenager she might have become if she
had lived. Are the visitors on the Red Line ghosts or hallucinations?
Either way, when Harry's team discovers the source of the visitations,
the MBTA declares it will bring them to an end. Alexandra has a
brilliant idea: Build Visitation Rooms that replicate the features of
Red Line train cars so that people can continue to meet their loved
ones. But not everyone approves. The Archbishop of Boston seeks to
get Visitation Rooms banned in Massachusetts. And a gangster who
frets that his victims might return from the dead warns Harry and
Alexandra: Cancel Opening Day for the first Visitation Room, or else!

BILLY DELAHUNT BOARDED A RED LINE TRAIN with his
mom at Boston's Downtown Crossing station heading
towards Harvard Square in Cambridge for his piano lesson
and then afterwards, she promised, to shop for a new
skateboard. Because their train car was almost empty, he
and his mom had no problem finding seats.

Billy loved to observe the other passengers. Sitting
across from him, for example, was an Asian lady, her long
dark hair carefully brushed and all in place, tidily dressed
for work in matching clothes, intently checking her
BlackBerry. A young woman standing near a door was

gripping a pole with one hand and the handle of a baby stroller with the other. Also standing near the same door was a grey-haired man in a blue blazer and red tie, white trousers, and brown loafers. At the far end of Billy's train car, a young man chatted with two women, all three of them probably students based on their ages, casual dress and backpacks. The women laughed at something that the man said, which Billy was unable to overhear above the *basso profundo* rumble of the train's steel wheels and the creaks and shrieks from the train car's undercarriage as it braked and swayed around turns, noises that were amplified in the reverberant Red Line tunnel.

Billy stared unblinkingly at his fellow Red Line passengers and being only eleven, he did not glance away even when one of them caught him staring. However, their faces revealed little beyond the obvious external clues; they were non-threatening, non-welcoming, and frustratingly for Billy's research purposes, blandly non-expressive.

Suddenly shattering the spell and causing Billy almost to jump out of his seat, the neatly-dressed Asian woman right across from him screamed, "Oh my God!"

She lurched sideways and stared transfixed at the empty space beside her and exclaimed again, "Oh my God!" and then, "Robbie! You've come back to me! Is it really you?" She began to sob, causing her eye make-up to run, which smeared glistening smudges on her formerly immaculate cheeks. "Oh my God!" she repeated. "I can't believe it!"

But Billy saw no-one sitting next to her, nor standing in front of her. There was no-one there, no "Robbie" nor anyone else.

He checked whether the woman might be communicating with someone – her Robbie – through a Bluetooth headset hanging off one of her ears, perhaps hidden under her dark hair, but her ears were ornamented only by small gold hoop earrings. Her hand clenched as if it were taking hold of something. "I've missed you so much!" she said, and then paused, looking at the space next to her, seeming to listen.

As their train approached the Central Square station in Cambridge, the woman stood up from her seat and pleaded, "Come with me, Robbie. Promise that you'll stay with me!"

The grey-haired man and the baby-stroller woman sidled aside to give her extra space at the train car door. They let her get out first, and then followed several paces behind. After the door slid shut, she turned back towards the train car. She looked surprised, and then distraught, and cried out, "Where are you? Robbie! You promised you'd stay with me!" Billy could hear her calling frantically, as the train began to move, "Will I see you again?"

Billy's mom was flipping through a free Metro newspaper that someone had left on a nearby seat. "Did you see the woman crying?" Billy asked.

"Yes. She was very emotional."

"Did you hear what she said?"

"Not really," Billy's mom said, "I was reading the paper."

"She was talking to someone."

"So?"

"But she was alone!"

"Maybe on her cellphone."

"No cellphone. No Bluetooth. I checked."

"Sometimes people just talk to themselves."

"Well I thought it was weird."

"You're weird yourself," his mom said and added, as the train slowed to enter the Harvard Square station, "This is our stop."

Once they were on the platform, Billy repeated to his mom, "She was really sad when she got off the train." When his mom did not respond, Billy pointed to an official MBTA sign attached to the red-tiled station wall, "See Something? Say Something!"

"That's for security. It's not about ladies on the train who were crying."

"I want to report it."

They approached a man wearing an MBTA uniform, including the official logo, a black T inside a silver circle, stitched on the right shoulder of his jacket. "My son wants to make a report," Billy's mom said.

The MBTA man listened attentively as Billy described what he saw. He asked for all the details that Billy could remember and took notes as Billy talked. He thanked Billy for his report and assured him that he would pass it along to the proper authorities.

"Satisfied now?" his mom asked, once they were on their way again. They were going to be late for Billy's piano lesson with Mrs. Fiona Lewis, who was a stickler for starting on time, so his mom hustled him to keep up with her as they climbed the steps out of the station to street level in Harvard Square.

After Billy's piano lesson, he texted his friends about the lady he saw crying on the Red Line, about how she was talking with someone who wasn't there, and about how the MBTA man in the Harvard Square station seemed really interested when Billy reported what he saw.

One of his friends responded, "Sweet!" and another replied, "Woo! Maybe she was talking to a ghost!"